The House with Old Furniture

by
Helen Lewis

HONNO MODERN FICTION

First published by Honno Press in 2017. 'Ailsa Craig', Heol y Cawl,
Dinas Powys, South Glamorgan, Wales, CF64 4AH
1 2 3 4 5 6 7 8 9 10
Copyright: Helen Lewis © 2017

The Author would like to stress that this is a work of fiction and no
resemblance to any actual individual or institution is intended or
implied.

A catalogue record for this book is available from the British Library.
Published with the financial support of the Welsh Books Council.

ISBN 978-1-909983-66-3 (paperback)
ISBN 978-1-909983-67-0 (ebook)

Cover design: Graham Preston Cover image: © Shutterstock, Inc.
Text design: Elaine Sharples
Printed by Gomer Press, Llandysul, Ceredigion SA44 4JL

For Stephen

Chapter one

I don't want to leave. I'm being ripped from the rock I cling to. A whirlpool of change drags me down, pulling me to the very bottom of its vortex.

I want to stay. I need to stay, clinging to all the memories made here, ensuring they remain sharp and deeply etched. Because if I go who will say – remind people even – that this is where we had our first row, over there in the corner of the garden is where the snowman you built stood for two weeks, and round that corner where the tarmac cracks you came off your bike, you still had the scar ten years later, that little white smile on your kneecap.

"They're here!" (I knew they would have to be eventually.) "Have you seen the size of the truck?" Finn runs through me and out of the door to greet the vast removal lorry. I almost smile. This is the most alive that I've seen him in months. He needs to escape the weight of sadness pressing down on our home; he needs to restart his life somehow. The lorry will block the road. I hear the neighbours tutting already.

So today we have to go, the tide has finally overwhelmed us and pushes me forward into the future, leaving nobody behind to mark the memories, the special, ordinary places we've been; no blue circular plaques mounted by the door to announce that Jesse Wolfe flew his kite for the first time right here.

See, it says it here in the diary: April 12 2010, MOVE. I've spent the last four months bypassing April, only writing in dates for May or March, birthdays, anniversaries, school breaks up, school restarts. Rhythmical things that always happen whatever our postcode – a postcode that's always been TW, maybe the numbers swap themselves around but I'm always TW, that's all I know.

"It's massive – have we got enough stuff?" Finn shouts from the gate. He's bought into the propaganda, how this will be a new start, the possibility of puppies and horses to ride because we'll have so much space – space unmarked by Jesse. And time, time with his dad, time to go surfing together and coasteering. Promises, promises, all gobbled up by Finn. Has he thought how he'll miss his friends, I wonder, and the everyday things that are always here that he doesn't even see until they've gone, like Willow and her café ("Here Finn try these, just made a batch, what d'you think?") and Gloria the crossing lady, the curry house at the bottom of our road, perfect for Saturday nights in, broadband, download speeds – and everywhere, in everything he touches, a trace of Jesse… He jogs back up the path, tugs at my sleeve. "Come on, they need our stuff." I don't want to see. I don't want to look, maybe then the lorry can drive on, block some other road. But it's too late. I can see it out of the corner of my eye, it's there. Finn crashes back downstairs with a box as big as him. "Here's my stuff!" He's shouting at an army of tattoos.

Those tattoos will want tea. "White loads of sugar love." I reach into the space the kettle sits in, it's gone, sugar dissolved, fridge sterile, unplugged. Our lives are boxed, labelled, stacked and waiting. Could I grab Finn now, hide away from the boxes, the tattoos; the traffic jam in our road? I think I sound mad, sound sad. I am.

"We'll start with upstairs, all right love?" He already smells of stale sweat – it's only 7.30am. He has a cartoon Mr Incredibles-gone-to-seed physique; I imagine him as a Dave – Big Dave, can move a piano, solo. He stamps upstairs – the grit on the soles of his shoes crunching into the stair treads. Each of his thudding steps scours out more of our presence. There are six coats of varnish on each of those steps, which makes them shine beautifully in the sunlight. We spent a whole weekend painting them together, foolishly, Andrew starting at the top, me at the bottom. Andrew spent most of the day marooned upstairs playing with Jesse in his nursery, over and over they played the music box that made Jesse laugh. I can hear the tune now tiptoeing downstairs. I wonder if the new owner will appreciate the scuffed boot marks. "What d'you want us to do with this lot, love?" His bellow makes me jump.

He's in Jesse's room.

"Leave it, leave it!" I chase his boot marks up the stairs. "Come out, please come out."

"Keep your bloody hair on!" Big Dave mutters past me, "You best tell us where we *can* go. Need to be out of 'ere by 12 – 12.30 latest, don't forget." I nod sorry and yes I'm up to speed on the time issue. I back into the no-go zone shutting the door. Sitting in the middle of Jesse's floor I pick up his T-shirt from the pile of dirty clothes he left, ball it up to my face and inhale. With eyes shut I'm sure, certain, that I can still smell him, he's still in there, still in here. I have no idea where to start, what is required of me. The door opens slowly, with great care, great caution.

"I brought boxes and…" A pen-stained hand passes me tissues. Finn sits beside me quietly, leans his head on my shoulder. "Jesse's looking forward to the new house, he wants the big room."

I want to scream, "Don't say his name!" I want to hold Finn and never let go.

"Ouch, Mum, don't squeeze so hard!"

I know that every night he comes in here, sits on Jesse's bed and tells him about his day, the things that Jesse's mates have done or said on face-space, the little injustices that I have dealt him. And he asks Jesse what he should do, how does he beat Luke at the hundred metres, what's senior school like – is Mr Hawks really that strict? I shouldn't listen, but I can't tear myself away, I can hear Jesse's replies as much as Finn can, I'm sure of it. And when he finally leaves Jesse's room, the shrine that I have kept for us, he wipes at tears.

"Love you."

"I know. Can I do his pens-n-stuff, Mum?"

"NO!" The word has burst out of my mouth before I can swallow it away; it's slapped Finn's face so hard his eyes are prickling. I take a hard long breath, holding till it hurts, we must take the shrine with us, carefully piece by priceless piece. "Sorry. Good idea Finn. Label the box though, don't forget. Make sure it says Jesse."

It takes six boxes to hold everything Jesse owned, touched, in his room. To me that doesn't seem enough to hold sixteen years of life. I want more boxes to throw my thoughts and memories into – we've even packed his bin with the screwed-up homework, the inky mess from badly behaved pens, the torn school tie we argued about…

"If you think I'm buying another tie, think again. You can explain to Mr Hawks, that's your fifth this term and your mum won't get you another."

"Whatever," Jesse grunted, bored like a Catherine Tate caricature. He slammed the front door so hard it bounced back.

"Shut the bloody door," I'd shouted. What kind of sentence is that to follow you to school? I shake my head, make my brain a snow globe so none of the thoughts can settle and suffocate me. I move the boxes onto the landing. I don't want the stale-sweat tattoo men in here; they'll squash what's left of Jesse.

"You want to take this old carpet?" I would take the paper off his walls if I could move it in one piece. "Yes," is all I manage.

The removal men devour the Jesse boxes. They move too quickly, carry too much, the top box falls, I haven't stuck it down properly and the bin explodes, spewing crumpled paper.

"Hey, this is just rubbish!" the guy shouts, annoyed. I snatch the box back, stand the bin up. To me it's Ming, it's Spode, priceless. All the brave-face tape I glued myself together with when I got up this morning breaks. I know I'm shouting at this man. I see he can't understand why he needs to put these boxes back. He wants to be angry, to tell me to fuck off but he's getting cash in hand at double time. Finn is frightened. Andrew arrives two hours too late.

"Everything all right?" Andrew only ever asks this at the

point of crisis, when nothing, not one atom of the universe is all right. It has a twang of annoyance, a why-can't-you control-yourself ring to it. I walk away, leaving him to his removal men. Finn has collected up all the precious crumpled treasure from the landing and is carefully repacking the "Jesse's things" box.

Time is running out. Twelve o'clock is sneaking closer.

It feels like we're deserting. Maybe we should have done this at the dead of night. It would have felt more authentic. Andrew is ironing and smoothing out problems; like Finn, he can't contain his excitement. He's itching to start our "new life".

"Happy?" He's holding the tops of my arms and I can tell by the squeeze that he doesn't want to know my true answer. He makes it sounds like more of a command: hit your jolly switch now. Pack away your troubles. Forget all about it. Count to ten and start again. I realise my staring is confusing him, but I can't believe that this is the person I have travelled through this year-long horror with, this whistle-while-you-work man. "Too late for second thoughts, come on, pack the last few things and we can get cracking." I pull hard from his grip; walk away, leaving him in the echo-chamber living room. The front door is irresistibly open; my feet don't want to stop so I walk on out. I have no idea where they are taking me until I reach the park, the bench: Jesse's place.

The After Place: after the row over the night before, after the first party, the first home late, always I found Jesse here. Sitting on this bench, kicking old fag butts and dust. And after Jazzy, their first break-up, his first broken heart, the only chance he had at heartbreak. I sit at one end to make space for his memory, there won't be these places in our "new life", places where Jesse was, where he is. I can feel his warmth coming up through the graffiti-gouged wood. His gum might be stuck under one of the planks I'm sitting on. He will have sat here and spat on the ground, boys do. There are blades of grass that have grown up through his saliva. I can't leave while he is still so fresh, so part of everything. Andrew doesn't understand, won't understand. He is glued to counselling guidelines, moving on, moving forward.

I am rooted to my home. I can't leave our child, leave all these places where he grew, these parks and streets that were his backdrop. I can look at the seesaw and watch him bounce up and down, and the roundabout where I can see him now, eyes closed, sitting in the middle then stumbling off like a drunk roaring with laughter at his crazy, lurching world. I come here every day to rewind, to relive the past, a past Andrew doesn't see. I can't leave. Andrew can.

And there, way across the picnic lawns, then the rugby pitches and the far wild grassland, my first, real home – Nana's house. It watches, broken and crumbling, sewn on to the edge of Marble Hill Park. With my eyes closed I watch her watching us, Jesse and me. I took him there so many times, and sat in the tangled garden telling him the fairytales that I made my childhood into, a total fiction that he adored. "Tell me more Mummy, more…" So I conjured up the magic potions Nana and I made together that turned nasty people into angels and pumpkins into coaches. She stands at the garden fence as she did every day waiting for me to come home from school. She waves goodbye. "Safe journey, Evie," she whispers, then turns and makes her way back up her garden to put on the kettle.

Andrew's voice travels across the open parkland. I can't hear what he's calling, just his angry sound. I don't have to hear the words: I know them, Alice-in-Wonderland-white-rabbit words: "We're late, we're late for a very important date." Jesse smirks, giving me the strength to open my eyes; he melts from beside me into the air, the trees, the dust at my feet.

Andrew's run out of patience. "Evelyn!" My mother used to snap my name off in full when she was angry.

"I know, I know, I'm sorry, I'm coming. I just had to say goodbye."

"To a bloody bench?"

"Yes to a bloody bench, and to the park and the fucking swings." The "fuck" was unnecessary but it did at least change his tone; stoke his anger. He's easier to fight angry. "What's the point of all this Evie? We've talked about this – you agreed to this – *you* said you wanted this, for Christ's sake." Actually *he said* I wanted it – *he said* I agreed to it. I just went along for the ride, said nothing, did nothing, hid and hoped it would all go away. "Stop being so selfish. Finn is waiting and the removal guys. Owen from—" I mute him, getting up from the bench, and snatch a brave daisy sprouting in the dust.

"Bye," I whisper. A breeze rustles paper leaves, let's pretend its Jesse waving us off. Andrew's Blackberry rings, he's back in demand, the space for last-minute fears disappears.

9

It's quarter to twelve, ping. Time is up.

We walk back up the road to the house. Our life sits swallowed up by an articulated Red Dragon. It says it's in safe hands, it says it right across the length of the lorry, Red Dragon Removals: *You're in safe hands*. The "safe hands", Big Dave and his crew, sit on the kerb drinking coke and chewing pasties from Willow's café. The café is just round the corner, most mornings it's wrapped in a scarf of hungry commuters. Willow runs it, the girl I sat beside the first day at school, stood beside the first day at ballet, stood behind in the sixth-form show. It was her dream, the café, the food, feeding people, so I shared that too. I made cakes, sometimes just ones for lunch but there were special orders as well, towers of icing and tiny little flower buds, sugar sculptures I could spend a lifetime spinning, and then I made the pasties. I used to make them every morning; traditional, curried or vegetarian. They sold out by nine o'clock. "I need two of you," Willow always chuckled. It's been a year since I made a pasty, since I made anything. I think of Willow baking on her own, singing along to all our Abba tunes, dancing by herself.

Fearless pigeons peck the pastry confetti at the removal men's feet. "Time to go…" is written in the air, in the dust on the windows, across the faces of Andrew, Finn, Big Dave and his safe hands. I have to do my "one last time" thing, Finn holds onto my arm to make sure I come back out. The house has become just a building – the home has been removed from it. Our steps echo in the hallway, the living room has glitter air; dust motes sparkling in the sun's beams. The kitchen doorway is dented with a height chart of

10

memories, I run my hand over the new-bike-for-Christmas gouge that's so deep the wood has splintered, a slither slides into my finger tip, the pin-point pain intensifying the memory. In panic I wrap my fingers around the wooden frame pulling to see if it will come away with me. Will I remember all these things, these tiny small details of our life without it there as a reminder?

It's stuck. It stays.

Standing at the foot of the beautiful shining stairs, my feet stall. I can't place them in the dusty prints of Big Dave. Too many rooms, too much life lived up there. Babies made, nurseries repainted into teen pads, dens, private keep outs. Arguments that burst into flaming rows doused and soothed away, a life cycle of two becomes three, four, becomes three, finally stops spinning. Someone else's history can be written on our walls because ours has been taken down, rubbed out. Finn tugs, I walk out backwards, eyes never leaving the top stair. I really can see Jesse, he's still standing there in a sloppy melting school uniform that slides from his shoulders, hangs from his hips.

"Don't worry, Mum, he'll come." Finn tries to reassure me.

"You think so?"

"Course."

Andrew is sitting in his snarling new 4x4. He does that watch-checking thing at twenty second intervals. Big Dave and his eight-wheeled red dragon roar into life, Finn and I stand in the road to wave them off.

There's a car sitting at the end of the street, it's trying not to be there, squeezed up tight to the kerb. I recognise them, her watch checks synchronised with Andrew's. The people who offered the asking price. She measured our windows, wanted bits of our furniture that weren't for sale because she liked our taste. She had those Barbie nails with tappy white ends, her kitten heels made the same sound as her fingertips. Eventually, she told us, Jesse's room would have to be the nursery; her husband shrank a little further as he followed her. I wonder if legally our house is now theirs.

"Time to go, guys," Andrew shouts out of his window.

"Coming," I reply, taking a deep steadying breath, the fumey air carries a deep hit of burnt garlic. The Indian is starting early today. The thought of curry lurches my stomach. The smell claws the inside of my nose, making a bitter taste. I want to spit.

"They've burnt the korma," I say to Finn (korma is his favourite, passanda for Jesse. I used to have the biriani, but I have Jesse's passanda now, otherwise the order looks all wrong.) Finn frowns, uncomprehending.

"What korma?"

"Can't you smell it, that burning smell?"

"You've lost it, Mum. Come on, Dad's about to blow." Turning our back on 34 Basset Gardens, we walk towards the car. A man-sized schoolboy nods as we pass him, his uniform the same as Jesse's was.

"See ya, Finn," he grunts and catches my eye, not sure what to say. There are two more boy-men and a girl imitating a goth-prostitute in the same uniform standing on the other side of the road watching us, watching Andrew in the car.

12

"Is it lunch time or something at school, at Jesse's old school I mean?"

Finn shakes his head. "Think they've come to say goodbye," he mutters.

"Goodbye? But we don't know them, do we – do you?"

"They know Jesse."

Four more teenagers amble down our road, they stand awkward and silent. Finn nods behind me to the other end of Basset Gardens: there are more of them, too many to count in a glance.

"Guys…" Andrew's past impatient.

"Wait Andrew, just a minute. Look."

He sees the uniforms ahead of him and filling his rearview mirror. "It's a bloody riot! This place is going seriously down…"

"Shh. They've come to say goodbye." I nod across the street: the goth-prostitute gives a small shy wave. I don't know what to say, which words to choose: See ya, goodbye, thank you.

"Thank you," I whisper up and down our road. "How did they know we were going today, Finn?"

"It's posted on Jesse's wall."

"His wall?"

"It's a computer thing, Mum, you won't get it."

The computer thing – I do get it.

Andrew revs up his monster as if a quick getaway is needed. The curtains at number 13 twitch in anticipation. I watch in the side mirror as we pull away. It seems as if a black wave

13

follows behind us and I'm sure that there, surfing down the middle of it, is Jesse.

Chapter Two

She *so* doesn't get it. She doesn't get *any-fuckin-thing*, not computers, not me, not movin', not Dad – most of all not me. It was all OK before – well almost, I mean she drunk, got all loud and lairy, then woke up messy sometimes, but now ... now Dad's the invisible man and she's ... she's rubbish. Like yesterday she was makin' tea and spilt the peas, they went everywhere – and that's her, bits of Mum everywhere. She sat there in the mess, not movin', not even cryin' – might've been another one of her blackouts, an' I thought, I don't care! Get up and be my mum again! It's not just Jesse that's gone, he's taken them all with him. Left me here alone, where everyone mopes about because we're all too sad to do stuff anymore.

So the thing I don't get is this movin' right. Isn't it like runnin' away? Everyone knows what happened, they all know Jesse's dead, so what's the problem? OK, get a new house here, in a new road, one without a Jesse's room maybe, but, like, go away, really away, I mean who knows anyone in Wales? I don't. And they can stick learnin' Welsh, or rugby. I guess there, though, no one's gonna keep asking how I am, how I'm feeling. No one there will know about Jesse, or give a shit about me.

The only thing that's quite cool is everyone sayin' goodbye and stuff, cos nuffin else about the stupid idea is. I mean I lose my brother so my parents think that losing everythin' else – like my friends and a place in the U11s' squad is going to make everythin' all right – dim or what. Anyhow, I now have 856 friends on facebook which is 302 more than Luke. I mean do they even *have* internet in Wales? Cos I have 856 people to message and I'm *not* writin' postcards. Bet you can't even download a film or anything. Wonder who Luke will be partners with in PE – wonder who I'll be partners with.

Shit! You should see the size of the lorry they're gonna move all our stuff in. It's definitely gonna block the road.

"Mum, they're here!" I gotta go see this.

Chapter three

I check my wing mirror again. The uniforms have gone.

"What are you looking for?" Andrew is edgy, in a middle-of-a-work-crisis mood.

The reflection of the final black shape dissolved around the last service station. I was just trying to decipher its outline, certain it was Jesse-shaped when Finn asked: "Leigh Delamere, is that French? It sounds French."

"Epic fail, Finn! We're in England, moron."

I waited for Finn to retaliate but, of course, half the conversation – the Jesse half – is in my head. Despite all of it, every little pain and loss and all that is rushing behind and away from us, I smile.

"Oh Finn! Leigh Delamere is English."

"Yeah? But it sounds French."

"You think?" Then he's gone, back to his buzz of DVDs, Nintendos and iPods.

Andrew mistakes my smirk. "Getting excited?" He glances over at me, relieved. I wish I could reach across the vast void of gear stick and handbrake to pat his knee and say, yes. He flaps a map onto my knees, gesticulating toward the Irish Sea. Outside the air is greying, the grass throbbing greener. We soar over the bridge crossing the Severn Estuary.

Hands-free, Andrew thanks the under secretary for persuading an over secretary to scrape and grovel to a minister. It's all double speak, a dialect Andrew works in at his precious Attorney General's Office, his true home and the place he'd rather be more than anywhere else on the face of the earth. Place names flash bilingually past. The chimneys of Port Talbot grab the clouds, pulling them down over their ears. The weather is paused on imminent downpour. Swansea crowds up and along the hillside to Llanelli, so many L's, in an endless grim row of two-up-two-downs. At Carmarthen, bricks run out, people stop living and only hardy farmers hide out in scattered dour stone heaps that collapse into rusted barns. Green intensifies, growing over everything with only a tiny snow shower of sheep here and there. And onwards still to a point where your toes are almost dangling in the Irish Sea and you can wave back to the Statue of Liberty. "Not much further…" Andrew mouths as Whitehall calls again.

"Are we there yet?" Finn shouts over something that's booming and destroying his hearing.

"Not yet." He's doing well – I make that only the eighteenth time he's asked, that's once every ten miles, once every ten minutes. He goes back to the rumble.

The place names are lengthening, the interruption of fields growing. Pembrokeshire welcomes us. Everything is narrowing, the roads, the daylight, the horizon.

The cat is sick.

The smell is so bad that Finn is sick. And then so am I. Andrew, who struggles with other people's bodily fluids hurries on until he and the sat-nav agree we are there. Almost. We scramble from the stench in the car into air so wet you can't see through it.

We are truly nowhere.

Have we fallen through a hole and landed in infinity, or maybe beyond? There is no view apart from an occasional tree claw that looms overhead when the thick air splits for a moment. Silence presses in hard, no traffic, no planes, people, buildings, everything has been absorbed into this absolute nothingness.

Eurig-the-Estate-Agent should be waiting for us with keys at the entrance to a lane, down the bottom of which waits our new life. A swift call made balancing on top of a log pile to catch a tiny wisp of signal clarifies that Eurig works Thursdays – it's Wednesday, he's at the cattle mart Wednesdays.

Andrew and I juggle his impatience and my urge to retreat. I can wait, find a B&B, go back. He can't. He needs those keys tight in his hand.

"Come on. Let's take a chance!" He's in the car before the end of his sentence.

The engine roars, decision made. Home, here we come. In rollercoaster fashion we tip steeply downhill on the dirt track. Down we bounce. To the right and down again. Sharply left, a steeper drop.

"Slow down, Andrew!" But he can't hear; he's fired with the race to the bottom of wherever we're heading.

Rocking and rumbling we fly down through a tunnel of trees, woods dripping the same slate gray as the track we're trying to stick to. Finn is gripping the back of my seat, his face pressed into the gap between me and his father, his expression says he's waiting for the greatest surprise he's ever seen. After three or four more veers to the left and right our tyres crunch on gravel.

"We're here – Pengarrow!" Andrew shouts into the collecting silence.

We're where? None of this is as before, as I remember the place from the house details or our viewing. The mist swirls open for a moment and a white cliff of a wall looms over us.

"Cool!" Finn erupts from the car and is swallowed by the air.

"Don't go far." I warn him but already he's dissolving. The cat escapes its basket and vanishes into the thick air before I can grab it. How is it ever going to find its way back, when it has no idea where back is?

The mist is so wet it lies over our faces and hands, picking up the hairs and leaving tiny beads. Finn is running and whooping, somewhere to the right of me. The air hangs with the pungent smell of garlic as if we've towed the curry house behind us, I can hear Jesse coming in from football and inhaling as he opens the front door "Can we have a curry tonight, Mum?" My heart skips a beat.

"Jess?" I call out to him. Has he come all this way with a memory of home?

Chapter four

D'ya want a look round? Come on I'll show you – it's cool!

See, my room, it's up these stairs here. There's stairs everywhere. This is the cellar, spooky, and up there's something else I don't even remember! No, not in there, that's Dad's room, get this, it's got a full-size snooker table. *Full size*! We had a go last night and my feet came off the ground when I went for the black – Dad said that was cheatin', said you gotta be real careful of the green maize.

Look in here, see, if I run fast I can slide the *whole* room on my knees. Have a go. Couldn't do that in our old livin' room. It's bigger than the whole of our old house put together. Our Christmas tree will be *massive* this year!

Come up here. Watch that step, it creaks – bit creepy, listen. So that one there is Mum and Dad's room, that's Jesse's and this, yeah, this is all mine, check it *out*!

"Finn!"

Gotta go – Mum's yelling. But up there's the attic, have a look if you want. It's gonna be my den. Mum thinks it's haunted but it's not, just Jess and me muckin' around that's all.

"Finn!"

This place! It devours you voice-first. Where's he gone now? I need him on a string; he's in and out and round and round all day long! Me? I'm overwhelmed, intimidated, bewildered, I can't take my pick. Last time I saw the house it was someone else's home, a bad taste place oozing sage green and old nicotine. Now it's doubled, trebled in size, even filled with all the boxes. Someone tell me, point me at a place to begin. Inside or out? The gardens have us surrounded, green closing in on all sides. Branches shooting their claws out, reaching to tickle and tap on windows, primroses explode from flagstones in the front, and there's an overgrown tangle of greenhouses, orchards, vegetable patches and herb gardens creeping and climbing out back.

Who's going to cut all that grass?

There are sheds spawning sheds awaiting mechanical man things; their doors flung open, hungrily demanding quads, ride-ons, strimmers, chainsaws – the ancient smell of two-stroke oil hangs like bad breath about them. Andrew's shopping list grows by the hour. And outbuildings, garages and barns, like a script description from *The Archers*. Why do we suddenly need all these buildings? We've managed for years with a house, a bike shed and a prayer for a parking space outside our front door. All this as far as the eye can see stuff, is ours, how ridiculous, insane: three small humans occupying one side of a valley, almost. I want our old house back; that was my home, not this, Andrew's vision of Utopia.

I hear Finn now. He's doing that sliding thing again down the empty living-room floor, his knees are red raw, jeans threadbare. Andrew and Finn seem in their very own version of heaven. I hear it in their sighs as they race up and down the staircases. The weight of the grief and memories left behind in London has lifted from them. Finn has found a den in the attic, which to me looks like a perfect hang-out for ghosts. But then this whole place echoes, it's empty and will be even when I have unpacked every last teaspoon.

And me? I still carry all the cares from last year and cannot let go of one. The only space that doesn't feel empty is the airing cupboard – the only cosy place I can find. Inside there's that smell, that fresh-from-outdoors with a hit of scorched cotton. That's just how Nana's kitchen smelled on washing day, the radio playing Vera Lynn *We'll meet again*... as she steamed up the kitchen. "Fancy a cuppa dear?" she would say at around 11, and in would come Papa magically summoned by the kettle, lighting his morning pipe puffing blue smoke into the steam. I sat on the high, high, be careful, red stool that stuck to the backs of your legs in the summer. We had coffee in beautiful, translucent, palest pink teacups – the last three of the set – wedding present Nana said, blown up by the bomb that hit Marble Hill Park.

That's how I feel in here, in the airing cupboard at Pengarrow, Nana-safe, cosy curl-up warm. The walls are lined with ancient timber shelves and in between you can read the story of this house in layers of old wallpaper and patches of paint from antique chalky palettes, little swatches of history. Just inside the door a list is pasted to the wall ticking off all that should be stored here, in elderly spidery writing no longer legible. Our bedding has been unpacked, ordered and stacked, pillowcases on the highest shelf, then sheets, duvet covers, towels, and on the other side table-cloths, odd napkins, no sets, just as if they too had been blown up in the war, only single survivors making it. Everything looking pressed, sharp edged and neat. I brush my hand over Finn's Arsenal duvet cover; it feels warm, just ironed and when I smell it fresh-outside is trapped in the fibres and the light scorch is still there. I could never get that smell in London, that cleanness.

"Evie, Evie!" Andrew's voice pushes under the door of my hideaway. Reluctantly I get up off a stool that's been used as a step for the highest shelf (pillowcase shelf) for generations, the backs of my legs stick to it. "Be careful you don't fall," Nana whispers as I open the door. My shoulder brushes the old list, the bottom three entries tear off and flutter in sycamore helicopter circles to the floor. I pick it up, trying to unpick the loops and swirls but all I can make out is "linen 28".

"Evie? Evie, where are you?" Andrew's feet on the stairs get louder.

"Here. I'm up here. Thanks for sorting all the laundry."

"The what?"

"The laundry, the washing – the ironing."

"*Washing*? Haven't even found the machine yet, let's do that next, thought we could make a start in our room, at least get the bed up. Can't face the airbeds for another night – back's killing me!"

"So the sheets, the towels and stuff…?"

"Not guilty." His phone rings. He moves over to the window, to find a signal or for privacy I can't tell. "OK, OK," he assures the caller, anxiously glancing in my direction; he's going to break another promise, I can feel it. Ending the call he turns to me. His face is flushed; it's the colour it goes when he's about to lie.

"Look Evie, I'm really sorry but that was the Attorney

General – another crisis. I'm going to have to go back to London in the morning."

"But you've got the week off. You booked it."

"I know. Hopefully I can iron out the issues and be back by Thursday, Friday at the latest."

"Friday!" The awfulness of this vast, vacant house towering in cardboard boxes for three days with only Finn and me bumping around is too grim to look at. But Andrew is in demand, in his favourite place, back amongst the happening.

"So, the bed?" He wields a power tool revving its motor, silencing me. At any moment he'll jump, feet wide apart, point at a spot between my eyes and grasping his "piece" with both hands, demand I make his day. When did Andrew ever use a drill? He gets people in to do that sort of thing.

"Evie? Evie?"

"Mmm." I'm sulking. For the first time in a long time I don't want him to go. I'm jealous of his freedom to dip in and out of this rural idyll. I can't believe that after only three days he has managed to worm his way out.

"Yeah, yeah the bed, it sounds like a plan."

I follow him and his weapon of choice up the ever-increasing staircase, three quarters of the way up, and I can feel a tightening burn at the top of my thighs. Our door has already been thoughtfully fitted with an authentic spooky creak – the floor lurches away from you sober or drunk, moaning and groaning at the centuries of footsteps it's had to endure.

"Ok, grab this – looks simple enough." With a rev of his

drill we're off, no instructions, just free-styling into a bed shape. After twenty minutes of finger-gouged swearing, the headboard is the bed-end, which is upside down, three bolts and a mattress are missing.

"It's four hours to London – we could come with you, leave now and we'd all be there for dinner."

"That's not helping, Evelyn."

I know, but my headache is back, and that awful burnt smell, can't even blame the Taj takeaway at the other end of the M4. If this is the smell of the country, give me back smog.

"I need Paracetamol."

As I reach the door, Andrew drawls, in his best American accent: "Hey, Evie!"

I turn, he's doing his *Dirty Harry* impression, feet wide, arms straight in front "Make my—"

"No."

"Why don't you see if you can find the box with your sense of humour in while you're down there," he calls after me.

"I've looked, but all I can find is the one full of bad ideas," I yell back at him but his drill is already revving.

The afternoon deteriorates into snipes and angry silence. Andrew's pissed off with DIY and its obsession with detail and small parts; applying his global overview skills fails on all levels. The mattress is lost. But Paracetamol are discovered hiding with the cooking brandy. By four it's unbearable. Andrew makes a very poor performance of yet more office catastrophes and ministerial tantrums that haul his

31

departure from tomorrow into now. I almost believe him, until he can be heard disappearing down the hallway suggesting Ottolenghi's for supper with his father.

"Dad's going, isn't he?" Finn is trying very hard not to be concerned. His voice hits every note of unsure.

"He's got to go back to London, love, see Granddad and work." I can't offer much we'll-be-ok, it'll-be-fun-camping-out-in-upside-down, mattressless-beds.

"Are we going with him?"

I shake my head. "He'll be back by Friday," I cross my fingers as I say this, praying this isn't the beginnings of a weekend-only Andrew. I slop cooking brandy into a mug and down three Paracetamol. "So where shall we sleep tonight, your place or mine, Finn?"

"Mine, mine! Sleep in my room, I'll go on the floor, if you want." Our relief at a good suggestion is equal. I take another swig from my teacup. Something is working, the alcohol, the tablets or Andrew's imminent departure I can't say, but the pain in the centre of my brain has turned into a low, almost comforting hum.

"OK, guys," Andrew breaks our little peace. "Got to make tracks. I've left a list of numbers on the table, you know, take-aways, doctors…"

"Take-aways?" A vision of the little wobbly Domino's Pizza boy on his dropped moped stumbles through my mind. "No one's going to deliver down here, and you have the car, I would say that makes us stuck as far as fast food is concerned."

"I've got a hire car being delivered in the morning,

remember – it's easy, automatic, please don't make this any more difficult. It's not my fault – and it's only for a few days." All of this is, of course, his fault. There are off buttons on mobiles – they are put there for family time, when work should take the hint and sod off. "Look I could call Mother, she could stay for a bit."

"No." No, no, no.

"She did offer."

Finn's face bleaches of colour. I can feel sweat.

"We'll be fine."

Andrew's face cracks into smiling relief, his ultimate deterrent wins yet again. One day I will be brave enough to face him down. That woman would never have three back-to-back days available at twenty-four hours' notice, it would be considered a social faux pas. Andrew scatters ill-targeted kisses and attempts not to rush out the door, throwing worthless phrases into the air.

"Look, just call if you need me back. I'll come straight away. Call the office number, you can always get me on that."

I have never once succeeded in contacting him on his office number; Caroline rules the telephone lines, and as she always explains, Andrew is busy, unavailable, and cuts me off before I've even managed a "good morning". We don't do small talk, Caroline and I. We maintain our hatred for each other. I married her Andrew although she gets to occupy most of his waking hours. Stalemate. I am walking back inside the house before his wheels begin to munch on gravel. Disgust is lurking somewhere with "you bastard".

Through the kitchen window I can see Finn still sat on the wall watching where Andrew left, the image heartbreaking.

"Hey, honey," I shout out of the window, "let's find something to cook and something to cook on." There's some excitement in my words that reach through his gloom, a switch is flicked and in he runs with all kinds of ridiculous solutions to our mini famine. I laugh, thinking back to Willow's café with all its organic wholesomeness. What would Willow think of me now? I couldn't face sorting everything in London, just packing it was a mountain to climb, so we're left with all the things I should've thrown out and nothing that we really need. Having never tried out-of-date Pot Noodle, frankfurters and processed cheese, with digestive and Nutella sandwiches to follow, I am surprised by how filling they are, and how quickly indigestion sets in. But then there was still one Christmas-pudding's worth of cooking brandy to soothe away the burn.

Chapter five

"*We'll meet again, don't know where, don't know when…*"

"Shhh, Mum," Finn murmurs, his voice thick from just this side of awake. I thought the song was in my head, music to fall asleep to.

"*Just close your eyes, Evie.*" Sleeping beside Finn has been our best decision since arriving; we feel secure, you can hear it in our breathing.

As we finally gave up on the day, abandoning the kitchen and the chaos exploded over it, we creaked upstairs, discovering two erected beds, both the right way up and made, just waiting to tuck us in. I turn my Andrew anger down to mute. But out of spite Finn and I drag mattresses, duvets, sheets and pillows up to his attic den.

Now all I need is for sleep to wash over me – the "on" switched off. That's where the song came in. The theme tune to night time, to lying awake waiting for someone to come home: the sound of Jesse's key in the front door, a slurred "Home Mum"; Andrew cursing as he trips over shoes in the early hours, my ma's heels clicking down the hall tiles. "Don't worry dear, she'll be back by morning," Nana would whisper as her cool, soothing hand stroked the hair from my forehead. "Your ma will be here by morning, you'll see."

"*Don't know where, don't know when…*" Nana hums on in an attempt to chase away my nightmares, but…

*

Once again the doorbell rings with the sound of the school break bell. The clock on the mantel ticks gameshow loud, counting down, running out. The break bell clangs again. I'm late.

"Mum, hurry!" Finn's face green and pressed against the coloured glass of the front door. *"Hurry!"* he calls.

"Slow down, Evie." Andrew's voice drawls behind me from a vast armchair at the dark end of the hallway.

"Help me, Andrew, the door, I can't open it." The tempo of the clock tick-tocks faster.

"In a minute, but we need to talk, listen…" Always I need to listen, but today there's no time, Finn knocks frantically to the beat of the count down.

"Mum, hurry!" I pull and pull. Andrew raises himself from the chair, frame by slow-motion frame. He holds out the key which, inch-by-inch, slides into its lock, the other unused keys jangling in excitement.

"Mum, quick!" It's almost impossible to squeeze past Andrew; the front garden has fallen away from the path, only a narrow beam stretches to the gate, so thin that my foot overhangs. Chips from the terracotta tiles crumble into the void that is sucking me down. The fence has been swallowed, there's nothing to grab for balance. On elastic the distance from door to gate has been horrifically stretched. I know the only way is to run and hope speed will carry me across the tightrope. Fear shakes the muscles above my knees.

"Faster, Mum, faster!" Finn is already on the other side of the gate, he flicks the latch, clinking metal against metal, louder and louder. He shouts over the clinking chinking: *"It's Jesse, Mum, it's Jesse…"*

My eyes snap open but the power is down to the rest of my body. The room, bed, heavy breathing beside me make no sense. Somewhere an emergency generator kicks in and feeling is instantly restored with a thump to my brain and in a slow buzz to my limbs. The deep breathing: Finn. The room: Finn's den. The thumping head: cooking brandy, but the chinking sound? Morning sunlight rudely pokes through the curtains. Grabbing yesterday's jumper from the heap on the floor, I pad downstairs, hop-scotching the creaky ones. I stop stunned in the hallway – there is a woman standing at my kitchen sink, elbow-deep in yesterday's pans, plates and glued-on cheese.

The woman at the sink has appeared from nowhere, a bit like the cat, which has returned and now sits at her feet.

My head's still humming a cheap brandy tune but I'm sure there wasn't a knock or a doorbell, just that metal china chink, the sound that broke into my dreaming dragging me from the nightmare. It made me think of weekends; it's the sound Andrew made in the kitchen when it was my turn to get up with the kids and I was too hung over to wake up. Andrew's back, that's what I was hoping as I came downstairs.

I know last night I locked the front door, back door, side and cellar door along with anything else that had a bolt, latch or catch. I did. I know I did. I had key-into-keyhole trouble, the last glass, one way too many. Finn followed me, glued, just in case, though both of us were absolutely not scared in the least. Of course this woman at my sink might have her own set of keys. But why? Some long-established arrangement; did we purchase home, land and a housekeeper? Or, no, it'll be Andrew interfering from two hundred miles away. I bet he's thinking, "She can't cope, let's send in the cavalry." I can cope, we can cope, Finn and I aren't bothered by a pile of dirty dishes.

Except, the woman in my sink – she's bothered.

She doesn't hear me; scrubs on, humming, swaying slightly, wafting wood-smoke and earth into the air. I stand, stunned, waiting for words to come, to be said. She works around the chaotic kitchen that's half lived-in, half just arrived with endless, secretly multiplying boxes in the way, waiting to trip you up. Except that this morning, with the sun floodlighting through the windows, the room now has a hint of home. It has warmth. It's waiting for pans and boiling, slicing and dicing. It's hungry for stew and soup and first thing in the morning loaves. The fire is burning. Some books have got themselves organised and found a shelf.

Her hair hangs in a red rope down her spine, escaping from a dirty scarf. The elbows that pump the water are raw and exposed from sleeves pushed up high. The tune she hums is so familiar, painfully I dig and delve to know where from. She's clothed in a whole family's wardrobe all tied up with a belt stopping any layer escaping; everything looks a hundred years old, worn to breaking point, repaired then worn out again. A heap of a person the colour of dead leaves.

Where the hell did she come from?

Why is she in our kitchen?

A burst of thunder rolls down the stairs behind me, and with failing brakes Finn crashes into my back, multi-tasking on his iPod. He'd not expected a road block in the kitchen doorway. He wriggles under my elbow into the room and

39

stops. His noise seems not to disturb the woman at the sink; it's as if we aren't here but are ghosts that she's unaware of. Finn stares, sucking her image into his brain, none of her makes any sense to him either. Eventually he turns to me and I read the "Where did she come from?" that shouts from his silent, mesmerised face. Shaking my head and shrugging is the only soundless answer I can offer him. He leans back against me, his warmth crossing over. I rest my chin on the top of his head, surprised again how little I have to stoop. His scalp smells of sleep and freshly washed bedding, I wrap my arms across his chest and we watch this woman, an illustration ripped from an old book and pasted into our kitchen.

Finn hums her song. I can feel the tune through my teeth from my jawbone resting on his skull. The woman at the sink and my little boy softly hum a song I know inside out and can't find anywhere.

She pauses for a moment, we hold our breath, maybe at last she'll join us. She looks towards us, but it's not us she's watching it's something out of the window, the wind-rosey skin at the corner of her eyes pleats as she smiles. She waves, dries her hand on her skirts, grabs something matted and knitted from the back of a kitchen chair and leaves through the back door, the one I locked last night. Freed from our spot we rush to the window. My heart grabs hold of the next beat painfully. Sink Woman links arms with a golden-haired man-boy. He's dressed up to play soldiers, uncomfortable in the dirty green serge uniform that hangs from him. His face is gaunt, pain streaked, twitching anxiously like a cornered wild animal. He attempts a laugh; it sounds so like Jesse's –

broken and unsure of which octave to aim at. They hug hard, then hurry off toward the nearby wood, Sink woman, our cat and a haunted image of my Jesse.

"Jesse?" Finn's voice is little more than a whisper, a flabbergasted whisper.

Chapter six

"*Mum*," I yelled. "Mum, c'mon quickly. They're goin'!"

"Jesse!" I called him. "Wait for me, Jess. *WAIT*." But Mum didn't come. He didn't wait. Mum's never quick enough. Never hears. Always turns up too late, too late to follow Jesse and that woman, the one from our kitchen.

It's like that first time I saw Jess again. I thought he'd been hangin' around at home – but every time I turned round – nuffin' there. Maybe he was just sussing me out. I mean it was only doors and lame stunts like that. Oh and nickin' my pens, hiding my homework – you know, just usual Jesse stuff. Well, we were walkin' along the towpath by Marble Hill Park, me and Mum. I was looking for river rats, the gross black ones Mum hates. Anyway, so she was talking on and on about stuff, I wasnt listenin', and when I looked in the park there he was sittin' on the swing, just like he always did, same swing, same everythin'! Once me and Jess had this competition on those swings to see who could swing right round and over the top. He looked weird on his own with none of his mates, just swinging real slow waitin' for me.

"I'm comin' Jess!" I shouted. It was definitely him. I ran fast as I could, I checked Mum was followin, but she was standin' watchin' me instead of looking at him. When I turned back, Jess'd left already.

Just gone, why didn't he wait for me? I called him...

Jesse was always like that. When we walked to school, Mum always told us, "Walk together along the main road." But he'd just go. I had to run to keep up.

Hey! Did you hear that? What the...? There it is again!

Wow, check that out, that's gotta be the biggest bird ever. What is it? So what was I saying, oh yeah, he's like Dad, walks fast, giant steps, I always have to run to keep up with him, but I don't walk much with Dad now, he's always workin'. I guess cos Jesse's not around Dad doesn't want to do the hikin' stuff any more. D'you reckon you could camp in the wood by Pengarrow? That would be so cool, Luke will love it. He's my mate in London, he's coming to stay in the summer, he asked his mum and she said OK. He texted last night. But it would've been cool to go with them – Dad and Jess. They went off camping, just on their own, I was too young, couldn't keep up with them. Well that's what Jess said. But like I said, if I run or walk really fast, I do keep up. I'd like to go campin' with Dad.

And then if Jazzy showed up on the way to school, well forget it. Jess really liked her. I mean *really, really* liked her. Mum *really* didn't. We came home from football trainin' once, Mum used to pick me an' Luke up. When we got home Jess-n-Jazzy were sittin on our wall, Luke said they'd been kissin' but I didn't see that. Jazzy starts askin' Mum who's she starin' at, don't think Jazzy knew we lived there too. Mum tried to be cool, but you know mums, they just aren't. She blanked Jazzy and told Jess to come inside. I was like thinkin' don't argue Jess, luckily Jazzy had to go otherwise things could've got messy, then it would've been all round school which would've been well embarassing.

Jazzy was in a gang. All her brothers were too – they were much older. They didn't like Jess, didn't like him likin' Jazzy. That's where the trouble started.

45

Dad warned him. He didn't like Jazzy much either. Anyway Jesse wouldn't listen and, like normal, our whole house turned into a war zone. Jess yellin' at Dad, sayin' stuff like he was racist and stuck up. And Dad tryin' not to shout back that he wasn't, and that it was all about "cultural differences", whatever. And Mum, well she yelled at Dad because she said Dad was "drivin Jesse away". She said we should ask Jazzy over, which was weird cos I thought Mum didn't like her, I mean Jazzy was well rude that time before. Mum wanted to "build bridges" she said, but I don't think Jazzy was into that kinda thing.

But that's what Jess always did. Turn up the volume all the time. Make everyone shout at everyone, even Grandma and Granddad. They were tryin' to make Jess go to Dad's old school. (Looked like the place from *Haunted Fang*, mine an' Luke's favourite film, well scary the first time you see it.) It cost mega bucks to go to this school and the uniform was well weird. And you lived there – only came home in the holidays, like prison really. Jess said there was no way he was goin' to that "shit-hole" to Granddad's face! But Granddad only told him not to be "narrow-minded" said he was "wasting his potential". That's the sort of thing Granddad goes on about all the time. Grandma tries to kiss and hug you loads and says stuff like "Darling how you've grown!" Jess does this wicked impression of her. I don't think Grandma and Granddad really get us, theyre stuck-up, in a nice way I mean, but you know? Granddad's on telly sometimes – in the borin' bits – news programmes and stuff.

No one said anything about me goin' away, not that I want to – but I don't want to waste my potential, if I've got it, you know, like Jess.

Wish Jess was here. I don't know how to do all this on my own, how I'm s'posed to handle Mum and Dad? Dad tries – but Mum never gets it, she always takes offence – like she wants to fight. I wish Jess never went to school that day, never went out with Jazzy. I want our old house back and my old school. And I want to know where Jesse has gone with that woman. I shouldn't have waited for Mum to come, shes so *dumb* sometimes.

"JESSE!"

Why didn't he wait for me?

"I MISS YOU!"

BREAD

4 oz yeast
2 Tabl s Dem Sugar   } mix + put in warm place to work.
½ pt. luke warm water }   USING DRIED YEAST

2 tablespoons BRAN.   } Put 50 gm of Yeast
1 bag wholemeal flr.   } ⅓/₄in ½ Tablespn Dem Sugar
+ white flr to 6 lbs   } FLR. 1 PT L W WATER
9 small teaspns salt   } Put in a bowl.
2-3 oz Lard.

add. Yeast. when frothy plus another 2½ pts warm water
mix with wooden spn until work able by hand.
keep folding over + pressing out until this is smooth.
Weigh up 1¾ lb for larger tins + 1½ for smaller tins — Greased
make into sausage shape.
Put in cold oven .... *Chapter seven* .... then change
loaves over top to bottom shelves. leave for another ½ hr.
If tops when tapped sound hollow, ie cooked at bottom
turn out onto rack

5. 1 lb oz flr.

knead

Stunned, I'm glued down to the ground in a freshly baked and abandoned room that's been astonishingly gathered up and sorted out, all the little "to-do"s done, cooked and washed up. This is a space we've passed through in the last few days, paused in for a while and completed some chores, but not yet a place I have taken ownership of, not a heart of this house. But this morning I see it's already owned, it's Sink Woman's space, an environment she's comfortable in. Things, our things, are where she wants them. Surely we were dreaming, seeing things? The last ten, maybe twenty minutes in this kitchen, was it all in our imagination? But this steaming mug of coffee planted on the table amongst papers, notes and a crumbling old book, the bread, warm, hacked into doorsteps waiting for the palest butter that's been scooped into a dish, the air so heavy with aromas that you can taste the flavours, these can't be imaginings. The crust is still warm – I'm chewing, swallowing.

"Mum!" Finn yells from outside, his voice is sharp and full of hurry up.

The song Sink Woman hummed hangs in the air like the smell of bread. I can't immediately work out where it's coming from. There's crackling and static sounds, it's my nana's radio! It's been dug out, dusted down, and now happily sings that, *Although it's heart is breaking, it's singing this cheery song*. That thing hasn't spoken in decades, I remember saying to Andrew that it died the day she did. He wanted it dumped, skipped, but I couldn't bear for it to go, too much of my childhood tangled up in its wiring. I was sure one day its voice would return. To me it's a sound that speaks of Nana and Papa and of their home; still around, even though they have gone. And now it's back with me again, my old friend, contentedly murmuring a melody.

The slate floor shines darkly wet, newly exposed by a tide of cleaning that has washed and scrubbed over every surface. Around the kitchen door footprints pad in two sizes. One set, Finn-sized, dash out of the backdoor, the other follows me over to the table. I move one foot to the other, repeating the pattern. Just two sizes of prints pressed to the floor when three different-sized feet have just walked here. How do you walk on a wet floor and leave no marks? Round and round reality my brain goes once again. Dreaming, real? Real, dreaming?

"Mum, c'mon they're going!" I know I need to go to him but I just want a moment, another line of song, a swallow of coffee, a bite of bread. This is so delicious, the taste of home, Nana made bread like this. Every Friday, breadmaking day, bowls of mushroom-plump dough idling in warms spots around her kitchen, a yeasty fug fermenting the air. If your hands were clean you could knead the dough, pummel and punch out all the week's disappointments. "As hard as you can now, Evie." Sometimes we made great giant loaves for Papa's cheese and pickle sandwiches, the sort he loved for his lunch down on the allotment. Other times Nana and I rolled round and around springy golf balls that puffed into soft, floppy baps – perfect for park picnics and feeding the pigeons. "Make sure they're all even now, Evie," Nana chivvied.

"Mum." Finn's voice barely pierces my reverie, I don't want to leave Nana's kitchen, I'm happy dreaming there. It's the place that's my home, where all my happy memories are kept. I want to scoop up Finn and take him back there with me now, stop him chasing after ghosts or angels or whatever these amazing people are who appeared from nowhere and don't leave footprints on wet floors. What kind of madness is this? I bury my head in my arms; it aches again.

"Mum, they're going." The bleakness in his voice finally rouses me.

"C'mon, Mum help him out," Jess whispers, his voice right there beside me. There's a warmth on my neck where his breath lasts. I reach into nothing to touch him and feel the coarse tangle of his hair, a slight grease on my finger tips. I draw in the emptiness to me hugging tightly, wanting to keep a bit to hand over to Finn to show him that Jesse still cares, still watches us. It's been so very long, such a long everlasting year, what I would give now to truly touch you, Jesse, just once more, just a last goodbye.

"Mum," Jess urges and I come back.

"OK, darling I'm going."

I take with me a handful of the air; somehow I will give this to Finn.

Finn is hanging over the big wooden gate that leads out and on into woods. He's pushing himself away from the post then gripping tight as he swings back with a destructive crash.

"JESSE! Wait for me."

"I MISS YOU."

It's unbearable, Finn's tone is the same as it was at the funeral.

"Don't take him!" Finn had sobbed as Andrew grabbed him tightly, stopping him running after Jesse's coffin.

"Bring him back Dad, *please*," Finn had begged. "*Please* bring him back." Finn dragged Andrew down with him to the ground, and he'd had to wrap Finn so tightly in his arms that he'd disappeared, only his begging sobs escaped, over and over. "Bring him back, don't take him." And from somewhere a deep guttural howl had risen above the people gathered there, hanging in the air, covering us all in despair. It wasn't until Andrew's mother pulled me from the yawning black mud hole that had swallowed my baby that I'd realised the howl was mine. In any quiet corner those words, "Bring him back," always poke sharply at my thoughts. I want to take Finn's grief, squash it into mine and smash it over and over like he's doing with the gate. I walk towards him, he glances down.

"Great timing Mum."

"They're gone?"

"What d'you think. He might've stopped if you'd called him. He never listens to me."

"Finn, that woman, Jesse, they can't be … they're not…"

"I *saw* him. I *saw* her. YOU, you saw them. Go on tell me you saw nothing … see you can't! So … so that means, it means something." He swings and smashes the gate again angrily.

"I just don't know, Finn. All this … this chasing Jess, it's just going to make it hurt again more – we'll be right back at the start and the pain will be as much as it was the day he died … I don't know who or what we saw."

But I know in my heart the truth is, it does hurt as much as the day he died, and even more than the day we buried him, it's a pain that is slowly intensifying as each significant date passes without him. The Jesse-shaped hole in our lives is growing and we are on the very edge of it about to fall in.

"I SAW Jesse."

"OK, OK, Finn."

"It was Jesse, Jesse hair, Jesse tall, Jesse's walk even. I saw him, and you saw him too, Mum."

"I … I saw something."

"You SAW Jesse!"

"Oh Finn, I want it to be Jess more than anything, more than anything in the world… C'mon sweetheart, smashing the gate's not the answer."

"But if he comes back I don't want to miss him."

"Finn, I think if he wants us to see him, then he'll come and find us."

"Do you?"

I cross my fingers in my pocket to help with my lie. "Course love. C'mon." I throw my arm round his shoulders, wishing he were three, four, five, then I could sweep him up and hold him squeezy-tight. I kiss the top of his head as we walk back up the path to the house, the sleepy bed smell is fading, his scalp is hot from his hurt and anger, his hair damp and musty.

"Want some toast?"

"OK. We got any chocolate spread?"

"Not sure, we need to get some supplies – maybe we could brave the village."

He doesn't bother with toast but grabs at the cut loaf on the table. "Mmmm, this is still warm, Mum. Tastes like the stuff Willow makes."

He scrapes a week's worth of butter over the slice, his bite mark perfectly preserved in the creamy pale spread.

"Ghosts don't make bread."

Taking another bite, I agree between chews, "They don't." I fish amongst the papers that have scattered on the table in front of us. They are yellowing, autumn-leaf notes. Some are brief messages, reminders, others addressed and dated, scrawled in the same way the laundry list in the airing cupboard is. This is someone's life fluttering before us, the ups and downs, forget-me-nots and to-dos. The scraps and notes have spilled from the old book tossed on the table, its pages are open half-wayish but flip back and forth undecided in the breeze from the open backdoor. Curious I pull it towards me, it settles, making a decision on a page marked 28th April. On one side there's what looks like a diary entry and on the other a remedy for headaches that makes my stomach churn. I thank the Lord for Ibuprofen. I read it aloud to Finn.

1 Sprig of lavender
3 Leaves of mint
Crushed root of ginger
Pinch of coriander seeds
  Half a quart of freshly boiled spring water

Steep ingredients in boiling water for ten minutes.
Strain the liquid through muslin discarding the herbs/seeds.
Sip the remaining liquid to cure the ache.

"All this needs is a leg of a newt and a wing of a bat – abracadabra, and we'll be able to turn pumpkins into fairy coaches!" I laugh.

"You need mice."

"What?"

"Mice. Mice make the footmen – remember? In that panto you made us go to – the mice turned into footmen." I smile, recalling the protests Finn, Jess and (come to think of it) Andrew had made about going. Christmas isn't Christmas without a panto, I told them, and dragged them off to Richmond Theatre to watch Cinderella. I think it was the Australian soap actress that held their attention not the whole "Behind you!" thing. It even snowed as we left. This year it was Jack and his beanstalk but we didn't seem to care if it was Christmas or not.

I turn my attention back to the book as Finn mutters off to get dressed. His speech is un-developing into teenage mumble. "April 15th" is scratched legibly across the opposite page but the handwriting underneath is an alien mess of tangled lines, thick and blotchy in places then worn to a hairline in others. Something obviously happened on that day as the first sentence ends in wild exclamations. There's excitement in the lines that make the marks; they're big and free. I can definitely make out "Came home" but the rest of it is a mystery.

The radio crackles and pops, hunting for a stronger signal. Briefly Chris Evans explodes into the room, "Right my friends, on this day in history…" static drowns him but he bobs back up, "So 15th April's quite an important day for all you…", and then silence, I'm left wondering what's so important about 15th April, because Chris Evans knows and so does the writer of this diary I'm trying to decipher. Finn is back; he looks much the same as when he left.

"Let's go to this village then, I'm ready."

I'm not.

After days of mist and rain the air in this spring sunshine is damp and heavy, the ground steams. The gradient of our track, now that we're walking it, feels close to vertical, I'm unsure that I'll make it up to the village. Hedges crowd over the path reaching out snagging brambles, bluebells push through primroses. We crunch upwards, Finn swipes at things with a stick he's found, slashed flower heads spray in his wake.

"When will Dad be back?"

"Definitely by the weekend, maybe even Friday night."

He slashes on. "And when does my new school start?"

"Monday next. One more week off. It's gone so fast – hasn't it?" He makes an indecipherable grunt.

"Are you looking forward to it?" He makes the same sound, it must mean shut up.

We meet three lolloping, curly dogs that remind me of a bunch of teenagers playing hooky. They check if we smell good – we don't, so they lope off. Minutes later a quad bike roars up and a wind-ruddy man enquires, "Seen any hounds?" We point him down hill – he tips his cap, blips the throttle and disappears, leaving us splattered.

We walk on – the lane bumps over a cattle grid joining a road, years of farm traffic and harsh frost have nibbled away at the edges of its ancient tarmac. A faded sign announces, *Llaneglwys Graban, winner of village in bloom 1978*. There isn't a flower in sight, the hedges are squared off viciously and the verges shorn.

The village is a triangle place, set around a road bent to accommodate a cenotaph, so that all the buildings can perpetually honour the dead. A tiny dark stone church waits for worshippers, its walls damp, moss greedily reaching up to its dead-eye windows. A store-come-Post-Office-come-garage faces across to a cracked and peeling pub that looks like the regulars forgot about it. A bypass takes life on to somewhere interesting while Llaneglwys Graban waits patiently for the last resident to turn out the lights, lock up and leave quietly.

"Well this is a hip and happening place. D'you think the queue will be too long in the shop?" I quip to Finn, but he's watching an old man who's walking towards us with an empty dog lead. The bent-over man is stubble rough, whippet lean.

"Heel, Brony." He snaps to the dangling lead and pulls at it sharply. "Hello, hello, I was just on my way down." He nods to the track some way behind us. A smile transforms his face into pleasant, friendly creases. I marvel at his ambition to walk down and up our track, certain he's incapable.

"Morgan." He holds out a crooked coarse hand. "Morgan the Milk they call me."

"Hello, Mr Morgan, I'm Evelyn Wolfe and this is my son Finn." I place my palm against his; he crushes my bones and lets go.

"Enough Brony, siT." He spits the T and snaps the lead again. Finn's face screams bewilderment. I babble on before Finn can ask about the invisible Brony.

"We've just moved into Pengarrow…"

"That's a big house for just the two of you is it?"

"Oh no, there's four – um – I mean three of us." My face burns at the error. "My husband works in London…"

"Ah, there we are then. That's a long way to go though, is it?"

Is it? There's not much to add to his statement, he's right it's too far. Morgan the Milk picks up a stick from the verge, waves it around then throws it. "Fetch, Brony," he urges empty space. "Stupid animal… So how's the old place?" He reads my confusion. "Pengarrow," he clarifies.

"Ummm, in a muddle at the moment! Boxes everywhere." He's not listening.

"Make sure you don't let that stove go out now – you got plenty of wood in?"

I'm not sure.

"Right! Well must be off. Promised my Merry I'd look in on the new folk moved into Pengarrow. My Merry says they're all the way from London town – more bloody foreigners I told her, thinking they has the right to move in an' take away what's ours! Still what's done is done, my Merry says. Long time ago now, what d'you think?"

I'm not sure how to answer, if he even needs my answer. "Quite right," he agrees with my silence. "Go careful now – mind the traffic – walking on these roads." Involuntarily Finn and I scan the deserted lane.

"Bye!" We shout to his back as he unsteadily rambles off down our lane.

"Does that make us the 'bloody foreigners'?" Finn whispers, relishing swearing.

"Possibly. D'ya think he'll be all right?" Finn shrugs a "how would I know" and we walk on the short distance into the village. The quad returns, the driver nods, three curly dogs jog beside him, heads hanging guiltily, and Morgan the Milk sits on the back swinging the empty lead with what looks like our cat on his lap. I watch Morgan the Milk turn and wave toward the church. I follow his gaze up to the open lych-gate where a woman with a rope of flame hair down her back and skirts the colour of autumn waves to him, then melts away between the gravestones.

"Was that Sink Woman?" I nudge Finn, hoping maybe to catch another glimpse of the Jesse look-alike that she had with her, but there's nothing to see.

1891

Chapter eight

ELDERFLOWER CHAMPAGNE

2 heads of elderflower   1 gallon water
1½ lb. white sugar   1 lemon
2 tablespoons white-wine vinegar

Pick the heads when in full bloom and put into a bowl followed
by the lemon juice, cut-up rind (no white pith), sugar and
vinegar. Add the cold water and leave twenty-four hours.

14
6. Elder flower
1½ lb. Sugar
3/lemons

The Post Office finds us! A jolly little van driven straight off the pages of a child's book appears. Finn rushes out to meet the postman as if he were expecting something.

"Hello, hello!" A Max-Boyce-look-alike booms from the open van window over the engine and a radio shouting the chorus of (*My, my, my,) Delilah*. I follow Finn at a slower pace, still munching bread and jam. For the third morning running a fresh loaf, butter and now jam were waiting for us when we got up, along with a fire in the grate and this morning some weird tea drink smelling of mint and ginger, that neither of us felt tempted to try. I feel like a wary Shoemaker's wife each day tiptoeing downstairs into a Grimm tale. I need to see our mysterious Sink Woman again, to hear her speak, just a 'Good morning', something audible, something to make our flame-haired Mary Poppins real. Last night I even left her a thank you Post-it. This morning it was gone just like her and the haunted Jess-look-a-like soldier boy. They've evaporated, Finn hunted every square inch of the house for them. I heard him earlier around six, trying to catch them.

"Is your Mam or Da in boy, I got something that needs signing for?" The postman gets out of his van, then notices me on the doorstep.

"Hello, hello!" he repeats

"Hello."

"I got a whole pile here, been waiting for you at the sortin' office, it has. Didn't realise you were here till Morgan the Milk told me. Hope it's nothing urgent!" He laughs, his grin splitting his face, his eyes disappearing. "So what d'you think of it? Nice to have someone back living in the old place after all that argy-bargy, it is."

I have no idea about the "argy-bargy", so I do a smiling shrug which he nods at vigorously, agreeing with me and handing over a pile of post for Andrew, all needing signatures.

"Well, if we ever manage to unpack all the boxes, it'll be great!" I add. "I didn't think it was empty though, I thought there was an old lady living here, the one that showed us around when we came down to have a look. You know, typical estate agents, double booked us, or something. It's a wonder they stay in business." His face is puzzled. Oh shit, I hope he doesn't know anyone in the business.

"Really? Now who was that then? No one's lived in Pengarrow for years now."

"Umm, I don't remember her name, she was really kind though, even made us tea and cake."

"Ah well, there we are then! Can't complain at that! Anyways, see you tomorrow then I expect." He expertly reverses the little van, zip, zip, spitting gravel and shooting off back up the lane.

Finn runs past me in the doorway with the mail hoard.

"Were you waiting for anything, love?" I'm surprised by his eagerness.

"Oh you know, something from Luke, or Dad, maybe." Luke would have face-spaced, if there was enough internet or whatever they do on phones and computers, Finn is hunting for something from Andrew because for this last year he's been Andrew's shadow, hovering a few centimetres from his elbow, constantly in the way. It's as if Finn can't let him out of his sight. I feel sick, Andrew isn't great with pen and paper, you're lucky to get *Ax* in a card, he's not one to ink in his feelings; my "stash" of love letters is nothing more than notes, backs of beer mats and un-sticky stickies.

"You could call him, Finn."

"What, Luke? Nah."

"No, Dad. I'm sure he'd really like to hear how you're doing."

"Maybe… Later." He starts to deal the letters. "Dad, Dad, Dad, he gets loads of stuff. That's for you, Dad, Dad… Ah, this is for me but I think it's from Grandma, look at the writing."

"What's she got to say?" I try to keep my voice light, stop myself from asking what the old witch is after now as he tears open the envelope.

"Umm, just wants to know about school, and errr, friends – have I met any, usual Grandma stuff." He puts on his impersonating Grandma voice, "Be a good boy, wash your hands, say please and thank you, wipe your bum, blah, blah, blah…"

"Finn." I warn, and know I should add that they love him very much and mean well, but I don't know if they do.

"She misses Jesse. She wrote to him and he wrote back, now she feels guilty and writes to me, but I'm not Jess." His statement sits blocking the air between us. "I'm going to sort my room. Can we fix the telly this afternoon, Arsenal are playing in the semis tonight?" He creaks upstairs not waiting for an answer. I pick up a photo of Andrew from a box

64

waiting to be unpacked, he's straight off a polo pony, windswept and exercise bright. "I need you, here, now," I tell the print. "You explain your bloody mother to our son, because I can't begin to." The picture has caught Andrew at the start of a smile, from memory I know that by the time he'd crossed the field and reached me he was laughing, full of victory. The grey hasn't begun at his temples and his forehead is a clean sheet, as yet uncreased by our life. This is my beautiful Andrew, the one I keep in my heart, waiting for his return.

I wonder if he does the same, holds the person I once was in *his* heart, hoping that I'll come back to him one morning without red-rimmed eyes, and this haggard face. That when he wakes up on the next pillow the girl he was smiling at in this photo will be there, wild hair with a life all of its own, fresh-air cheeks and a head full of nothing but love and the birth of our first child.

"Evie, Evie, wake up! Let's run away, get married on some island, you know, all bare feet in the sand!"

I'd laughed and turned over to face him, "After, wait till the baby's here," I'd answered, too tired to open my eyes properly. "Spoil sport!" he said as he kissed me.

Andrew, Andrew, where are you? Where is this printed man, dark and wild, free and lustful for life? When I first met you your parents had you all neatly tied up with Caroline. Oh God, Caroline! On paper she was so perfect for you and the career they'd mapped out for you. Your mother was in matchmaker heaven! What a find Caroline was, a Lady or Honourable something! And so eligible with that brilliant legal brain, able to slide the rich and successful out of tricky little situations, and all that inheritance just sitting there, waiting to donate itself to your father's 'party'. Didn't her parents own a lot of Suffolk? Why is she still everywhere? Whichever way I turn there is fucking Caroline ready for me to trip over. I don't understand why you don't tell her, Andrew; tell her to go chase after another unavailable husband.

She's back again, for God's sake, how could Andrew have given her our new address? I roughly tear the expensive handmade card from its thick crisp envelope.

Darling Andrew, Finn
and Evelyn
Wishing you good luck in your new home. Can't wait
to see it!
All our love, Caroline, Angus, Archie, Agatha

I put the card back in Andrew's post pile, the wishes aren't meant for me. I trace the line of Andrew's mouth on the photo, his lips stretched to smile, his chin covered in heavy black stubble. Closing my eyes I remember the sensation of it as he brushed, scraped against my cheek, warm and almost painful. He'd breathed, "I love you", words made of air, barely audible. He'd held me tight, too tight, forgetting there were three of us hugging. He'd smelt of horse, warm leather and hot skin, and tasted salty when I licked the tip of my tongue under his jaw line, along the sharp hairs there.

That was the first time I met your parents, that

unforgivable afternoon, I tell his photo. You failed to mention they would be there, in that damp tropical heat of the marquee, celebrating your team's polo success.

Polo? In my world, Polos are a cure for bad breath. You'd kept us as your dirty little secret – you bastard! Would there ever have been a right time, maybe not? But to choose such a public setting, one so alien to me: to put us all in the same ring, blow the whistle and let the fight begin. You introduced me by saying "Mother" (and who speaks like that anyway, where was my alarm bell?) "Father, this is your future daughter-in-law. And…" You smoothed your palm down over my rounded belly. "…first grandchild." God, you were so pleased with yourself. I'd never met that other peacock-self: that proud, under-handed self. Your mother's gasp was pure horror, as if she'd been shown a terrible image of her son's future, and that picture was me. Your father, the smug, self-satified, Right Hon Rufus Wolfe, MP, loomed high and dark over us all: a storm cloud shadow that always hangs in the background of our life. If it were socially acceptable I'm sure he would have growled, low and displeased: a sound to make the ground vibrate. I had never slapped a face before; your stubble spiked my palm like a thousand pins. You made me into a person I wasn't that afternoon; made me defensive, out of place, you tortured me and you didn't even use my name.

Did it sting, that slap, like my humiliation?

Still staring at Andrew's photo I reach for my coffee, it's gone cold. I take a mouthful. Ergh! I've grabbed the wrong cup, it's the tea left earlier by our mysterious visitor. "Gross, that's disgusting!" I'm about to spit and remind myself I'm not eleven. I swallow and wish I'd pinched my nose to block the tastes. Ginger leaves heat in my mouth, mint makes my nose tingle, but the sensation isn't completely awful; it's weirdly soothing like my nana's hot lemon and honey remedy for a sore throats which burnt like hell when you drank it but left a comforting numbness after, although that may well have been the large splash from Papa's 'pick-me-up' bottle, the one with a grouse on the front, that she added secretly. I want to be back there with her now, safe and loved.

Gently my temples begin to tingle as if the opposite of deep heat has been rubbed there – deep cool. Andrew's grin in the picture widens a little and I can hear his low bass chuckle. A sound I love, almost animal, a sound to wake up to: "Come on sleepy head, you'll miss the day," said with a laugh around the edges. "D'you remember when you said that, Andrew?" I ask his picture, you said it a lot I know, but that morning in Queen Charlotte's, I couldn't open my eyes they were glued shut with anaesthetic. "Hey, I've got someone you need to meet," you whispered in my ear, and Jesse's tiny hand gently flapped at my cheek. I was so angry with Nana, that's what dragged me round. I'd told her absolutely *not* to contact you, after the polo, and your parents, I'd sworn never, ever to see you again, I hated you. "We're not your possessions, things to be used for point-scoring in some stupid family feud," I hissed, stumbling from that bloody polo match marquee. They all watched – all your upper-class phoney chums, silently enjoying a sordid little spectacle. Some hooray clapped and brayed a cheer.

Jesse and Nana had better plans. "Children need fathers," Nana said each evening as I returned from working with Willow in her café.

"Well, I didn't!" I'd snapped.

"Just speak to him, Evie – don't make the same mistake your ma did."

And I stormed and raged at Nana, about that "mistake", how could I ever understand what Ma had done wrong if no one ever told me?

"Tell me Nana, where is my dad? Who the hell is he, just tell me!" I threw something that broke, but I can't remember what because Nana and I got to this stalemate often.

"See, as I said, children need their fathers," she would say and turn her back on me to carry on with whatever she was doing. And I never did see, never was convinced, that I needed anyone else. On this she was wrong. But that's how I ended up in the maternity ward with a little angry red sparrow baby, mouth open demanding more, and an uninvited Andrew, tousled and bursting with pride.

I chance another mouthful of the "tea". It's a little less grim now I'm not expecting coffee. I hold the liquid on my tongue building the ginger heat, fuzzing the mint in my nose, until I have to swallow almost choking. The roof of my mouth prickles, the same sensation Space Dust made when we were kids, or champagne – if you squash a mouthful up with your tongue you can hear the bubbles popping. Before I met Andrew I'd only ever tried the elderflower kind. Nana had a huge white bridal tree of it at the bottom of her garden.

"Only collect the flowers on a hot sunny morning, that way the flavour comes out," Nana said, brushing the bugs from the tiny scented bouquets. We always opened a bottle for Nana's birthday, the Queen's and mine. Papa opened something darker, deeper, full of autumn on his birthday.

But you and your kind, Andrew, prefer the "real" version of champagne. "What a shame this isn't from the Reims region," your mother recoiled as I presented her with my Tesco ten-pound special bottle at the Sunday lunch ceasefire your parents had begrudgingly invited me to. She quickly let go of it, leaving it on a windowsill as if contact might cause some awful disease. The food was all tiny and precise, the conversation rehearsed; a battery of questions designed to fully expose each and every one of my inadequacies. Your mother, Amelia – she finally was able to introduce herself although my name escaped her for most of the ordeal – didn't eat a mouthful, just sipped at her Reims region champagne, which I quietly prayed would choke her. Yet another spectacle you let me wade into with no clues on the depth of what was expected of me.

I still prefer the elderflower variety.

I found a recipe for it in the old book that was left on the kitchen table. Yesterday I flicked on from the April 15th page to see if I could understand anything that happened in May and there it was at the beginning of June:

Elderflower Champagne

50 elderflower heads (If you pick the flowers in the morning they should smell slightly of bananas; if picked in the afternoon/evening there will be an aroma of cats piddle! Both work, but bananas are best.)

6 lb caster sugar

15 tablespoons white wine vinegar

50 pints cold water

11 large lemons zested and juiced

Pick the elderflowers when fully out and shake to remove insects. Place the flowers in cloth bags and seal. Place the sealed bags in the water, with the sugar, vinegar, lemon juice and zest. Mix well, cover and stand for 3 days. Remove bags of flowers and strain into bottles and cork. Leave the bottles in a cool pantry for 2 weeks.

If I can find someone to untangle and translate this for me I shall lay down some for my birthday, and Nana's, I always toast her on her special day.

I take another sip of "tea" now hardly noticing the strange taste, just enjoying the sensation; it's therapeutic and quite relaxing. Returning to the post I select another letter, from my pile this time, it's franked London, and I smile at the swirling address full of extravagant looped letters: this scrawl I can decipher. What does Andrew need to write that he can't phone about? The envelope is wedding-invite thick, the edges sharp ready to cut a tongue or slice a finger. Inside is a single yellow Post-it with a swirly "Sorry I had to go, back Friday promise. A x" There's a pressed white daisy, paper-thin, stuck to the back – my favourite flower – I wonder where he found that in Whitehall. I stick it on his photographed nose and hunt down my mobile. There's no signal in the house, the stone walls are more than a foot thick in places, handy if we're ever invaded by the Irish. Outside I sit on the front doorstep and press six, Andrew's "only use it if it's an emergency" office line. I miss him – a deep-down hurting miss. It's almost an emergency, this is the first time in a long time that I have to tell him I need him, I do love you Andrew, I do, it's just that I can't find it sometimes, it gets lost under all the other crappy feelings we throw at each other. The phone rings twice before a crisp, sharp voice sings into the receiver.

"Andrew Wolfe's Office, how may I help?" Caroline giggles, role-playing the demure secretary – badly. What the hell is she doing there? I'm about to cut her off when I hear him.

"Caro, just hand the phone over, that's my personal line." There's rustling as the receiver is exchanged. "Hello… Hello?" I've lost the words I needed to tell him, Caroline has knocked them flying. I'm back to angry with him again.

000 Tot. about 50,000
pounds. Gill
A Slater 1.0.9ᵈ — 2b.

Chapter nine

Awsome! You are not gonna believe this, no way, listen right – my dad – who happens to be the coolest human on earth, has only gone and got me – check this out … my own, my very own HORSE!!! Oh my god this is so gonna blow Luke's mind when I tell him, my own horse, forget stupid hamsters, or dogs, this is outta this world, man!

He's 14.2 hands, that's how you measure horses, in hands.

His name is Ginger, which is totally gay, so I'm changin' it, maybe to somethin like RED WARRIOR, or Flame.

He's brown, well Dad said you call it chestnut, he knows loads – well everything really, about horses. My horse has this wild tail and mane that's all different colours. He really likes me already.

I don't know where Dad got him, not in London, don't think they sell horses there, but when he came back today, Dad had this new car, which is for Mum, which she wasn't even very pleased about. It wasn't her favourite colour so maybe that was why. But still he did try and it's way cool, and then he had a horsebox with Ginger, I mean Red Warrior. At the moment he's in the field next to our house, Dad can already ride so tomorrow he's going to teach me. Dad's even won trophies and stuff, he showed me photos when he won at polo, mum was in them but she doesn't ride, I'll teach her when I know how, then she won't feel left out.

Not sure that Mum likes horses, she didn't want to sleep in the stable with me an' Dad. Think she's pissed off with Dad – well Dad and Aunty Caroline. Don't know why Dad hangs out with her, Aunty Caroline's sooo boring.

Anyway – Dad doesn't have to go back to work for ages, a week at least, so by the time he does I will be able to jump and everythin' on Red Warrior. We're gonna race as well, here you can take horses on the beach and just ride and ride and ride, awesome.

I got up early this morning, before anyone else. Tried to sleep in the stable but agreed with Dad it was too cold and the hay was too itchy, we camped out in my den instead. Anyway I got up early to check on Red, I think he was in a mood cos he just faced the corner, wouldn't turn round or anything like he was pissed off, probably because we didn't stay out with him. I bet he was lonely. I called him, but nuffin', then from absolutely, completely nowhere that woman shows up, the one in our kitchen. I wasn't scared or nuffin', just made me jump. This time though she actually talked to me.

"Here, give him this." She gives me an apple, shows me how to hold it out, and he came over, like nuffin' was wrong at all!

"Hes a fine horse, boy, all yours?" She talks weird like she's singin or somethin. I told her my dad got him for me, and that later today he was going to teach me how to ride. "Might take more 'an a day," she said.

"No way." I told her my dad has won cups. "Best give him a brush so he's ready then." She goes and she gives me this hairbrush but with no handle. She did one side I did the other. We made him shine.

"Don't fall off now, Finn, you go careful now."

"How d'you know my name?" I asked her because I've only seen her that one time. She says nuffin' strokes my hair – weirdo. "I'm Alys," she goes, then off she walks.

"Hey, where's Jesse?" I ran after her. She walked real fast; she didn't hear me, just opened the gate and disappeared into the trees again. I was gonna run after her but I needed to be ready to go riding with Dad when he got up.

Dad takes ages to wake up, think he must've got cold in the den and ended up with Mum. He looks well wild when he finally shows up; his hair is sticking out everywhere.

"Cool hair, Dad!" He didn't get the joke. I made him a sandwich to hurry him up, he's so dumb he thought Mum had been making bread.

"Nah, Alys does it," I told him, but he didn't know Alys.

Borin', can't go riding until we've gone and got my new school uniform, how dumb is that. But we're gonna get me a riding hat, so not so dumb.

Chapter ten

August

Book 12.85

Oh God, I don't believe this! Andrew the prodigal father returns with, not only a new car as a peace offering, but also, a sodding pony! What the hell is he thinking? I'm already angry. This morning I stoked my rage writing a list of his misdemeanours, so that in the unlucky event of stupid tears, I could refer to it and remain "on message" when I confronted him.

Yesterday afternoon I couldn't stand on the doorstep watching Andrew and Finn any longer, I felt my presence might be construed as some kind of "congratulations what a splendid idea". I smashed in through the front door slamming it with more force than it had seen in its entire three-hundred-year life. I threw myself down at the kitchen table teenage-style with another headcracking ache developing at my temples.

"What the hell is he playing at?" I hiss at the scrubbed tabletop. Nana's radio quietly hums something tranquil and soothing. It doesn't work.

"Maybe it'll help the boy." I look up and Sink Woman stands in the kitchen doorway, basket on arm in about-to-leave mode, my anger dissolves any amazement or surprise at her sudden reappearance.

"How?" I snap at her. "Finn hasn't the first idea about horses, come next week Andrew will bugger off back to Caroline and their beloved ministers while we'll be stuck here with a pony to look after. How's that possibly going to help him or me?" I can't bear to think of Andrew rushing back to Westminster, cajoling obstinate ministers to his way of thinking. And that Caroline slipstreaming his every move, smoothing the way, embedding herself ever more in the role of Mrs indispensable.

"Have some tea. Give them a while, you'll see." I look down to find the tea and when I look back she's gone. I sip some, it's that weird stuff again with the ginger that warms you, then chills you with mint; I could perhaps do with a larger cup.

"How cool is that, Mum? I wish Dad had got me a horse." Jesse whispers so quietly I know I'm thinking him.

"Arrgh! Stop ganging up on me. Wouldn't have fitted in the garden back home though would it?" We laugh, but mine is forced.

"Still, it's a cool thing Dad's done; Finn loves hanging out with him, now they'll have loads to do together." Jesse sighs. And, of course, I see briefly into Andrew's logic; now they'll have loads to do together, which is all Finn needs and wants right now – time with his dad – his dad and his pony. I have a brief stab of jealousy – I want that time with him too. I drain the cup and walk over to the kitchen window, watching them, their voices clear, carried in on the late afternoon breeze. The pony has been coaxed from the back of the box and in the sunlight its coat shines the conker colour of Sink Woman's hair. But the most blinding thing of all is the sheer joy blazing from Finn's happy face.

I'm witnessing love at first sight, an instant attraction in the flick of a horse's tail. Obediently the animal follows Finn and Andrew into the field at the side of the house, they close the gate then lean on the fence to watch it. On cue the pony careers off sideways, flicking and bucking, twirling in the air it might as well have shouted hooray! Finn does, Andrew laughs.

"Best go in and find Mum, shall we?" Andrew nudges Finn.

"Did she know? You know ... about getting the horse?"

"No it was a secret between Granddad, Aunty Caroline and me."

All my favourite people tied up in one gunpowder plot, I wonder why I couldn't have been consulted.

"Mum's gonna be well mad!"

"I can handle it. It won't be as bad as the time I forgot my keys and I got home in the middle of the night!"

"Did she go crazy?"

"Ballistic." I can see Finn wince and they walk on in silence toward the front door bracing themselves for my wrath. I'm furious that I will be cast as the villain, I'm deciding on my opening line when Sink Woman intervenes...

"Here, give them this," she whispers. "It's bara brith." A large loafy currant thing cools on the windowsill. I turn in time to see the red hair disappearing again from the doorway. I try calm breathing, inhaling the smell of the bara brith which is delicious.

They slink into the kitchen with smiles they can't hide. "Hungry?" I ask, turning my back on their smirking faces. Neither of them can speak because if they do a thousand horse words will fall from their mouths and they won't be able to stop laughing with complete delight. So we all pretend for a tiny while that there isn't a pony staring in through the kitchen window.

Refusing to acknowledge the pony I spitefully pull everyone back to reality for a moment. "Right Finn, school uniform." I feel like I've just walked into a teenage party and turned on the lights, all the excitement in the air rushes for the door.

"No worries, we'll get the uniform and then we can pick up a riding hat and maybe some boots on the way home." Andrew snatches the problem and with his sleight of hand turns it into a treat.

"Cool, let's go now!"

"Finn it's five. I meant tomorrow. Tomorrow you need to get your uniform."

"Glass of something, Evie?" Ever the magician, Andrew intervenes, plonking a bottle of champagne on the table, from Reims, not elderflowers.

"Are we celebrating?"

"Of course we are!" He takes three mugs from the draining board ignoring my frowns on the amount he pours into Finn's cup. "To Ginger!" Despite myself a smile creeps to the corners of my mouth.

"To Ginger." I clink his mug.

"Red Warrior!" Most of the champagne slops on the floor as Finn enthusiastically smashes his mug against ours.

"Red Warrior," Jess whispers deep inside my head just loud enough for Finn to hear – I can tell by the grin on Finn's face.

The dastardly duo decide to spend the night in the stable with the pony, no one consults me, or the pony, which is just fine, I'll carry on with my Caroline rage all by myself. Having ripped open a selection of boxes *not* marked *CAMPING STUFF*, they unearth sleeping bags and torches needing fresh batteries. I hadn't even realised we had stables, those buildings had come under my shed category, how handy that they already had hay and saw-dust, or had that been organised before our arrival along with the pony purchase?

I feel inconsequential; more and more of my life is being decided without me. When were my decision-making capabilities quietly removed because someone had decreed I was no longer capable? Is this how it starts? With people suggesting what would be good for you, gently guiding, pointing out possibilities that slowly become "This is what we are doing." Uncomfortable memories of Ma bullying Nana seep into my mind – that year Ma tipped our life out all over the floor…

…"I'm fine just as I am, Martha. I manage very well on my own, thank you." Nana assures Ma. Ma had been wheedling and nagging Nana since Papa's death two years before. She was after something, money probably.

"Manage? Mum, that's the third bloody time you've put the electric kettle on that gas hob! When are you going to listen? When the house is burnt to the ground?"

"Martha, don't! It's that new-fangled oven I'm not used to it, and whoever heard of a plastic kettle? No wonder it melts! I don't know why you had to do away with my old one."

"Because, Mum, it didn't work! No one uses Rayburns anymore. No one has coal delivered. You're living in the dark ages. And no, don't bother to thank me!"

"I liked the dark ages."

"Oh, for God's sake, Mum! You're being childish." Nana muttered something about Ma behaving like a hypocrite. Ma was the child – she'd spent all of her 40 years successfully evading maturity. All of her energy, was focused on her universe – on her airbrushed world of advertising where each catchy slogan, each carefully considered word, can transform its creator from a mere copy editor into a creative diva. Ma was good. She had imagination. With a clear head she could crack a campaign for a new catfood in a few highly paid hours – with a clear head. She reigned supreme, eight-out-of-ten of her slogans became household sayings. They paid her more, so she asked for a raise and celebrated, a lot. They created a monster, Nana explained. They gave her her own office. She celebrated more, rolling into work straight from the night before, personal assistants (the little people as she liked to call them) scattered in all directions to source something stronger to keep her up – lubricate her creativity. The advertising world of the eighties applauded a wild child, but a spoilt brat who messed with deadlines, who couldn't form two words quickly enough got moved from the high-profile campaigns, dropped by clients, fired.

Ma wouldn't give up. She carried on moving in her big-time circles, hungrily chasing the scent of the next great campaign – sure she could win the business. The people inside those circles mostly ignored her; she was "unreliable", unwelcome – no longer "one of the creatives". With a clear head she may have found her way back, may not have slept around with so many creative directors, not ended up a single mother with no real employment, broke, drunk, and lonely. I wanted to be enough company and Ma tried, really hard sometimes, to let me be. And then she found something else to celebrate.

Ma had just met a pinstriped, cash-flash, city trader, ten years her junior, and already she was ringing wedding bells. Overnight her wardrobe shed twenty years, her heels rose inches, along with her skirt hems. When she came back to Nana's, she drained the hot water, filled the air with Anaïs Anaïs and stripped the place of cash. Then without a thanks, or sorry, or see you in a couple of days, she would vanish, her sweet sickly perfume hanging in the air the only confirmation that she had really been there.

Ma spent my childhood falling in love with unsuitable men: too young, as in this Mr Trader, too old, too stoned, broke, violent. Every time romance hung around, Nana and I crossed our fingers hoping, and every time they turned out to be some loser with an angle. She never did bring home the mystery man who was my father, the knight I dreamed would return to care for us all. At night I practised mouthing the word Dad, enjoying the way it felt in my mouth. I played out the way he would sweep me up and hug me at the school gates – the way Willow's dad did when he was home on leave. My dad would be the tallest, the strongest: he would lift me so high I'd collect the clouds for him. But Ma would never say, not a name, a surname, a photo. It gave her power, the power to hurt and manipulate, to make so very many broken promises.

Ma and her trader realised what a gold mine Nana

occupied on the edge of Marble Hill Park, with its perfect leafy postcode. They had measured and surveyed and planned to demolish Nana's house, turning it into an open-plan living space with deck and mezzanine. There was even space for a studio for Ma. Trader had promised to back a new advertising venture, to feed her big city clients. But study their blue-prints as hard as you liked, there was no granny annexe.

"Where will Nana and I sleep?" I asked Ma and Trader after the grand unveiling of the plans at a tense meal in Nana's kitchen.

"God, Evelyn, why do you have to be so nit-picky? See the bigger picture, I'll be working again!" I'll be loved again was what she meant. "Just look at all the beautiful space we've created. Christ! You could fit your entire class in the dining zone!" Ma was nervous, edgy, high on something. Nana and I were obviously not supposed to sleep anywhere in these spacious, class-accommodating plans. I could imagine that I might be allowed in the 'guest room' when the guests didn't need it, but would the invitation extend to Nana?

Staring very hard at Trader I asked again, "Where will we sleep?"

"Hey, this is getting heavy guys. Martha, let's check out, head into town get some real stuff down us." He said this holding up his glass of elderflower champagne. Nana had broken all the birthday rules wanting to make a good impression on Mr Trader. So, halfway through supper, Ma and Trader abandoned us. Nana sat opposite me. She swallowed repeatedly, smiled and reached for the elderflower to top up my glass.

"I do so hate wine snobs." She forced a giggle and I made myself laugh with her. "Hang on, d'you hear that?" And so began our game that we still played, especially when disappointment sat down with us for dinner. It's my earliest memory, and even as a teenager still was one of my favourites.

"Yes quick, get to the shelter!" I replied grabbing my plate and glass, Nana rushed as fast as she could to the sink, filling the ever-waiting Thermos with cold water. Then we were off, out of the backdoor, torchlight sweeping ahead of us to the bombshelter at the bottom of the garden.

Papa built the shelter before the Second World War; it's not really underground, the ground sort of comes up to swallow it. The old heavy wooden door had been replaced with a pretty glass panelled one now that the risk of bombs had passed. You could sit, quite invisible to the outside world, watching out over the Park, viewing the wild life carrying on, day in night out. There were two camp beds, the original canvas army issue kind, a little stove, lighting (although Nana and I preferred candles) and best of all the radio, singing us to sleep during night raids. Nana started the game with Ma and a few times, the best of times, in between Ma's deadlines, we all played it together, Nana, Ma and me.

We do both *know* it's a game.

Nana tells me tales of the real explosions ripping up the London sky leaving it to smoulder like that evening, as the sun burned its way down to other side of the world. She was such a good storyteller that she made the air-raid sirens whine as we snuggled down for the evening in our blankets, the cold water in the Thermos magically warmed through into hot chocolate. We shared it out between ancient tin mugs, warming our hands, blowing cocoa steam into each other's faces.

And that night, when Mr. Trader visited with his blue prints, we were just settling down for the night with the Glen Miller Band crooning gently, when footsteps crunched down the garden path.

"It's the air-raid warden, or maybe Nazis," Nana hissed. "Turn out your torch."

"Mum … Mother! Evie. Are you out here?" Ma's voice shattered the game into a hundred tiny pieces of reality. We both groaned and pulled grim faces at each other, knowing we were in trouble. We listened to discontented rustling and the odd swear word before Ma appeared the other side of the glass doors, cross. "What the hell are you playing at, it's nearly midnight."

"Hot chocolate?" Nana offered her a battered tin mug.

"It's water, Mum. Stop it! Evelyn, get in the house now, you're bloody old enough to know better. Right – tomorrow morning we're off to Little Haven, no arguments." She hustled Nana back up the path too quickly. "See, it's obvious you can't cope."

"I cope just fine, Martha!" Nana snaps, trying to tug her elbow away from Ma's clamp but failing.

"Don't be ridiculous, Mum, look at the pair of you."

Nana brakes suddenly refusing to move, glaring up into Ma's face.

"If I'm so bad at managing, why d'you leave Evie here all the time you're swanning around with Mr Wrong? Not scared I might neglect the poor girl or d'you just not care?"

"Oh very witty, Mum. I only leave her with you so that you're not on your own, someone to keep an eye on you in case…" Ma pushed her on inside.

"In case I conveniently pop my clogs and hand over the house and all my worldlies?"

I hover in the dark kitchen doorway hating the words being thrown around, the angry viciousness of it all.

"The house, Mum, for what it's worth, is just a crumbling heap. It's far too big for you anyway. You're being selfish and stubborn as usual. I can't be here every five minutes, putting out fires, making sure you sleep in a bedroom."

"You're not here from one end of the month to the other! Then you only show up cos you want something. Wasn't born yesterday, Martha. And the house is fine for the pair of us."

"Evie doesn't live here, it's temporary, remember? Like I said, till I'm settled, then she'll live with us."

"Us! What? With that spotty teenager you brought to supper? Don't make me laugh. He's only interested in a good time and making a killing on the property market."

"You bitch! I don't deserve that." Ma raised her hand to hit Nana. "No wonder my life's such a screw-up. Have you ever supported me in anything, eh? Ever?"

"Well, I can't say I was a fan of the drugs, or the alcohol, or come to think of it—" The smack finished Nana's sentence for her. I stepped forward out of the dark to protect her, but she shook her head at me and stared hard into Ma's face. Ma dropped her hand from its slapping position.

"You truly are poison. You know I can declare you insane, go to the lawyers and just get the whole thing signed over to me. Then off with you to the old folks' home, and outta my hair. I can do it, Mum." She snaps her fingers millimetres from Nana's nose. "Just like that!" Nana stands firm, she seems to stretch up a few inches or maybe Ma shrinks.

"Nothing to sign over Martha, all taken care of." Ma's mouth flapped, she forgot to make sound. "Evie's in charge, it's all hers, the house, savings, any jewellery that you haven't already helped yourself to. The whole shebang! I know she'll keep the place just the way it is, not go ripping it up for a swift buck!" She spins on her carpet slippers and joins me in the doorway. We walk up the stairs together holding hands, never looking back at Ma, who's frozen to a cracked tile on the kitchen floor. I feel Nana's heart pound through the palm of her hand.

I wake the next morning to taxi rumble. Looking down from the bedroom window I watch Ma pull Nana by the elbow into the black cab. A note waits angrily on the kitchen table: *Gone to see Little Haven, old folks' place, back by lunch.*

———

It's beyond dark, thick and black when the bedroom door moans open. I think I hear Red Warrior the pony whickering from the field. Boards creak as feet make their way to the bed. I hold my breath trying not to sniff; the ugly images of Ma always make me cry. They stamp all over the happy days, her sober days when she came back and stayed for a while trying very hard to be a mother.

"Never settle for ordinary, Evie," she would say. "Be extraordinary." The mattress dips down on the empty side of the bed.

"Evie? You awake?" Andrew whispers. I turn over towards him still so angry, wanting to reject him. He rustles under the duvet and reaches out, pulling me to him, tucking me under his chin, my face resting in the hair on his chest. I breathe in his skin smell that faintly hangs onto the morning shower gel and the hay he's just come from. Anger runs away through my fingers, I don't want there to be a Caroline squeezed between us.

"I missed you." His words are hot on the top of my head. I want to stay here in this safe place, in this moment, but still the little malcontent that's moved in with my thoughts nags: ask him why is Caroline always there, answering his mobile? Sentences muddle up in my brain, but all that comes out is, "And Caroline?" He exhales, releasing his hold slightly.

"What can I do? Caroline and I work together. That's it; you know that. And she's happily married to Angus, you know that too. Thursday she popped in on the off chance I was free for lunch, but the Japanese Ambassador had beaten her to it."

"Why can't you just tell her to back off?"

"I don't need to tell her to back off. She's my colleague, she's very good at her job Evie, and they're friends – her and Angus, I mean we were all at Oxford together."

"Are they? And they're large donors to your father's party too, that you can't afford to upset?" He pulls away turning onto his back. I imagine all the clever responses running round his head as he tries to find a right one simple enough for me to understand.

Eventually he says, "Yes." He pauses then hurtles on, "And I feel guilty for leaving her like I did, it was messy, and I hate the way she can get between us still. But there's nothing going on, nothing, everything is in the past. Please, Evie…?"

I roll over to his side resting my head in the dip between his chest and shoulder. His heart thumps an agitated beat. I stretch up to kiss the tiny silver scar on his jawbone and then the one on his shoulder, souvenirs from school days. Andrew sighs, a breeze from the open bedroom window collects it, taking Caroline-talk away into the night. I draw my fingernail down his arm to his elbow, his skin raises in a thousand tiny bumps.

After, lying tangled up in each other, with sleep hanging heavy on my eyelids I can hear the faint song… *But I know we'll meet again, some sunny day*… a cool hand strokes the hair strands from my forehead …*keep smiling through*… "Evie shhh go to sleep now." …*Just like you always do*…

Chapter eleven

I hate school, hate it. The uniform we got last week is totally gay, real itchy. What's the point in sending me to this place when I'm only here for a term, not even a whole one. How stupid is that? Why couldn't I just hang out at home with Red. That's what Mum and Dad are doing, hanging about being all lovey dovey, back to how they used to be. That's all I want to do, not the lovey stuff, just stay home with them; it's so unfair.

And I don't know anyone here.

My teacher is OK, I s'pose. I mean he's about eight foot tall, he's massive, but speaks really quiet so you've gotta listen all the time to catch what he's telling you otherwise you go wrong. There's not many in my class, loads less than my old school. Don't know why Mum thinks that's good; you get picked on all the time to answer stuff.

I can't play rugby. Everyone else can, even the girls! How wrong is that?

I can't speak Welsh, it's stupid, more stupid even than French and that's well stupid.

I can't stand that cawl stuff we get for lunch all the time, its mingin', errr water with bits in – disgusting.

By lunch today I've had it – I can't do it any more. They don't lock doors or do buzzers or anythin' here, not like my old school. So when they ring the bell I decide it's home time. All I know is home is downhill. This dump's at the top, the bus hardly makes it. I mean yesterday it was sunny while me and Mum waited for it to come. By the time it got to school we were in fog, it was freezin', didn't even bring a coat. So out the gates an' downhill I go. It only takes fifteen minutes on the bus so how long can that be walkin' – nothing, I think. Cos I'm going down and the bus is goin' up, simple!

Everywhere you look here it's green fields, or fields covered in shit, that is so totally gross, it stinks. They actually get all the cow shit and spray it everywhere. There's no shops, no houses, just green, green, green and the smell of shit. What was Dad thinking, he said this would be a cool place to live – derr, I don't think so.

Crap, I didn't see this from the bus, there's three roads so which one? Downhill, downhill, down, it's gotta be ... that one, that goes down most. I wish I'd stayed for lunch first, I'm starvin'.

Wonder what Luke's doin' for lunch; wonder who he has his sandwiches with now. And it's football training tonight at home, I mean old home. Bet Ryan is playin' striker now. I was way better than him and he knows it. Loser.

I don't remember any of this. Don't think the bus comes down here. Crap. I've been walkin' ages, my feet hurt, didn't need new shoes, my trainers fit fine, Mum makes so much fuss. "Got to make a good impression, Finn, blah, blah, blah," she goes. Want to fit in – no I don't. I want to ride Red that's all. And if I can't I might as well go back and live with Luke and go to my old school cos there ain't no point in stayin' at this one. I hate it.

Where *is* this place?

I haven't even got my phone to call Mum, Mr Evans took it, bet he keeps it, probably took it cos it's better "an his. Loser.

I think I'm lost, shit.

In a minute a car will come and I'll ask them for a lift, they'll know Pengarrow. Gonna ask in this farm, maybe they'll give me a lift, I don't mind if it's in a tractor, saves walkin'.

Come on, I can't knock any harder. Idiots. Where are they?

"Hey hello, where'd you come from? OK, OK, down..." Shit, how d'ya control dogs. "SIT. Yeah good boy, no, no sit, I said sit."

"Brony! Brony! Stupid animal. Brony!"

Oh God, it's that mad bloke Mum and I met when we went up to the village – Morgan thingy!

"Ah there you are. Come. Good girl. So what d'we have here then. A runaway?"

"No."

"I see, no school today then?"

"No."

"So the uniform?"

"Jeans were dirty."

"Ahh."

Then Morgan thingy just sits on the doorstep with me. I thought he might take me home, have a car or somethin. But I like his Brony, she's real friendly. Wish we could get a dog like her, Dad would love her. But Mum ... hmm, maybe not.

"Which way goes to my house?" I ask him.

"Ahh now then... You're miles off." And that's all he says. What help's that? Miles off, I'm really, really hungry, and he looks like he's gonna sit here all day.

"So … I gotta go," I tell him.

"Where?"

"Home – Pengarrow."

"Oh, I know. Big house that for a small boy, my family used to own that place, some smart London bugger stole it off us."

I don't know what to say, he seems cross now.

"Not far from here, Pengarrow. Down that lane there. I'll show you, if you like, I'm on my way there to milk the cows."

But we don't have cows.

Chapter Twelve

1½ cup. Flour S.R.   **DUMPLINGS**
¾ " Suet
Soda Salt
Mix dry, then add water gradually, until dough.

We've composed a rhythm to our days at last, a sense of things in their place. I put Finn on a derelict school bus each morning, crossing my fingers that at least the brakes passed an MOT recently. It's 'not cool' to be driven to school because "everyone gets the bus". So we stand back while Finn tries to fit in. He *seems* to like the school, the teacher.

The electrics trip. We replace another fuse.

The Rayburn goes out. We relight it.

Andrew and I have breakfast together, a new experience. In our other life, Andrew was gone before the day had even got itself organised into morning. His Minister's greedy with his time, breakfast together was as rare as an eclipse – only when a birthday or anniversary fell on a Sunday without football or tennis did it occur. Eating together full stop was something that needed to be logged in a diary and double entried on the evil Blackberry, otherwise policy-making and Bill-writing barged everything out of the way. I always imagine Andrew's cabinet ministers as a row of fat angry babies banging on their highchairs and demanding another bite out of him, while he marches up and down issuing laws sent from on high – from the god, Attorney General, himself. How furious they must be that I have him and they don't.

Over cereals we challenge ourselves to one packing case each emptied and re-homed a day. I'm ahead of target, Andrew is behind. This morning, sitting on the edge of the day together, he puts his hand over mine, his palm warm on my skin. It reminds me of the day he strode into my life: a complete stranger who walked up and covered my hand with his. All my how-dare-you's lay abandoned in Ward D3, heaped beside Nana's hospital bed. She'd been admitted with pneumonia, I thought it was a flu, I'd given her honey and lemon for a week, but at least now she was peaceful; someone finally coming up with the right formula of drugs to smother her pain for a while. I'd needed a different set of fluorescent lights to slump under. On the ground floor, by the entrance, nasty NHS orange tables gathered trying to look cheery and café-like. The WRVS had stopped volunteering for the day, washed up and left the vending machines to it. So for half an hour I sprawled in a chair designed for discomfort. I may have fallen asleep, or wandered off with my imagination somewhere that took me away from the endless bleached blue corridors squeaking with footsteps. That's where I was, head sticking to the partially wiped table top, arms crossed in front of me, hand resting in a coffee ring.

Did I hear him first or I feel him first?

"Are you all right?" His warm palm brushed over the back of my hand. Was it his touch that brought me round or his voice? Exhausted from the days of absolute nothing, I didn't open my eyes or even answer, my mind sucking on the flavour of his words. He sounded grey, married with grown-up children, a man who would read the news.

"Can I get you a drink or…?" he asked. I lifted my head, opening my eyes to thank this someone-else's-dad, but I looked up at Andrew; a ghostly pale, dark-haired man dressed in a flag-bright T-shirt, still carrying a riding hat.

How vivid he looked against the background of shambling washed-out pink and grey dressing gowns. We offered each other our visiting credentials; he had accompanied his polo teammate – suspected concussion achieved falling from his horse. I'd never met anyone who played polo. He called his teammate a chum at one point, another new experience, I thought chums were locked securely between Enid Blyton's pages. His other worldliness fascinated me, his total unawareness that real life – the life say, that I led, was any different from his. He kept his hand over mine and listened, only once breaking eye contact to offer a handkerchief that smelt faintly of horse…

———

Yesterday, we explored the nearby town, Arborth, the whole place looks like it might slip into the harbour with one hard shove. Sugared-almond-coloured shops with caviar prices clung one to another toppling down the steep cobbled high street. Cars queued impatiently to be somewhere else, jammed behind delivery lorries three sizes too wide for the narrow street. Bakers baked fresh bread air, piled Welshcakes, bara brith and scones in impossible towers. The butcher hung out his corpses and the this-n-that shop spilled buckets and spades, dustbins and washing up bowls out over the pavement. It felt like we were tourists, mooching in, mooching out. I bought a postcard, I thought I might send it to Willow. Wishing she were near, I wanted to know how she was getting on with the lunch-time rush. And who made

102

the wedding cakes now? I wondered if a postcard could fill the gulf between us. I could hear her humming 'Dancing Queen' as I sent my thoughts to her.

Andrew and I ate sandwiches in a tiny rainbow café built into the harbour wall, every colour, everywhere. We watched the sea lick around the stones below. After lunch we walked round the harbour wall, along the cliff path and scrambled down to the little beach hidden from the town. Like teenage elopers we ran knee-deep into the sea fully clothed just because we could. I felt within touching distance of relaxed, not somewhere I had been for a very long time. And now I sleep. Deep dark blue sleep, that is empty and quiet. I thought I had forgotten how.

In the morning, the woman cleaning her teeth back at me isn't black and white, yesterday's sun has burnt her nose. Andrew and I spend whole hours together talking over a meal, just this-that rubbish, light nonsense with no consequence; I'm remembering this Andrew – I welcome him back with all my heart. The Whitehall white paper man is fading – his phone has been silenced; his ministers herded off to cause someone else headaches.

Today we had a picnic.

Tomorrow I have my first riding lesson.

And I wrote something on the calendar. A date I didn't want to forget. It's the second calendar we've had since Jesse died, which until today has been empty. Below a picture of an otter on May 14th it now says *Quiz Night, village hall*. We won't go, we're not quiz people, but we could, if we were. May 14th isn't significant; we've never been here before on

103

this day. There's no history. If we went to the quiz no one would look at the three of us, pouring all the sympathy they could squeeze into that one glance; they wouldn't whisper and nod towards us, or rush to give us the best seats at the front. No one would know about us. We are just the new people. The 'bloody foreigners'.

We are anonymous.

This was what Andrew had meant, his new start. I don't know how to tell him it looks like he might be right but I must find a way. Yesterday it was lunchtime before Jesse popped into my thoughts and then only because we were eating doughnuts sitting on the harbour wall. I managed to eat mine without licking the sugar from my lips, a game Jess always won. I smiled when I thought this. I smiled thinking of Jesse. I wanted to add this to the calendar too.

We make sure we're back at Pengarrow by three to meet Finn. I lurk a little way down our lane; being met by your mum is 'not cool' either. Andrew says I should leave him, let him walk down by himself, but that seems like I'm abandoning him a bit. The bus struggles home, dumping Finn in clouds of blue diesel. He flops down its steps and scuffs to meet me. He lightens up the further down we stroll, refusing to speak of his day at school. As we round the final corner he races on to the fence, hugging Ginger, or Red as the pony's been renamed.

Andrew and Finn play horse, no one mentions homework, supper happens. I tried a recipe from the old book yesterday – Beef gobbets. I didn't tell them what it was called. I think it said:

Cut a piece of beef into pieces the size of a pullet's egg (I guessed at that). *Put them into a stewpan. Cover with water, let them stew, skim them clean, and when they have stewed an hour, take mace, cloves, and whole pepper, tied loosely in a muslin rag, and wild garlic. Put them into the pan with some salt, turnips* (no turnips so chucked in some spuds) *and carrots pared and sliced, a little a bundle of sweet herbs* (no idea what these are so used basil), *a large crust of bread, an ounce of barley. Cover it close, stew till it be tender.*

It tasted of the countryside around us – rough and coarse and sweet. They ate it, Andrew and Finn, wiped their bowls with Sink Woman's bread; we could have been eating at any point in time in the last one hundred years and I felt in touch with the house, I glimpsed how things were – should be.

Then sleep.

Sink Woman has gone. I miss her.

Jesse is quiet.

Andrew will have to go back, this pretend existence is just a little dream I'm holidaying in. But there are half-made plans to cut London days. Andrew is ignoring Caroline's calls, I know it's her I can read it in his face; yesterday there were just two.

The phone goes. One-thirty, Caroline's first call of the day? We ignore it. I take another bite of cheese-on-toast, it's Y Fenni, we bought it from the cheese shop in Arborth, a Spanish man runs it, said it was good for grilling. I was

thinking I must send some to Willow she would love it…
Last ring and the answerphone will dump Caroline at the
back of all the other messages we haven't yet deleted.

"Hello, hello, Mrs Wolfe, this is Arborth School. We've
got a bit of um … a situation … um Finn seems to have
gone missing, could—"

"Hello…" Andrew snatches the receiver. "What d'you
mean he's missing … yes, I'm his father … where the hell is
he?" That hand comes up, grabs hold of my heart squeezing
hard, my lungs won't completely fill with air. I pant, frozen,
watching Andrew erupt down the receiver. Not again, not
again, don't take our other boy, my chest hammers.

"Evie, Evie!" Andrew is shouting at me, I try to
understand what he's saying, "Did he take his school bag
today?" I can't remember; I'm replaying Finn running out
the door to catch up with Jesse and Jazzy that last day they
all went to school together.

"I can't remember." I can't remember, I can't, I fight very
hard not to rock on the chair, but I can't remember.

"…Don't panic? Are you insane! My son's missing!"
Andrew is shouting, I catch the fear in his roar. Then he says
"police". I can't stop the scream that my entire body makes.

"Where is he, Andrew? Where's he gone?"

"He's going to be OK." He holds me tight, I can't rock
held like this and that helps us both. "I'm going to drive up
the lane, see if he's made his way home." He holds my face
staring into me looking for comprehension. "Evie you wait
here. Do you understand that? He might call, or turn up,
or the police…" I nod I understand his "stay here" but I

don't understand how Finn can just turn up from six miles away. Isn't that too far for him to walk, would he even know the way? There's a frantic key hunt for a bunch that's sat amongst our lunch. Andrew runs out of the door, crunches gears and, spitting gravel, tears up the track.

I stare at the table, the room: it has an, "everything-is-all-right" feel to it, newspaper half-read, hardening cheese on toast, tea cooling. I shake, my teeth rattle, my skin is covered in a thousand pin points of pain. "Where are you, Finn? Please don't have run away." I stare out of the window, the pony comes to the gate staring too. Looking at the horse, I voice my thoughts. "He'll come back, he'll come back for Red."

"Don't panic, Mum." Jesse whispers. I want to feel him squeeze my arm.

The phone goes, making Jesse jump, "Have you found him?" I shout at whoever is phoning.

"May I speak to Evelyn, please." I slap a hand over my groan. Why is *she* calling, now of all times? All I can do is slam the receiver down on Amelia Wolfe, Andrew can explain to his mother that this is not a good time. I'm still holding the receiver down when it rings again.

"Andrew?"

"It's Amelia, is that you Evelyn? What on earth is going on…?"

"Just get off the line." I scream, giving her another receiver slam. For a dark moment I wonder how it would feel if I wasn't smashing phone on phone, but phone on flesh. Defiantly it rings again.

"Get off the—"

"Evie? Evie, what is it?" Thank God, it's Andrew.

"Your mother! She keeps bloody calling."

"Shit."

"Have you found him?" I plead.

"Not yet, I'm going to follow the bus route up to the school. Call me on my mobile if you hear anything. I won't be long. Stay there though." I nod, but he can't see. "Stay *there*, Evie." I stay for an endless time of nothing at all, running from the open front door to the back door, calling Finn's name, which bounces back at me from the other side of the valley unanswered.

I *need* to do something – anything: the stables, check, his room, check, outbuildings, cellar, loft, check, check, check. Just come home, Finn. I have nowhere else to hunt. Outside the smell of burnt garlic burns my throat, inside tears sting my eyes. I sit on the front doorstep frozen in panic, willing Finn's hiding place to jump into my mind.

"Milking time soon."

The sing-song voice springs me from my mental location hunt. I look up at the figure standing in front of the sun, a fire glows around her head, light shining through red hair. How am I supposed to respond to that, it's a nonsense! Like I did to Amelia I want to cut off Sink Woman.

"Won't be long now, don't fret, *cariad*." She pats my shoulder, her expression blacked out by the light behind her. She smells of wood smoke. I expect her to turn and melt into the sunlight but she sits down beside me to wait on the doorstep. Her hair brushes my bare arm, her smokiness

108

settles around us. Red whinnies, nodding his head over the gate. We wait, the three of us.

"They're late, then." Sink Woman sighs. Impulsively I look at my watch, it tells me two o'clock, but that, to me, is neither late nor early. "Ahh, here they come now." She gets up and heads round the side of the house toward the garages. Red calls out. Inside the house the phone demands attention. I stumble in through the instant sun-blinded-blackness, fumbling for the phone.

"Evie? Is he back yet? I'm at the school, the police are on their way to you. Evie are you there?"

"Yep. No sign of him."

"Has he phoned?"

"No, nothing, it's just…" I'm about to tell him it's milking time and realise my insanity. Am I so desperate that I'm clinging to the words of Sink Woman? I mean there's not a cow in sight. But I'm sure I can almost feel Finn trudging down the lane. "I think he'll come back for the horse," I ad-lib.

Andrew mumbles something exasperated under his breath, "Just stay put, the police will be there any minute." He's gone before I can answer. I walk back out into the brightness; a place behind my left ear is screaming panic. I carry on trying to ignore it. As I sit on the doorstep again a collie crashes down the lane barely making the final corner. It charges me, ears, tongue, tail flying. A police car follows in a poor second place.

"Mrs Wolfe?" An officer unfolds himself to an impossible height from the car. He walks towards me, his arm rigidly

109

outstretched like a sword. He crunches bones in my hand. "Inspector Craig Jones." He nods but I'm not looking at him I'm watching the black curls bouncing down the lane behind him. Inspector Craig Jones looks surprised as I run past him, catching his elbow with my shoulder.

"Finn!" My boy breaks into a run. We smash together. I pull him down with me falling to my knees. I breathe him in long and hard, deliberately taking a mouthful of his dusty hair. The collie joins in uninvited.

"Brony, off now girl." Finn pushes her away. "Morgan the Milk's looking for you." The dog spins, sprinting back up the lane.

Chapter thirteen

Whatever they say, I am *not* going back to that dump of a school. It sucks. End of.

Finn will have to go back. But we have the weekend as breathing space, bargaining time. Inspector Craig Jones has folded himself back into his squad car, adding us to the bottom of his at-risk registers. Amelia Wolfe has been appeased, reassured and safely tucked back into her South Kensington wonderland. We've done the across the table stuff with Finn, I watched the words bounce off him.

He wants to ride his pony.

He doesn't want to go to his new school.

Andrew completes his lecturing, convinced he's got his point home. Now they're playing Wild West in the paddock, jumping Red over poles, higher, faster. I'm sliding back into prisonguard uniform, it's like being back in London, after Jesse. How will I be able to let Finn out of my sight?

Brony the black and white collie reappears, trotting up to the fence where I can see Jesse standing, watching his brother crashing wildly over homemade jumps. The dog flops head on paws. Jesse reaches down stroking her ears.

Picking up the crumbling book that has become a kind of comfort blanket for me, something solid and real in all this turmoil, I sit on the frontdoor step, staying close to my family. I'll look through it for the elderflower recipe; it's nearly that time of year and maybe I'll find something for supper again. The sun is warm, hung low with a golden filter. Swallows shrill and shout, swooping and chasing in crazy arcs. An outsider looking in would think us tranquil, settled. I wish they were right.

The book creaks open, its spine aching after all these years. I turn to the first page, not having started from its beginning before. It says *Alys Thomas, 1897,* but the Thomas has been fiercely crossed out and Morgan is scratched into the paper. I run my hand over the ink feeling the scarred surface. "Hello Alys Morgan," I whisper. Evelyn Wolfe, 2010, I write under her name with the tip of my finger. She has filled most of the book but the blank paper at the back calls out scribble over me. Her pages are squeezed with reminders, fragile scraps of linen, dried crumb dust, flowers, lists and, squashed down page edges and handy gaps, a running journal that stops August 15th 1916. It's May 12th, what were you up to today Alys Morgan a hundred years ago? Carefully I flick through a life-time in notes, bread recipes, invitations, skeleton leaves, remedies and jottings, onwards to the May 12th 1916. I stare at the scratched script trying to learn the loops. Slowly some words identify themselves, she writes: *I pray that Nye will never return to France.* There's too much panic in the next sentence, I can't read it but I can see the anxiety in the marks, when I run my finger over them the pressure is deeper. She finishes with: *I can't bear to lose him again, he's too young. Surely someone can stop this.* Poor Alys, I feel her fear, I know the shape of it and how it tastes. I wonder if Nye found an escape or whether he's another name carved somewhere in France. The rest of the May 12th page is filled with lists, the writing small, half-hearted, Alys's mind clearly on the week ahead, like mine, Monday: Andrew returns to London, Finn to school and now, maybe, Alys Morgan's Nye back to France.

"Mum, Mum, look at me!" Finn's voice brings me back into today. He's on Red, riding in circles around the paddock fast. Closing the covers on Alys's life I run to the fence.

"Andrew, is that safe?" I shout but neither of them can hear me; their excitement drowns me out.

"Any minute now…" Jesse laughs beside me. And like a ping-pong ball popping along the table top Finn bounces in the saddle, into the air, and on to the grass. Andrew shoots me a stay-put look.

"Hey! Big guy, nothing broken, ehh?" Andrew stands Finn up. "That's it, straight back in the saddle, there's a good chap." He lifts Finn up onto Red. And off the pony skips again with Finn, who's holding the reins in both hands now.

"D'you think it's time to come in?" I ask.

"Five more minutes," Andrew shouts.

I go back into the house, too sensitive for Andrew's schooling of hard knocks, making myself trust in his judgement. For distraction and to drown out the "trot-on"s I return to Alys Morgan. Imagining the horror of a mother fighting to stop her boy returning to the trenches, maybe to his death. How many women did just the same with their sons, husbands, fathers, uncles and on through every layer of male relationship? Her swirls and scrolls uncurl to say: *How I have missed him. When he left he was my boy, now he's a frightened man in uniform that I hardly know.*

"Walk on." Andrew's command issues through the open kitchen window.

Flicking back a few pages a letter slips out, a child's handwriting carefully crawls across the paper.

Dear Mami

I'm sorry. I had to go. Please understand. I'll be fine, they're putting all us Dyfed lads together, Carmarthen Pals we're called, 15th battalion, Welsh Regiment. How grand! I'll be standing there beside Ellis Hughes, Dai Howells, Idris and Evan – the whole village Mam, I had to go. I couldn't wait back home, I need to be a part of it too, see a bit of the world, make something of myself. We're in Rhyl and next week a place called Winchester, then France, imagine Mam, a foreign country. Food is good, and the pay is twice that of the railway, Idris says. I'll write again soon. Please don't worry Mami and say a prayer for us all.

Nye

How old were you, Nye, when you signed up to see the world, I wonder? I pray you're not on that village cenotaph. Did it take long to get used to his going, Alys, to ignore his empty place at the table, empty shoes by the door – his coats and hats hanging, waiting?

"He was but a boy. I told him, you're too young at sixteen to fight." I look up from the letter in surprise. Sink Woman sits across the table, eyes fit for crying.

"Alys?" She lifts her chin a little, the movement dislodging a tear. So you're Alys Morgan. Sink Woman has a name. I have a hundred things to ask her but only one is important, "Was he all right?" Tilting her head she blinks in slow motion, disturbing other tears that wait to fall...

"Mum, Mum, you'll never guess what I did." I jump at

115

the noise crashing in through the kitchen door. When I look back for Alys' answer an empty space replies.

"Alys, was he OK?"

"Who? Was who OK, Mum?" Finn is impatient, he has successes to boast. "Guess what, actually you'll never guess." I'm exhausted watching him, he's exploding with achievement, covered in grass and shiny with sweat. My head's still stuck in the conversation started with Alys. What happened to her Nye? "Mum, guess!" Finn shouts, his noise finally pushing the others aside.

'What, sweetheart, what on earth have you done now?"

"Only Jumped Red over a two-foot fence, totally wild or what!" He'll burst – there's no room left in that body for any more pride.

"Oh my goodness, weren't you scared?"

"No way, it's like flying, it's awesome. Dad says Red can jump at least four foot, maybe more!"

"Wow! Bit dangerous though?"

"Don't be a wet, Mum." He throws himself into a mess on the chair where Alys was just sitting. "What's that?" he nods at Nye's letter that I'm still holding.

"A very old letter from a boy that ran away to fight in the First World War."

"Cool, can I see?" I hand it over, telling him to be careful; the paper looks like it has been handled endlessly. "How old was he? Did he get shot? Did he shoot any Germans?"

"Finn! Don't. He was very young, very frightened."

"Wuss! That must've been so cool, to shoot Germans. Or stab them with bayonets." I'm stunned briefly by how he can switch from the real life horror these weapons have caused our family to the comic book adoration of them.

"Finn, stop, it must have been terrifying?"

"Nah, no way, I'd love it!"

"You wouldn't. You'd be scared stiff, cold, hungry, knee-deep in mud. Rats nibbling at your toes, and Germans trying to blow your head off. I can't see any cool in that."

"That's because you're a girl." This conversation has stalled in a cul-de-sac of ten-year-old boy rubbish. He starts to read, it takes him a while to decode Nye's handwriting, halfway down he looks up in surprise. "I know this! This is our topic in school, Mr Evans told us. There was this guy General, Admiral Major something, errr, oh yeah, Kitchener. He's in these posters, YOUR COUNTRY NEEDS YOU and he's pointing out. He thought it was good to put everyone from the same village in the same army bit. Pals regiments, so you like fight with your mates. But then when they all got killed, there was all these villages left with no men! Derrr."

I relish this sudden spy hole into Finn's school world, I want to hug him and say thank you, but he carries on. "Hey d'you remember when Jesse said he was going to join the army?" Could I ever forget that evening? Sitting around a table in Pizza Express on a rare Friday night together playing happy middle-class families. We hadn't even got as far as the pizza, Andrew was busy with the, "So how was school guys?" and Jesse just threw it across the table. "I'm joining the army." Andrew choked on a dough ball, Finn sent his coke flying.

"No listen – I'll get £800 a month, in six months I can buy a motorbike and insure it!"

"I thought Dad was gonna explode, he was so mad." Finn giggles at the memory.

"It wasn't Jess's finest hour." I agree. The Pizza Express in Richmond is noisy; even when quiet, sound bounces off the public-loo-white-tile walls, letting you in on conversations you're not invited to. But that evening the place fell silent, people tried to pretend they hadn't heard, weren't listening in, and failed.

"Motorbike?" Andrew hissed. "You won't get to ride a motorbike, you'll be stuck in some roasting hell hole fighting The Taliban. And when they've blown your legs off and you come crawling home, what will you do then?" Jesse stared down at his drink.

"And what did Dad say to that woman on the other table? 'And you can…'" Finn begins.

"Finn? Think it's time for a shower, don't you…" Andrew appears stealth-like behind him. Andrew needs Jesse reminiscing clearly sign-posted, dropping Jess's name into a sentence still makes him freeze a year on.

"OK, Dad. Can we jump Red again tomorrow?"

"I would think so. Off you go now." Obediently, for once, Finn heads for the bathroom. I sit with the memories he's left behind. Andrew certainly had been angry for about a week. They didn't speak.

Jesse threatened to leave home.

Then Andrew's father, Rufus Wolfe, the lurking shadow, stuck his nose in.

Officer training, Rufus pointed out, could be an excellent career choice, missing Jesse's protest point completely; he really wanted a Yamaha YZF-R125 not the chance to shoot the Taliban. Jesse switched career paths from war hero to rap artist and started writing lyrics about gangs and guns...

"What are you humming?" Andrew asks, bringing me back. I hadn't realised I was making a sound, just running the lyrics of Jesse's "dead cert smash hit" through my head.

Hey boy, yeah you boy.
March the beat man, ignore your heat man
Stand straight an' learn to hate man,
Don't rock that line cos it's all just fine
Pull the trigger, don't stand and figure
Go from zero to superman hero
Hey boy, yeah you boy.

I remember Jazzy chanting the words, swinging her long bare legs as they dangled over our front garden wall. A black boy beside her, in enormous jeans that piled around his enormous trainers, made a beat noise into his fist, a clone of him mimed drumming, the group bobbed in time. Mrs Dennis opposite at No 13 watched everything, started another letter of complaint.

"I was thinking of Jesse's band," I answer Andrew.

"Why?"

"Oh, I don't know really." I could show him the letter from Nye, tell him about Alys, say I was just wandering past memory lane but Andrew isn't in listening mode, he's afraid we're about to talk Jesse and he can't do that. Brony dog tick-tacks into the kitchen, lifts her head, sniffs the tension and collapses by the Rayburn.

"Hey! What the bloody hell…? Where's *that* come from?"

"'That' is Brony, belongs to Morgan the Milk. He used to have cows down here apparently. Mad as a March hare now, but nice enough. Finn and I met him last week in the village."

Andrew claps his hands, "Go on shoo, stupid animal." Brony opens an eye briefly.

"Ahh, leave her, she'll go when she's ready." But he can't. He pulls Brony by the collar, "I'll run her back up the lane in the car, won't be long."

The car crunches out on the gravel. Sitting alone in the kitchen I return to Alys' book, looking for nothing in particular. Nana's radio gently crackles back into life – an over-jolly tune marches over the airwaves and around the table carrying the sound of men whistling off somewhere. I've flicked through the pages stopping in May, *That Meredith Roberts was back again today,* Alys writes, *asking after Nye, speaking from under her eyelashes, just the same as tha' mother of hers…* Nothing really changes does it Alys, I reassure her pages, you should have met Jazzy! I read on: *Nye says he going to marry this one, and what does he know about life to get married, he's only a child. If his Da were here now…* Alys's fears are so familiar. What did you do Alys, how did you keep hold of your boy, I wonder?

"I didn't," Alys replies, crossing the kitchen with a wooden board of bread and cheese in one hand and a bottle of black

120

liquid and two glasses in the other. She clinks the glasses to the table glugging the purple black wine into them, blackberries and the end of summer evaporate in the air. I sip, it tastes as if it's just been picked from the bramble bush.

"Cheers!" I lift my glass to her.

"*Iechyd da*!" she answers. Now that she's sitting opposite I've lost the courage to question her further, not wanting to make her run, disappear again, her company right now is as warming as her wine.

"So, did Nye marry that Meredith Roberts?"

"Ha, the floozie! Chased after one of the other village lads. Daft *mochin* had to marry her in the end seeing as she was a bit too free an easy with her favours!" She saws off a hunk of bread and passes it to me. Footsteps march across the gravel outside, I look out the window to see five boys in khaki, they're whistling the same tune the radio's crackling.

"They were all too young." Alys mutters following my gaze. "Here I'll get another bottle of this." She heads out of the kitchen door dissolving into the darkness of the hallway as Andrew's car pulls up. His door slams, he flops back into Alys' chair, picks up her half full glass.

"Cheers." He lifts his glass to me. "Mmm, that's nice. What is it?" He doesn't wait for an answer. "Anyway found the old Morgan guy in the pub. You're right, he's insane, said he'd see me at milking time tomorrow. Reckoned he'd be down for six!" There's the tick-tacking sound again from the hallway, Brony slinks back in through the kitchen door, returning to her spot by the Rayburn.

122

Chapter fourteen

So, Monday is back.

An excuse of a day sketched in pastel, then scrubbed out again as a grey mistake. Air falls, drenching everything in cloud. The wind's given up and the sound of outside is smothered.

Andrew has gone back, safely tucked up with Mummy and Daddy or maybe Caroline, I refuse to wonder.

And the school bus took Finn back.

A deal, struck late yesterday evening – "no school, no pony" – seems to be holding, Finn left this morning and, as yet, the school haven't phoned to report him missing.

And Nye Morgan? Did he go back to France this morning?

"All gone," I whisper, remembering how I used to say it to Jesse and Finn as they sat in their highchairs blowing raspberries back at me through whatever puréed mush I'd managed to coax down them. "Clever boy, all gone!" Except there's no relief, no achievement in this morning's "all gone", it's an empty loss. Even the view, with its layer upon layer of fields and hills, spotted with sheep and trees, has all gone. Just a blank day, waiting to be drawn in. Not even the birds make a suggestion, life is on mute.

Silence only adds to the grey air, to its opacity, it stretches out, swallowing the hours ahead whole. The peace builds to a point where my ears replace it with a bright and sharp ringing.

I imagine Andrew at his desk hoping it's his not hers, and Finn lined up in assembly.

And Nye Morgan? I pray he's not slopping across the Channel as I think.

I stand on the front-door step snapped off from human kind. The "nobody can hear you..." saying runs through my head and I scream out "Andrew!" as loud as I possibly can, because I can. The word suffocates in front of me dripping silently to the ground. I wait but nothing is coming in this half-lit day. Five minutes take an entire morning to pass. Sitting down on the doorstep I shut my eyes feeling the mist's moisture that's caught in my lashes, cold rain tears amble down my cheeks, I wipe them on my hugged in knees, fighting the sense of abandonment. I sit hoping the house has something to say. Nothing.

Some auto-reaction makes me stand eventually and open the front door, its old iron hinges moan at the disturbance, the sound a welcome companion in this gloom. Closing the heavy door behind me I lean back against its ancient wood, rubbing the back of my head across its deep rutted grain hoping the vibration will kick-start an idea in my brain. Nothing.

In the kitchen Andrew's wine glass from last night waits for me on the table. His lip print makes a smile below the rim. I'm standing where he stood as he scrubbed himself free of horse and Brony dog yesterday evening. With hands still wet he turned arms wide. "Come here," he said softly and I pressed hard into him, touching as much of me against as much of him as I could; feet alternating, the outside of my calf warmed through by the inside of his, knees squashing painfully. His arms wrapped too tightly around me, his soapy palms soaking through my shirt. "Don't go," I whispered into the bones of his chest. He kissed the top of my head. And this morning he left.

At least in here there's sound, ticking, clicking, electronically created sound, but company at least. I sit in the chair where Andrew had his breakfast much earlier, his toast crumbs litter the table. Licking the tip of my finger I press down on them and pop them on the tip of my tongue. He's left his coffee cup: black oily liquid reflects the overhead light. This is the kind of thing we argue about: "We don't have people that 'do' in this house, Andrew. How hard is it to clear a table?" and finishing with, "I'm not your bloody servant, you know." But he forgets these things, thinks he's back in the ancestral home, maybe thinks I *am* the bloody servant.

The wine bottle and Andrew's glass watch me from behind his cup. A dreg of blackberries waits in the bottom of the glass; picking it up I put my lip to the print of his, tip and hold the wine on my tongue forcing the blackberry sensation up through my head. And the heat of it warms my throat as I swallow. I grasp the bottle, "So what!" I voice silently, and pour in an inch, maybe two. The kitchen clock ticks, tutting loudly that it's only 8.45am. "Shut up," I tell it, and gently and quietly Nana's radio hums into life sprinkling notes on the air. I take my glass as a partner because Willow is at the other end of the M4, and *pas de bourrée* around the table. "Again, again!" Nana would've shouted at us. "Straighter Evie, your feet are limp kippers," Ma would've scolded, always criticizing and finding fault. "At least I try to dance!" I yelled back at Ma once. "You call that dance?" she sneered, leaving the room. "Your mother was a beautiful dancer when she was a girl – her teacher

126

thought she'd go far, 'She's extraordinary,' she told me. Such a pity," Nana sighed. So instead she pinned her hopes on Willow and me making the Royal Ballet. I drain the glass before adding a wobbly pirouette. "Out of practice, Evelyn," I scold myself. Drawing in tight, hardening the jelly of my stomach muscles I try once again holding the *relevé* perfectly before closing *in fifth*. I curtsey to the audience, scooping the first of the bouquets thrown at my feet.

As I finish my reverence to the Upper Circle there's another power cut. The fridge freezer sighs in dismay. The room swoops into dimness; even on a bright day, lights are essential in here. The clock ticks on, smug with its battery heart. Now at least I have a task to perform today; hunt the fuse because I don't like darkness, even dimness. I don't like silence. I won't sit here, won't be left here in the dark. Not again – never. Nana said, "No one will ever leave you on your own again in the dark, Evie." She promised. And she shouted it at Ma.

"It's all right for you – you've got Dad. I'm on my own – I've got deadlines to meet. Can't drop everything at five and come home. She's not hungry – there's telly – she's fine!" Ma slurred bouncing off the hallway walls and out the front door of the mean, dingy little flat we lived in, somewhere near a tube station I remember, with lots of blackened towering buildings looking down on us. "Not fit for rats," Papa said and they took me back with them to their house on the edge of the park. I remember how green and clean it all felt and how quiet without the tube train growling beneath the ground. Ma didn't show up for a week – and then she forgot to take me back with her, left me on permanent loan with Nana and Papa. "It's better this way…" was the only answer all three of them gave when I asked about going home to my ma.

The fuse box is in the cellar, standard positioning for any good horror movie. It's too gloomy to make out anything in particular down there, so I remove a random fuse from the long line of them – they all feel about the same. I'm sure house-type fuses are a set size, a set amp-ness or whatever they're made in. There'll be a man, in a shop in Arborth, that will know all these things and he'll point me in the direction of a replacement, this I reassure myself as I hunt for the car keys. They've camouflaged themselves amongst the Sunday papers that still sprawl on the table with Alys's book, my security blanket I carry around. I use her book now to help me remember all the little forgettable things that melt away in a day. Like now, I must note the power cut, in case a pattern is forming, a fault recurring. This way my time is memo'ed, I can answer the question "What did you get up to today?" There's a small list to refer to; there was a power cut, a fuse blew, I went into Arborth, I found the shop with the man that could sell me the right fuse. And I will know which is the right fuse next time.

The phone rings, its call leaps out of the silence, making me jump. It could be Andrew, I will it to be him, but when the answerphone bites into the ringing the caller remains silent, there's maybe the hint of a sigh, a female sigh that no one has answered. The caller and I wait, then the line returns to its purr.

128

Deciding whether to get washed and dressed before I go fuse hunting takes more time than it should. Is there anything wrong with joggers, Andrew's fleece and a baseball cap (Andrew's as well) I debate with myself? They smell of his aftershave and hay, like he did last night. Staying like this keeps him close, so I finally arrive at a decision; go as I am.

The phone rings again. It won't be Andrew and I can't listen to that sigh again. The car keys materialise in the middle of the table. I snatch them and hurry out from the dark of the house that's pressing in on me.

I blank the car, I will not allow it to unnerve me with its four-wheel-drive, low ratio levers. I passed my test ten years ago: surely a car is a car, gears, pedals, fuel, stop and go. But there wasn't much point in owning a car in Richmond, buses stopped at the end of our road, trains rattled past the bottom of the garden and there was no chance of a parking space outside your own front door anyway.

"But we might not always live in London," Andrew said. I thought he was joking. He bought me driving lessons for Christmas; a card with a car on the front all wrapped up in shiny paper: "Happy Christmas Evie, twenty driving lessons with Fast-Trak driving school." It took me forty. I didn't get out of second gear for the first ten lessons; the traffic was so bad. "What's the point in driving a car?" I ranted at him having embarrassed myself again by stalling on the Hammersmith flyover during lesson eighteen, "It's quicker by bus!"

I hate driving. There's so much to concentrate on, there's no room left for conversation or the view passing by.

The car is kind, helpful even. It happily starts and slowly, carefully, creepy-crawly we scale the lane, up to the tarmac. The overwhelming smell of newness inside the vehicle is suffocating, I indicate to pull out of the lane sending the windscreen wipers into monsoon panic and narrowly miss Morgan the Milk dragging his empty dog lead. Hurriedly rolling down the window I shout; "I'm so sorry, I didn't see you."

"You watch out for my dog now, lad! You need to slow down." I apologise again. He leans in the window, disregarding personal space, "You lost or something? Who you looking for?" His speech spits through his missing teeth, saliva landing on my cheek.

"I'm just off to Arborth…" I'm about to explain the fuse when he walks around the bonnet and opens the passenger door and arthritically climbs in.

"OK, so it's easier if I show you the way." I'm so horrified I can't think how to tell him to get out – gently or otherwise. The new smell is suffocated under a wave of farm stench that is so thick I can taste it. "Mr Morgan…" A quad bike turns into the road from a farm gate opposite, the wind-ruddy man nods at me and three lolloping dogs scatter around the car, pissing on the wheels.

"Ahh here's the boy now, thanks for the lift." Morgan the Milk swings back out of the car door, with a crunch of joints and a cheery wave. Hauling himself up onto the back of the quad, he calls the dogs and off they all go in the direction of the village. For a while I sit half in, half out of our lane, too stunned to drive on. Picking up my mobile I dial Andrew, ignoring the flashing low battery symbol. After two rings my call is answered.

"Hi, you'll never guess what just happened!" I gabble at Andrew, taking a deep breath to rattle the rest of the story out, except I notice there isn't anyone listening. You can hear when someone's listening to you, but silence has answered my call. The phone beeps: its battery has had enough and just before the call is cut I'm sure I hear that briefest of sighs again.

Chapter fifteen

I could almost feel that sigh on my neck, sure it left a warm dampness. My heart pounded and I launched the car in the direction of Arborth at high speed. I crashed into the town, gears wrong, speed misjudged, final hairpin unexpected. I parked across the lines up against the harbour wall facing out to the indigo sea. That sigh whispered over and over in my ear. I silenced the car, but the sigh still whispered. To cut out the sound and calm myself I watched the sea, but my mind was jittery so I grabbed Alys's book opening it at:

May 28th 1898
He lied.
Like Mami said – they all lie my girl, you watch my words, Alys, bach.
No trust to be had in any of 'em.
And every little thing, all those 'my cariad, my dearest' – lies!! Lies, lies… How could he?
He promised me – on his very word – he said, then broke every single one of his foolish words. Sorry! Ha! Sorry, he said, as if that could save my breaking heart, and those crocodile tears running down his face, the filthy liar! I hate you Auden Llewellyn-Rhys, you hear? Now the coward's disappeared! That won't hide what you are Auden Llewellyn-Rhys! Nothing, that's what, less than nothing to me! I'll forget you, if it takes the rest of my days, if it's the only thing I ever do I will forget you.

I re-read Alys's words for a third time. Sneaking into her life, her torment helps me hide from my own. Now I want to backtrack, to find out what this Auden lied about but I feel grubby rummaging through her despair for what seems like my entertainment, my little break from reality.

A stiff breeze blows, shaking the car and whipping waves that now lick up the harbour wall. The sky hangs darkly, sulking at the horizon, boats rattle in the crook of the harbour. The little town rising up from the sea looks less inviting today, quieter than when Andrew and I visited last week, when we played tourists. Nothing spills out onto the pavements tempting you to buy; the risk of rain is too great. Blinds are still drawn down on the baker's, and the butcher looks to be delivering elsewhere. Arborth is saying go home, the wind whistling, "It's shut."

Pulling Andrew's cap down harder I'm about to put Alys's journal on the passenger seat but then can't bear to leave her there on her own, I fight the book into my bag, as old receipts and sweet papers escape on the breeze. The allsorts-of-anything-and-nothing-that-you-actually-need shop is halfway up the main street, which would be called the High Street in any normal town, but here it's called Dark Street. Standing at the bottom staring up at it, I wonder why. A handful of salt spray hits my back. The air seems almost purple. I remind myself it's May, and wonder where the swallows have blown off to. Back in Richmond, Café Rouge would have its too tiny tables out on the too narrow pavement, Waitrose would already have introduced its new picnic range, summer would be there. When did it ever get here? The trees look still asleep, a few raggy daffodils hang on in a flowerbed here and there. The feeling of being in a totally different country is overwhelming.

At the foot of Dark Street, standing guard, is the town cenotaph, weathered, and soaked wreaths rot around its base; the list of the dead rise up on each of its four sides carrying on beyond my eye level. Is Nye Morgan's name resting here? I circle the stone needle for the M's. Thirty-two Morgans lost their lives in the two great wars, including three 'N Morgan, Private'. I run my finger over their engraved names to see if I can feel Nye in one of these entries. I'm sure these aren't Alys's N Morgan – I hope. I walk on up the hill, the names of the dead watching me go.

The man in the allsorts shop has a cold. His already large nose is swollen and red. His business day has barely started and he looks ready to close, he rattles his local newspaper irritably as I approach. I ask about fuses and lay my example on the counter. Without looking up from the obituaries section the man grunts, "All sold out."

"What even these?" I hold up my fuse.

"Yep, even those," he replies without a glance. "Anything else? Only I'm closing." He walks round me, flips the sign over on the door to closed and sniffs out through a doorway in the back of the shop. The lights go off. Behind, where he's just been sitting, is a board hung with every shape and size of fuse. After a few minutes of measuring mine against his I find an exact match. I leave the £1.20 for the fuse on his counter, I count the twenty out in one pence pieces – it makes me feel better like I've equalled his rudeness. He watches me leave from the doorway at the back, rattling his keys, impatient to lock up.

To be doing something I carry on up to the top of Dark Street where the shops run out of steam and a little park waits, circled by old higgledy-piggledy houses leaning on each other for support. They look out to sea, staring towards Ireland. The wind whips their telephone wires, sending a whistle back down the hill. From here I can see along the coast as it arcs in wide ragged-toothed bays. Tankers make their way toward Milford Haven, grey as battleships. I can see so far, a vast distance out, and out to the very point where the sea changes to sky. My eyes ache with the limitlessness of it all. I flop onto a park bench that's waiting to catch me. *Fuck off dylan hughes* is artfully carved near where my hand rests, full-stopped by a hardened lump of grey gum. I think of Jesse's bench in Marble Hill Park, hoping it's lazing in the sun.

The weather has crept in through the holes in Andrew's fleece, I'm cold and start back down the hill with the racing breeze pushing me on faster. The car waits lonely across the parking bays – waits to take me back to an empty Pengarrow. I'm not ready to cut myself off just yet, so I chance the rainbow harbour café again, the one Andrew and I had lunch in last week; it's still hanging on to the wall almost floating out to sea. *Lisa's* it says on the sign over the door, and she waits behind the counter clouded in frying and coffee and something that's just boiled over and burnt. Her face is flushed – the café is empty. It feels lonely and dull today; maybe it was Andrew that made it cosy and inviting last week.

"*Boreda*." The questioning note in her voice is pretty sure I'm not local.

"Hi." I answer sounding too English and out of place. But I can't help thinking how Willow would love it here; it's so effortlessly retro it looks like nothing has changed in here for at least the last forty years. Willow would order a latte with cinnamon sprinkled on top, I copy her, but Lisa looks insulted at the cinnamon and hands me a milky coffee that's only loosely related to a latte. I take my mug to the same table Andrew and I shared, it's hiding in the corner, its empty chairs looking out to sea. I sit with my back to Lisa and take out Alys's book. The smell of ancient dusty lavender catches on the air as I re-open at May 28th 1898. Auden Llewellyn-Rhys what have you been up to, what lies did you tell Alys, I wonder, flicking back a few days.

May 21th 1898

It's so hot – only May, and Cradog's fields are already burning brown.

Mrs Ebsworth moans all morning about the amount of lemonade the Judge drinks – 'Does he know the price of lemons?' she shouted at Idris Jones the butcher boy when he delivered, like he would know!

No sign of Master Auden today, Mam said they left early – London bound the coachman told her. He never said he was going away – not for too long I hope, there's so much we need to plan. I shall burst if we don't tell someone soon. I'm sure Mam knows something – don't go getting ideas above your station, my girl. No good will ever come of it – you listen to me now Alys Thomas, no good at all. Whatever promises he's made they'll be forgotten on the morn you mark my words, and you'll be left looking foolish. And if Mrs Ebsworth ever gets wind of it, she'll have you out of those kitchens quicker than you can skin a rabbit!

Oh Mami, I told her, don't go on so, but she fixed me with that look of hers, the one that goes through you like one of her darning needles. She doesn't understand. He loves me! Auden Llewellyn-Rhys loves me, Alys Thomas, and I love him back with all my heart.

Got a clip round the ear from Mrs Ebsworth this afternoon – drawing hearts in the flour stead of finishing the tarts. She sent me up to the village to order beef for the weekend – the Judge has invited some fancy London folk for the weekend, another endless shooting party. Anyway he forgot to warn Mrs E and now she's all in a lather I can tell you!

I guess Auden won't speak with the Judge until after the weekend now. I do wish he'd hurry up – I can't wait much longer. I suppose I will have to stop work in the kitchens, I wonder what I shall do with all my time…

"Can I be getting you anything else?" I jump, I hadn't heard Lisa approaching, too engrossed in Alys's diary. "Another Laaartey?" She draws out the word, I'm sure there's mocking in her tone.

"Um … thank you." She eyes Alys's book, scribbles

something on her little pad and disappears, leaving me to dive back into Alys's words. Her story is captivating.

May 25th

Oh my, I've never seen so many trunks and hat boxes! Mrs Ebsworth went quite pale. Are they taking up residence? she wailed. Poor Mrs E she does flap so, it's a wonder her heart don't give out!

The first guests have arrived, we had eight extra for luncheon, a right lah-dee-dah bunch! A Lady Isabella someone or other and her parents, my, does she have airs and graces – didn't touch a bit of Mrs E's asparagus tart and she has her own lady-in waiting who we now have to feed in the kitchen and find a place for her to sleep.

Auden's still not home.

There's talk of a big celebration come Saturday, not a shooting party after all then. The Judge is going to make a big announcement so Levi Hughes the gardener says, though how he would know I can't tell. I do hope Auden makes it back in time!

35 now it is for sit-down dinner this Saturday evening – half of Pembrokeshire is coming! Mrs E has roped Mami in to help us in the kitchens, there's to be drinks on the lawn, canapés, lobster, would you believe, strawberries and so on. The Judge has even borrowed two extra boys to wait, off Major Cadwalader from neighbouring Trewern. We haven't had a dinner like this since her ladyship passed away – been so quiet these last six years, we only ever seem to cook for the Judge and Master Auden.

Good news! Levi Hughes says Auden will be arriving this afternoon – I hope I get to see him.

Lisa breaks a plate, I lose my place in Alys's world. Her excitement at Auden's return bounces off the page. I imagine her running into his arms, hiding in the gardens somewhere for a stolen kiss, then I see the clock. Time has blown away on the sea breeze, I'm late – Finn will be waiting.

He refuses to make eye contact as I stall in front of him. He's sat on the doorstep kicking the dust. "Good day?" I ask, he mumbles something to his knees, the tone angry. I only catch the "What's for tea?" part. I want to tell him it's not actually me that says you have to go to school, Finn. Then I remember my list of to-do's for today: new fuse, something for tea, I've forgotten that last bit.

"I'm going to see Red," he shouts over his shoulder, aiming his school bag at the front door.

"Not going to change your uniform?" I call back but he keeps on walking.

The kitchen's dull and overcast, it smells dusty. The only sign of Alys today is another bottle of blackberry wine left on the dresser. I head for the cellar and fish about in the freezer, surely there must be something in there I can catch for tea. It's too dark down here to see much at all, I act blind man with the fuse box, carefully feeling my new version into each slot, trying one at a time. Nothing. The electricity seems to have run off with Alys. The freezer is full of things melting, so everything is for tea. And for the first time since we moved in I am grateful for the Rayburn chugging away in the background; I have no idea how that thing works, but clearly it doesn't involve electricity. I light emergency candles, turning the kitchen into a shrine.

Eventually Finn comes in wearing most of a hay bale. He slumps into a chair shedding dry grass over the floor. "Why have you lit all those candles?"

"Fuse blew after you went to school. I got a new one but it's not fixed it. Have to call someone tomorrow, I think. So did you have a good day?"

"No."

"No?"

"No." There's really nowhere else to go with this conversation but thankfully Nana's radio breaks into Finn's re-gathering gloom, crackling it away with a jolly tune. Bing Crosby urges us to "Accentuate the positive." And the Andrews Sisters remind us to "Eliminate the negative." The Rayburn breathes out the smell of things incinerating.

Half scalding myself I rescue three Findus pancakes (filling unknown), a fishcake and four fish fingers, a pile of round things bread-crumbed which I'm hoping are mushrooms, a family sized apple strudel, a garlic baguette and 24 mini party pizzas, a lamb chop and an individual portion of chilli from the belly of the Rayburn. I add a "Tah-dah!" as I plonk it all down on the table in front of Finn.

"Who else is coming to tea?" he asks bewildered.

"Just you and me and maybe the ghosts!" He laughs and

I pour a splash of blackberry wine into his chipped creme-egg mug. "Cheers!"

"Cheers." The pancakes turn out to be minced beef – Andrew's favourite. We put them in a bowl for Brony dog, who wolfs them when she shows up, letting herself in to sleep by our Rayburn.

The candles illuminate the kitchen giving it a rosy glow, it could be the heart of a home I think as I top up my glass again and try to stop hoping that Andrew might call. Nana's radio has moved onto its collection of Glenn Miller, and Finn and I dance around each other as we dump dirty dishes in the sink for the washing-up fairy. I don't mention homework; he doesn't mention the empty wine bottle.

The grey has been peeled from the sky leaving it red raw. Finn and I stand on the front door step to watch the sun bleed into night. It's OK now for me to put my arm over his shoulder and for him to lean into me.

"Love you."

I tell it out to the sky, he puts his arm around my waist.

"I can feel your bones, Mum."

I squeeze his shoulder, "Me too." I kiss the top of his head, smell hair and grass. The phone rings, cutting the evening.

"I'll get it, it'll be Dad." He runs away, stretching out my heart that was holding onto him. I follow him in.

"There's no one there. Hello, Hello? Dad?"

I take the receiver.

"Hello?" It's another non-call and just as I'm about to put the phone down I hear the sigh.

"Mum, you OK? Was it Dad?"

"No love, wrong number I guess. Why don't you give him a call anyway?" I pass the receiver over to Finn and amble over to the sink contemplating the washing up.

"Mum, this isn't working. It's dead."

"Of course, the electricity is off isn't it?" And our state-of-the-art, answerphone come email come what's-the-weather-like-today gadget needs more volts to run than a small city.

"So how did the wrong number call, Mum?"

Chapter sixteen

Mum won't wake up. I mean she's not dead or anything. Looks like someone's thrown her on the bed, she's too spread out, over my side. I pushed her in the night but she flopped back so I pulled my mattress away a bit, to get some space.

She was drunk. I'm not a kid, I know this stuff. I hope she doesn't get like before. That was really bad. I'd get up in the morning and she'd be splatted on the sofa, like hangin off it, one time she'd chucked on the floor – gross. Dad tried to hide it but Jess and I knew. He carried her upstairs. Gave Jess pocket money so we could go out so she could sleep the next day. He told us she wasn't feeling well. He pretended. We knew though. I saw him crying one time. I felt bad – wanted to shout at Mum – but he made excuses for her. He played this game where he said we'd both get £1 each for every bottle we found in the house. I tell you she hid them well, there was even one in the loo cupboard – I found that!

Then Jesse died and she stopped, which was kinda surprising.

But then she stopped everything, speakin', eatin', like livin' even. No hugs. Didn't even try to kiss me. She might as well've been dead like Jess.

Seeing her like that this morning you know when you shake someone hard and they just grunt, and smell bad, spooked me, cos Dad's not here and he knows how to sort this stuff. She had dribble down the side of her mouth.

Decided not to hang around waiting for her. If she can't be bothered to get up on time I'll sort myself out. I can get to school. I don't need her.

Tried cold garlic bread for breakfast – it's mingin' – but cold pizza is OK, and so is apple strudel. And seeing as I'm on my own Pepsi out of the bottle will do, if she's not here she can't tell me to use a glass. If you drink a pint of Pepsi quick, you can burp the alphabet.

And the phone is working again and so are the lights. So I call Dad – I bet four rings and he answers. One, two, three, four, five, come on Dad, six...

"Hi, Evie?"

"No, it's me."

"Hi Finn, everything ok?"

"Yeah. When are you comin' back, Dad?"

"Gonna be a few days yet I'm afraid Finn. Next week, I hope."

"Not by the weekend?"

"Don't think so, old chap."

"Oh ok, gotta go, I'll be late for school."

"Hey cheer up. Look we'll ride when I get back; how is Red anyway?"

"OK, I gotta go I'm late Dad. Bye."

Why is he never around when you need him? I reckon he loves work more than anything, well more than us anyhow, funny how he could always take time off for Jesse though – so unfair.

Chapter seventeen

Sunlight is laserbeaming into my brain, singeing holes in that grey pulp – it hurts. My head is hanging off the mattress onto the floor, the air is heavy with garlic again and I can't yet locate my legs.

"Finn?" It must be close to getting-up time. "Finn?" I chance an eye open, wishing we'd shut the curtains last night. But he's already up. The mattress on the floor of the den beside me has all the evidence of a child's occupation, but no child, just a dog-eared Malorie Blackman novel, a torch and two Crunchie wrappers. He must be having breakfast.

Surprisingly I'm still dressed, I was convinced I put on PJs. Was sure I cleaned my teeth, changed, got into bed – but honestly I can't remember that much, we were both so tired last night, best sleep for a long while, no dreams storming around my head waking me up in the small hours.

God the house is noisy today. The radio alarm in our room is waking up an empty double bed. Finn's iPod doc is pounding and every light bulb blazes competing with the sunshine. It takes me a long time to realise that at last we're reunited with electricity!

"Finn! Power's back on!" He can't hear. I switch the TV off in the lounge as I pass. Did we watch TV last night? And the washing machine and tumble dryer are whirring away in the utility room, completely empty. The kitchen is busy too with the mixer whipping fresh air, the phone's ringing and the coffee machine is perking something and I don't even remember unpacking it, but the room is empty. Do I answer the phone or locate Finn? Phone I decide.

"Hello?" I'm braced for the sigh.

"Evie!"

"Hello! How are you, can you come home yet?" Andrew's voice is like a cool wet cloth to my pounding head.

"I wish. How are you both getting on?"

"Oh, all right, no electricity yesterday, but all back on today. Even got some sun. You?"

"Frantic. The Minister wants to make some last minute changes before the final reading, far too dull to go into, but it does mean I'm stuck here for a bit longer than I anticipated." In the background Caroline chirps away, it's as if she wants me to hear her, know that she has Andrew, can see him, touch him... "How's Finn?"

"OK I think. Still hating school, why?"

"Oh, nothing really. He called this morning – sounded a bit low. Just wish I could see him, I do miss you both ... terribly." Caroline calls him; she's telling him they're late. "Look I've got to go, meeting starting in five, they've already put it back from ten o'clock." Put it back from ten o'clock echoes around my dull and aching head, I glance at the kitchen clock, its pendulum swinging like a finger wagging, naughty, naughty, it's five-to-eleven! "Evie? Evie – you still there?"

"Errr, ummm, yeah sorry." I can't admit to him I've only just got up and have no idea whether our son got himself to school or not. "Look I gotta go too Andrew. Please come home soon. Please."

"As soon as, I promise. Bye."

"I lov—" But he's gone. Needing to track down Finn

immediately, I telephone the school. Why do school secretaries always make you feel like you've just walked out of year one? "Of course he's here, Mrs Wolfe. They're having PE as we speak. Is there anything else I can help you with?" She might as well have said, "Any other members of your family you've mislaid that you'd like me to find?" And I could have told her to return my husband at her earliest convenience.

I feel like shit. Useless shit.

How could I sleep through Finn getting himself to school? I banged my head a few times on the kitchen table, the pain deserved – needed – to remind me not to mess this up. Finn is a precious treasure I have to keep safe –stop the world from taking him back and burying him deep in its earth with his brother. And I want to scream at Andrew that the task is too much for me on my own: I just can't be trusted to get it right, can't do it by myself. Burying my head in my arms, tears burn down the sides of my nose. I repeat Andrew's name over and over, banging my forehead on the table in time.

"This isn't the time for feeling sorry for yourself, girl! All this needs finishing up before luncheon, d'ya hear?" I look up to find the kitchen table laden with half finished baking; mixing bowls with batter, eggs separated, cream unwhisked, pastry balled ready to roll but no owner of the voice. An apron waits on the table at my elbow. The smell of roasting meat pushes the earlier garlic tang aside. Outside a man shoves a mower up and down the lawn in front of the house. From deep down the hallway the voice on the edge of angry shouts, "Jump to it then, girl!"

And I do. I don't know why, I'm muddled, lost and a little scared, but beating and rolling, whisking and stirring takes the edge off my uselessness, eases my longing for Andrew to return. By twelve there are cakes, meringues, three asparagus tarts and four strawberry and rhubarb pies in the Rayburn, a milk pudding settling in the pantry and cheese straws cooling on a rack by the open window. The man and his mower are still passing by. My head is aching but I feel good, I've done something, completed the task, the banquet is ready. I feel like I'm back in Willow's Café, this is what I'm good at.

I sit down with a cuppa, just for a break, I take Alys's book with me to the back doorstep where the sun pools for me to sit in. A light green leaf breeze tickles the pages to and fro it can't make up its mind which bit it wants to read. I step in and open at May 28th 1898. Immediately I slam the book shut but the sentence I've just read is already burnt on my retina.

...I am so very proud and happy to announce to you all my dear friends the engagement of my son, Auden, to Lady Isabella...

"No!" Escapes from me. Back inside the kitchen a heart wrenched from its foundation howls in agony; there's an explosion of plates and glass smashing, the screaming tears above the sounds of destruction. I scrabble to my feet stumbling back into the room but it's already obliterated, food is running down every wall, the floor crunches with broken crockery, flour billows in the air as eggs drip from the window, despair covers every surface. Frozen, I can't believe my eyes.

"Alys?" I gently call out to her. "Alys?" Sure this must be her doing, but only the sound of something spilt and dripping answers. I stand up the bottle, another one of Alys's powerful blackberry wines. Slopping what's left into my empty teacup, I down it in one gulp and crunch across to the sink to fill a bowl and start on the devastion.

I wash and scrub and scrape for hours, but it looks as if nobody's bothered. Things are drying, sticking on tight, I could work all night and not make it halfway through this mess. My hands are raw, the knuckles skagged over and over as they catch on broken glass. I sit up against the wall for a bit, resting my arms and back. As I've worked I'm sure the sound of sobbing escapes from the pages of Alys's journal. I rescue it from the back doorstep, holding it close like a broken child. I cry with her.

...Mrs E sent me – they needed more strawberries. Alys, see to it quick now girl – the Judge was chinking his glass with the great silver spoon we use for trifles, like a bell it sounded, hushing all the guests. I remember how bright the ladies' jewels flashed around their necks, funny that I should remember that. Then the Judge steps forward, red and grinning...

I am so very proud and happy to announce to you all, my dear friends, the engagement of my son Auden to Lady Isabella. He says it like the fat cat he is. Then from nowhere he plucks Auden from the crowd like he's a prize bull for showing. Auden looks at me just once then takes the hand of the lah-dee-dah girl, a fairy from a picture book she is. Isabella, my darling. He says kissing her hand.

I didn't even know that he was back from London – not a word.

I couldn't help myself; suddenly the bowl of strawberries was too heavy. The crystal went off like a bomb and I didn't even realise the scream was mine. I ran to the kitchen – couldn't stop – swept the table of everything, pies, tarts, everything! I wanted it all destroyed the way I was and never once did I stop my scream, not even when Mrs E slapped me hard round the face...

Oh Alys, what a terrible, terrible betrayal, how did her heart ever heal? Her painful words make the memories of my awful day in the marquee flood back, after the polo match, when Andrew introduced me to his parents. Sometimes there are days you know that you shouldn't start. You wake up and there's lead in your belly holding you under the duvet telling you, "Hide, stay here, stay safe." But of course none of us listen, we drag ourselves out and onwards, careering towards the oncoming disaster. I arrived at the polo field with only Andrew's words, "Come Evie, it's great fun!", which the uniformed man on the gate didn't accept as a substitute for a proper printed invitation. Unfortunately, Andrew had seen me arrive so my escape was cut off.

There was a dress code – I had broken it.

I watched birds of paradise women flit from group to group, giggling, twittering, and Andrew gliding in and out weaving a social circle I would never be part of, and all the time sitting at his shoulder was a golden creature, small and delicate and in possession. He turned eventually to her, their heads glued but their gestures angry, arms flying, shoulders hunched in, braced for attack. She threw her drink in his face and stormed off into a clucking group of equally beautiful women who swallowed her and wafted off to the marquee.

I stood alone at the rail watching grown men and chestnut ponies charge up and down chasing a tiny white ball, with my unborn baby galloping in time with his father on his horse. A man in an ancient straw hat offered me a deckchair, but I couldn't imagine ever being able to extract myself from it, I thanked him and headed once again for the exit and my familiar world on the other side of it. Three feet from the gate a barrier of words came down: "Evie! Evie! We won! Did you see?" Andrew's face shone like the winners' cup. "Hey you're not leaving, are you? Stay, go on, just a little while – it'll be fun…"

The drink-throwing-golden-girl stood in my path as I ran from the marquee after slapping Andrew, a day of exits barred. She'd been crying, her face bloated and blotchy.

"September 12th was to be our wedding day!" She spat, her tone unclipped and not much different from mine. "He said he needed time though, wanted to postpone for a while." Her words made a sense but not one that I knew, I wanted to ask who needed more time until Andrew called from behind me and I watched her face drag down in despair as she looked towards him.

"Did he tell you about us?" Her question was a desperate whisper.

Dumb, shaking my head, all I could repeat back was, "Did he tell you about us?" My hand protectively rested on my pregnant belly. Andrew arrived too late at my shoulder. His presence ignited her.

"You and your bastard will need this!" She ripped at her finger and threw a tiny ball of lightning at me, which caught me on the cheek before falling to the ground. An obscene sized diamond lay at my feet. I think I heard Andrew whisper her name. "Caroline…" I'm sure he said as I ground the ring into the mud before walking away never once looking back…

Finn's gasp made me jump; I was touching the small c-shaped scar on my cheekbone thinking about that awful day. I hadn't heard him come back in from school, so engrossed in the past again that I'd lost all sense of time.

"What have you done, Mum?" he shouts, staring at the broken dish and pie that I didn't even realise I was holding. I raise my other hand to my face, wiping something that is dripping from my hairline. I try to calm my breathing and realise that there's a gash across my right arm, just above my wrist. It looks deliberate, looks like I meant something by it. I want to tell him it's all an accident.

Chapter eighteen

OH-MY-GOD, OMFG. Shes gone MENTAL. The place is wrecked. She's drippin' in stuff and there's food smashed everywhere, EVERYWHERE! Theres even somethin' drippin' off the ceiling. And her arm, all that blood, I can't look – feel sick. Shit. I yelled, "Why can't you be NORMAL?" And then she tries to make out she didn't do it. Well who else d'ya think did it, Mum, there's only you here? Alys she said – Mental! Stop doing this Mum, STOP.

I made her cry. It felt good. I wanted her to get up, to not be drunk, not be weird. I wanted her to do something about her arm – hide it, stop it bleedin'.

The place smelt winey again. She smelt winey again.

What do I do? If I call Dad he'll go crazy, she might go away again like before when she was ill, Dad'll have no choice – like last time, she could be dangerous, then what? I can't do this. Fucking hell. *They're* s'posed to look after me. I don't understand all this stuff – it's grown-up shit.

I leave her to it, I asked Red what I should do, he said give him more apples.

"Jesse, help me. Come back and help me for fuck's sake."

Chapter nineteen

"Finn! Finn. Come back. It's not what you think. Finn!" He's out of the door faster than a swallow. He thinks I did it, thinks I smashed the kitchen up – he thinks I've gone mad.

I find him in the stables talking to his pony. "She's gone crazy, Red," he whispers into the animal's neck.

"Finn. Please, let me explain."

"Just leave me alone, Mum."

"But Finn, please, let me show you, see here in Alys's book." I try to show him her tormented scrawl, "Finn, see, in 1898…"

"Yeah, 1898 Mum, it's 2010 if you hadn't noticed. Just go, leave me alone."

"Won't you come back inside?"

"No. I want to ride Red."

"But Dad said to wait didn't he?"

"Whatever." He grunts, turning his back on me, full-stopping the conversation. If he were small I could scoop him now out of his desperate place, hold him to me so my heart could beat through my ribs and his, let him know I'll make it all right, I will, Finn. But he's ten not five. Defeated, the kitchen drags me back to the mops and buckets. The phone is ringing, ringing, ringing.

I lift the receiver, suddenly it weighs a ton, "Andrew? Andrew is that you, please come home, I need you … Andrew?" Static crackles back then a slow intake of breath

"Oh Evelyn, what have you done?" The voice sounds like Andrew's mother, the mocking hint ever present in her superior tone.

"Amelia?"

162

"Oh Evelyn, what have you done?" Now the voice changes, it's sharp, nagging and Caroline. Terrified I bang the receiver down hard. Immediately the ringing begins again – without hesitation the phone goes in the bucket, bubbles burst to the surface, popping little rings toward the ceiling. I turn my whole attention to the still-sticky floor. I put an empty bucket in the sink and begin to fill it again. I glance out the window but instead of a golden sunset three figures glare back at me, arms folded, heads slightly tilted. I know they are a reflection of my mind, I know that Amelia Wolfe is not stood out there with Ma and Rufus Wolfe hanging back in the shadows. They begin to shake their heads in disappointment. I rip the ancient dusty curtains closed, shutting them out. I fiercely spin the knobs on Nana's radio, desperately needing a happy tune – it stays silent. So I imagine Willow into being and tell her all about the rainbow café as I slosh soapy water over the floor.

Finn stays out until the dark turns up. I know he's starving, but he's pretending indifference, and half-heartedly makes his own sandwich with un-smashed leftovers. He won't look at me. His last mouthful is barely chewed and he's heading upstairs, mumbling goodnight. I want to race up behind him, chat in the dark under the duvets, prove it wasn't me, make him understand I'm not a crazy woman, but I have to clear all this away before we start on another day. The hot water runs out. By midnight I have the floor under control and the walls aren't running with rhubarb, but the ceiling still hangs as a challenge.

I want to speak to Andrew, pour a glass of something from a bottle we're sharing and rest my head against his chest, let the rhythm of his heart soothe me. Be on a beach somewhere far, far away, watching stars wink on the sea, go back to Royan where we stayed before Jesse was born. Next week seems so very far away, can we wait for him that long? Retrieving the phone from the cold grey water I check, stupidly, for a dial tone. Nothing. I hunt my mobile and track it down to yesterday's coat pocket. Rummaging in an unpacked box I un-knit a charger cable from headphones, string and three random USB cables. I plug in the handset breathing life back into the dead lump of plastic. The screen flashes the annoying jingle, jangles:

C U soon Ax

Pings. I run my fingers over his letters whispering his name softly, rolling it around my tongue. I have a physical pain where his hand should be stroking mine, should be gently touching the cut on my wrist and a place on my cheek burns from the imagined brush of his lips. My fingers run over his keys and press before I can stop them. His answer wades through from a deep unconsciousness.

"H-hello?"

"Hi. It's only me, I just needed to…"

"Evie? Everything OK?" His voice is all slurred from dreaming.

"Yep, Just wanted to hear you, that's all."

"But it's like … three in the morning, Eve."

"I know, I know, I'm sorry. Go back to sleep – Andrew, I love you."

"Mmm, me too, call me in the morning, hey?" And just as the phone bees buzz down the line – there it is – that sigh and – I'm sure, I'm not imagining it – a little high-pitched giggle.

"Andrew! Andrew, is Caroline there? Andrew?" Only the buzz answers my questions. In the middle of the now-clean kitchen table a bottle of dark liquid waits with arms open and a clean glass to chat with. The first glass I dedicate to the bitch Caroline, the second to my lying husband, then Amelia Wolfe, Rufus Wolfe and the last glass to Ma, may she rest in hell. By the time the bottle is empty daylight is timidly edging round into the kitchen. To make it up to Finn and banish the three hours till he surfaces I start to bake. His all time favourites are Brownies, can't find any walnuts or a proper recipe so I freestyle a bit, but they look about right. Jam tarts are always a winner; I'm not sure Finn will appreciate the gooseberry jam filling them but it's all I can find. There's enough oats to make flapjacks and pastry and eggs to make lemon meringue pie, which was Jesse's favourite, warm with the lemon running, I cut him a slice as soon as it comes out of the oven; a rack of cookies cool by the window, with a batch of scones. I'm contemplating a quiche, when the swallows get up.

The sun is low and climbing, burning through the orange air. Finally I'm tired, as wrung out as the mops leant against the wall. I make tea and sit on the back door step to watch the day organise itself into morning. I take Alys's book with me for company. Quickly passing over the entries I read yesterday, there's nothing written page after page, it becomes more of a scrapbook. A torn square of fine, once-white cotton with tiny daisy embroidery is stuck down beside a circle of paper flowers that have been flattened by the weight of words resting on them. There are no labels or notes, just a tiny date written at the bottom of the page, 12 September. Our wedding anniversary, the day Andrew should have married Caroline, but I stole it from her. I gently run my fingers over these treasures and something tells me Alys intended to wear these on her wedding day. The ribbons that hang in a tangle from the paper-flower headdress are yellowed, brown stains up the length of each one. The ancient glue holding the circle in place gives up and it comes away in my hand, I can't stop myself placing it on my tangled, matted hair. As it rests there I hear her with that sing song voice: *Auden Llewellyn-Rhys loves me and I love him.* Round and around her little tune goes, on and on to the smash of the bowl and the scream. I scamper back to the kitchen to check it's my mind smashing and screaming with Alys not the kitchen again. The kitchen is still, organised and quiet.

Putting her book on the table it falls open at its own chosen place, she's written one line right across the centre of the page:

July 12 1898 – I felt the babi move today.

Chapter twenty

Mmmmm something smells good. Smells of brownies, I was gonna run down quick to see, then I remembered yesterday. Remembered Mum's gone mad, remembered her arm... Makin' brownies isn't gonna fix it, how stupid does she think I am, like you can make everything all right with cake! I pulled the duvet over my head. Why can't we go back two years to before Dad got this job and Jesse was still here being an annoying prick – WHY?

She didn't come to bed last night. I thought about checking, but then I didn't want to see any more, didn't want to find anythin', I mean what if she was drunk, or she'd spewed everywhere or ... I don't know. So I just waited but she never came. Think she's stopped sleeping ... like before. So I started thinking how do I get help? Before in London there was like loads of people there – I mean too many really, always coming round to check we were all OK cos of Jesse. I mean Mum's mate Willow was there all the time. I know it pissed Dad off cos he thought she was a weirdo, but I thought she was cool. She just kinda knew what you needed. Didn't keep askin' you how you were or how you felt. She just turned up with cake and stuff and made me tea and held onto Mum. Not in a lezza way, just a cheer-up way. And Mum cried and talked to her – only person she did talk to – instead of sittin' an starin' – doin' her zombie face. Maybe I should call Willow, she'd know what to do.

Cos here, it's good no one knows about Jesse, but there's no one checking Mum, only Dad but he's not here. If I phone him its questions, questions, questions about stuff I don't even know, I mean I got no idea how Mum's feeling – apart from crazy and sad, I guess.

Shit, there's a spelling test today, meant to learn them last night, thought I'd cheer Mum up and ask her to test me – why do grown-ups like that so much – weird? Well it's gonna be her fault if I fail, she screwed this one up.

"Loser!"

"Shut up, Jesse." I hate it when he talks in my head and I can't get rid of him, he stays there all day sometimes and then I get told off for talkin' in class, and they laughed at me yesterday when I told him to fuck off and leave me alone, I got sent to Mr Jones' office for swearin' and Jesse spent all afternoon laughing at me.

"Go on then gayler, I'll test you."

"Don't be stupid Jesse," I told him, "What d'you know about Welsh?"

"More than you, by the looks of it dick'ead."

"Piss-off. I'm going for breakfast!"

"Watch out for the crazy woman." And then he was gone.

And I wished I could just disappear the way he does.

I knew she was still crazy before I got in the kitchen. She's standing there – right – dancing with a broom, singin to that ratty old radio, with a wedding thing on her head.

So there's one empty bottle on the table and it's only breakfast. How drunk does that make her?

"Gettin' married?"

"Finn! You made me jump." She doesn't even take the thing off. "I made some brownies. Want one?" Oh, she's drunk – since when was brownies for breakfast OK, what about cereals and juice?

"All right." There is food everywhere, last night she'd thrown it all over the floor, this morning she's made it all again like its a party. "Who's comin'?"

"No one, thought I'd use up some stuff. Make something you and Jesse, I mean something you like." The brownies are good – no nuts – how I like them. Her lips are black from wine, I don't want to look at her – her eyes are pink. "I could walk with you up the lane to catch the school bus if you like?"

"No, You're OK, I can manage." She tries to smile but it's wobbly. I think about saying thanks for the brownies but then she's gonna think everythin's OK, which it isn't, so I try to ignore her. I got hours before the bus arrives, well at least twenty minutes but it's too weird in here with her so I get my bag, I try to get out of the kitchen before she kisses me but fail. She stinks of wine. I hate her for that, why can't she just be a normal Mum – drink coke or something.

I start walking up the lane. It's hot already. I'm gonna get Dad to sort this, I can't do it, but as usual no answer when I call him.

"Answer your fucking phone Dad!" I shout. All I ever get is, "Hi sorry can't take your call please leave me a message."

"Answer your phone, Dad."

At least Brony cares 'cos she jumps out from the trees. I chuck sticks for her, but she's crap she ignores them.

Bus is late.

BREAD

4 oz Yeast.
2 Table sps Dem Sugar
½ pt. Lukewarm water

Mix & put in warm place to work.
USING DRIED YEAST

50 gm Dr Yeast
½ Tablespn Dem Sugar
1 PT L W WATER
Put 2 t/s in Flr.
Put in a bowl.

2 tablespns BRAN.
1 bag Wholemeal Flr
+ white flr to 6 lbs
9 small teaspns Salt
2-3 oz Lard.

add Yeast when frothy plus another 2½ pts warm water
Mix with wooden spn until workable by hand.
Keep folding over & pressing out until mix is smooth.
Weigh up 1¾ lb for larger tins + 1¼ for smaller tins - Greased
make into sausage shape.
Put in cold oven [illegible]
loaves one on top to bottom shelves, leave for another ½ hr.
If tops when tapped sound hollow is cooked at bottom
turn out onto rack.

Chapter twenty-one

5. 1 oz Flr.

The second Finn slams out, off on his own to school, the phone starts – even after its dunking, even without power. Sometimes there's a message – the same two voices, shrill nagging, sometimes just silence. I leave the receiver off the hook but their voices ring around the room. Their reflections, the three of them, Ma and Amelia with Rufus standing guard, still look in through the kitchen window. I shut the curtains on them, but feel their disapproving gaze through the material.

I am so very tired. Everything is heavy and weighed down and I no longer feel I have the energy to drag my limbs around with me. It's 8am, Finn has gone, I see in his face that he can't bear to share a room with me, I have six hours before he returns – six hours, and not a thing to do. I'm not needed. I wish I could put myself on stand-by, shut down, so that my brain knew it wasn't needed either, stop its thinkings, its little voices, the painful memories it throws around because it has a will of its own.

In once-upon-a-time when I functioned, at this point every morning, I would have achieved two packed lunches, dispatched children and be already elbow deep in dough and jam, eyes weeping from onions, fingers purple from the red cabbage waiting to be coleslaw'd, happily making in the tiny kitchen at the back of Willow's café: in my other life as that other person, before. Willow Green is my best friend. She's a rainbow person tie-died in a hundred colours of skirts, beads and bangles. Hide her in a dark corner of your memory, and when you take her out again her glow is even brighter. She is my only true friend. I think when I was young Ma moved us so many times, chasing one job after another, that I never had the chance to keep friends. Not until Nana and Papa stepped in, hauling me off Ma's destruction express, did I find her, a someone to stick to.

And Willow found me so we stuck together.

She was my partner in PE when the girls that won didn't want us on their team. She was my partner at ballet classes when Nana finally said I could go. Willow showed me which foot to point when left and right were still a muddle. We stood together in the playground when they called us names, and went to detention as a duo.

"Come back when you're ready," she said when I phoned to tell her about Jess – she already knew though – saved me from having to use the words.

I thought it might take a month or two for the numbness to pass, to want to work again at something, create beautiful towers of sugar for marshmallow brides. Willow did all the food for Jesse's awful after thing; that people can eat at a funeral is anathema to me. But they did, everything – gone. Six months passed, at home we ate microwaved things or forgot. Willow appeared magically at our front door with stuff that boys devour, chatting to Finn about music, gigs, football scores and things in his language, she kept him afloat in normality. Andrew thought she was in the way, interfering. Willow always thought he was a pompous prick, someone who came between the two of us. Gradually Willow's weekly calls came once a fortnight, I forgot to return her messages. Then we moved. I sent a change of address, last week she sent a "Good luck in your new home" card. It said:

"Miss you, miss your terrible singing, miss dancing. Feels like half of me's gone. Café's too quiet, and the food doesn't taste the same any more. You know there's always room here for you and Finn, always xxx

PS
Any chance of that walnut loaf recipe, and maybe the toffee cake — regulars still ask. Off to polish our glitterball, love you girlie. Wx"

I could do that. Find a pen, a piece of note paper and the memory of making Nana's walnut bread, write it all down and post it to Willow. Maybe.

All this time in between Jesse with us and Jesse gone has been filled with different kinds of nothing: empty spaces where people popped in to check you weren't crying, that you were dressed and didn't have scarecrow hair. But here there aren't any popping people; the ones I didn't want but now need desperately. Now it's me and nothing. It's a year, three months, eight days and one-and-a-half minutes since I've been all right left on my own. I can't stop my mind wading back to that moment…

One minute.

Fifty seconds.

Thirty.

BANG.

"Stay with me, Mum," he whispered, gripping my arm, pain wracking his chest, blood soaking the school shirt with the ripped pocket dark black red.

"You too Jess, you stay too," I pleaded into his hair, cradling his head in my lap. But already he'd gone. And all around, everyday carried on, parents trying to drop off the children, couriers chasing deadlines, joggers after a personal best and in the background the growing sirens closing in from every direction.

The dug-up memories have left an outline of Jesse's body in the kitchen, I can't bear to be in here for a moment longer. I grab Alys's book and run upstairs, the wooden treads moaning at my speed. A plan is forming to write back to Willow so quietly and carefully I open the door to Jesse's room, Andrew calls it the study, but Jesse needs a place to keep his things, Andrew can study elsewhere. As the tape rips off the first box, a cloud of stale Lynx deodorant escapes, one of Jesse's favourites– chocolate something or other – it smells as grim now as it did when he walked out of the door wearing it. A pad of doodled paper sits at the top of the box and, just below, a grotty Sports Direct mug minus handle clutches a graveyard of pens. I choose a chewed biro that I roll across my top lip imagining it in Jesse's mouth. After opening several other boxes, I find the one with his bedding in. Wrapping his duvet around me, I squash into a corner of his new room to write.

What am I going to say to Willow? I could phone her but that's too involved, she might ask questions, things I can't answer: "How's Wales, then, Evie? And Finn?" She wouldn't ask about Andrew. What can I tell her? My phone won't stop ringing, my mother is staring at me from the front yard, Wales is a new shoe that's a size too big, and my husband is missing, quite possibly with his ex-fiancée. Oh, and my son can't bear to share the same room with me. No, much better to write, keep those cats in the bag.

Starting a letter to someone you should never have stopped speaking to is complicated. Dear is too formal, but can I race in with Hi Willow? So I try:

Missing you too, Willow. Missing the café, and of course the dancing. Been cutting some mean moves to Nana's old radio which I finally got to work – sure she's watching over me, just need my dancing partner... Anytime you happen to be passing...

So that Walnut loaf – if I remember rightly:

10oz flour plain
tsp baking powder
2oz butter, 4oz walnuts chopped
and don't forget buttermilk, that's what Nana always used.

Make it like a scone mix, use buttermilk to bind, into oven 20 mins. But watch yours because some days it's a furnace and others, well, let's just say the fridge could do a better job! Unless you finally coughed up and got someone in to fix it.

Will write again soon. Don't forget me Willow, loving you too.
   Evie x

For safe keeping and until some envelopes materialise I push Willow's letter into the back of Alys's book, secure with all the other precious papers there. I miss Willow, she was like a reflection of my soul; sometimes we didn't even need to speak, she could hear my thoughts, give me an answer before I asked the question. We've known each other since we were six, since that day I stood with Nana shivering outside the village hall waiting to go into my first ballet class. Willow was short and round, her little skirt stuck out straight as it tried to cover her bottom, I was too tall, my knee bones rubbed even though my feet were six inches apart; Miss Walls winced as we tumbled through the door.

How we twirled, out of time, on the wrong foot and in the wrong direction, we were in heaven. As we struggled up the grades Willow stretched out into a lean liquid mover, I didn't really change except my tallness changed to shortness as Willow grew past, my knees still bumped. Eventually Miss Walls didn't have to shout so much, I stopped getting the boy role in the Christmas performance, and Willow got the lead. We darned our first pointe shoes together, stitched sequins, pinned up each other's hair and dreamed of the day when Mikhail Baryshnikov would *jeté* into class to *pas-de-deux* into the sunset with one of us.

Dancing soothed away the hurt, the rejection Ma left each time she appeared when another job vanished, then disappeared again when a new one started. Willow sprinkled sparkles over our teenage years when Nana struggled to keep up, or just plain didn't understand.

"You're dancing in a disco competition in black bin liners

and fishnet tights. Do bin bags constitute a costume?" They certainly do we explained afterwards, dancing round Nana's kitchen table with our under 16s Disco Champs trophy, Shalamar blaring out of Willow's ghetto blaster. I sat up with her all night after her rejection letter arrived from Ballet Rambert, helped her cut her ballet shoes into a thousand pieces. Dancing got moved to a Saturday night in one seedy nightclub or another. Willow only danced as a mating call, writhing for some male attention: most Saturdays she was successful, most Saturdays I came home on my own.

Cocooned in Jesse's duvet, hugging Alys's journal, the past is exhausting me, I give in to sleep, '*I'm gonna make this a night to remember*,' still boogying round my brain.

Sleep keeps me until three, I awake hot and confused with a hangover strength headache that has no reason to be there. I have no time to wash or change the clothes I think I've been wearing and sleeping in for at least two days. Finn has just started to walk down the lane from the school bus drop off as I arrive on foot.

"Hi sweetheart! Good day?" His grunt sheds no light on good or bad.

"Can I ride Red when I get home?"

I want to groan like him, I can only say no to this, it's like he wants to fight.

"Not tonight love. Dad's not here, you know that." His pace speeds up a little so that he's walking two strides in front of me. We walk this way home with me shouting conversation starters at his back and Finn grunting. He throws his bag on the front doorstep, not even bothering to come in and heads straight over to the stables. Red whinnies and Finn starts up a stream of animated horse babble. I'm jealous of the horse, of the attention Finn can give it, when a sentence about his day was too much effort for me. Hurt, I return to the kitchen to watch the happy couple. Supper is a fairly silent affair.

"I failed Welsh. Mr Evans wants to see you." I'm so relieved at conversation that I don't have the heart to chastise.

"Right. Did he say when?"

"No." His chair scrapes, he makes to leave.

"How long am I going to get the silent treatment, Finn?"

"I'm not doing silent treatment."

"So what's going on then? I mean I can barely get a word out of you."

"I don't see why I can't ride Red." I'm relieved it's the horse he wants to talk about, not me or last night.

"Well, can you put the saddle on by yourself?"

"Yeah – well sort of."

"Sort of isn't safe is it? That's why Dad said wait. He'll be back in a few days, so you can make sure you've got the whole tack situation sorted, then I'm sure, next week, you can do your own thing, ride when you want."

"Whatever. Got spellings to learn." Within minutes of his departure, loud indistinguishable music thumps on the ceiling and I wonder how he'll learn anything over that.

Washing up, I watch out of the kitchen window, Ma and the Wolfes have gone. A boy with golden hair walks to Red's stable door, for a moment I think it's Jesse, then he glances nervously over his shoulder showing himself to be Nye. The horse accepts an apple from Nye, who once again checks behind him as if he's being followed. By the time I've put the plate in the rack to dry he's disappeared into the yellowing evening. Around ten the music stops, no "Goodnight" just the dark and Finn's silence. When I go up to check on him, he's flung across his mattress in an awkward star, my mattress has been pushed up against the opposite wall, he might as well have shouted: 'I don't want you in here!' I get Jesse's duvet on the way down and drag Nana's old rocker from the furniture waiting to be sorted in the lounge, I pull it in front of the Rayburn and rock the rest of the night away to the soft hummings of Nana's radio. Around five dawn starts bleaching the night. I scribble another note to Willow enclosing the toffee cake recipe, which I've now remembered. Finn passes through for breakfast, it's an event of few words, he eyes me suspiciously. I feel guilty.

"You didn't come up last night."

"Didn't want to disturb you. How did the spellings go?"

"OK." He makes to leave, and my heart sinks with the six hours of waiting for him to return.

"I'll meet you off the bus." He looks me up and down, trying to pretend he's not. I realise I must look a bit wild and smile at him, he's embarrassed and hurries out the front door, shouting goodbye over his shoulder. I mean to head for the bathroom, but the phone starts ringing and the answer phone takes over:

"Evelyn. I know you're there. Speak to me Evelyn." Amelia Wolfe, Andrew's mother. She has a voice that pulls

180

your spine taut. Everything in the kitchen stands to attention. I picture our joyless greetings as we both try to avoid physical contact, her spiked fingers finding their way into the painful spaces between my bones as she briefly grasps me in a chilled hello. A woman made of angles and points; I imagine her internal organs cast in glass and wonder how much strength I would need to shatter her.

She hates me.

I have her son. I've ruined the perfect future her and Rufus had mapped out for him. And now she thinks I'm doing the same to her grandson, and she will never forgive me for that theft.

And me? I hate her right back: her disapproval, her judgments from on high, the whole superiority of her.

I grab Alys's book and run for the stairs leaving Amelia to shout at an empty room. "I shall have to come down…" I hear her threatening. In Jesse's room it's safe and quiet. I huddle into his duvet quickly sleeping deep and dark until a memory dressed up as a dream rudely interrupts. I'm standing beside Andrew in Richmond Register Office, my dress, though, is made of the fine embroidered white cotton from Alys's book and I know as I reach to my head that I'm wearing the paper ring of flowers and ribbons. Willow is there dressed as a rainbow. The door bursts open and in they hurtle, Amelia, Rufus and (lurking as a backdrop) Caroline. They know of lawful impediments stopping the service. As I run from the room Caroline shouts after me, "You can't trap him…" I don't hear the rest as it's drowned out by the sound of Alys smashing crystal.

I wake to the sound of Finn returning from school, slamming the front door.

"Mum! Mum! Mr Evans picked me for the rugby team! Mum!" Blurry from sleep I stumble downstairs to celebrate with him. Over oven chips and Jammy Dodgers Finn patiently explains his version of the rules of rugby leaving me utterly confused. The earlier heat from the day has boiled over into rain, we muck out Red together, talking mostly nonsense. Being together even in horse shit is a delight. I want to savour every second to help me through tomorrow when he leaves again. Around eight we give up on the day and head up to the den with cocoa. Finn suggests we restart *Harry Potter and The Deathly Hallows* as neither of us can remember which chapter we'd previously got to. He wants me to read to him. He wants me.

We sleep like normal people, all through the night. In my dreams I can see the winning post, one more day and I have dragged myself through my first solo week. "I knew you could do it dear," Nana whispers in my ear. I wake up with a Friday Fizz, bacon sarnies for breakfast and I can tell I'm too bright – I make Finn wince.

"Don't walk up the lane with me." He pleads, ketchup dripping down his chin.

"But it's such a lovely morning." Like me the weather's woken up, found the breeze and persuaded the sun to come out. "Go on … I won't come right to the end."

He looks me up and down, mouth slack, eyebrows joined. "Mum…" Is all he says –it's my scarecrow hair, it must be.

182

"OK, OK, see you after school then." He grunts a reply. I'll take it as goodbye-Mum-have-a-nice-day. As the front door slams behind him the phone starts to ring an Amelia Wolfe ring. I run for the bathroom, chancing a glance in the mirror, a wild stranger stares back. Her colourless skin and dead eyes unnerve me. The hot water is set to awkward today – closer to freezing point than is comfortable, but I will not give in. I break the first comb I try, and the brush just gets stuck in the mat that was my hair. I'm being practical when I grab the nail scissors. Why is hair so difficult to cut through? It's very hard to keep each chunk an even length when you have to saw through it. When I finish, the basin is full of what looks like a mountain sheep's fleece. I don't look up just in case that stranger is still watching me. "Oh my!" Nana exclaims in surprise, when I turn round, "Still it's only hair, it'll grow back."

I am clean top to toe, my skin stings, I glow a just-scrubbed red, but it's done, If the checker-uppers popped in now I would tick all of their boxes. I am back to fight the world, today I shall tackle the lounge but first a climb up the lane to the village – we're out of milk.

"But maybe a hat, dear?" Nana suggests as I head downstairs.

Chapter twenty-two

ELDERFLOWER CHAMPAGNE

2 heads of elderflowers
1¼ lb. white sugar
2 tablespoons white-wine vinegar

1 gallon water
1 lemon

Pick the heads when in full bloom and put into a bowl followed by the lemon juice, cut-up rind (no white pith), sugar and vinegar. Add the cold water and leave twenty-four hours.

14
6. Elder flower. 2 heads
1¼lb. Sugar
3 lemons

I hate rugby. Stupid game. I definitely did not miss that tackle. They scored because that fat git Tomos Waters can't run. I'm not the last line of defence – I'm fullback – derrrrrr.

When I get back home Brony's waiting, "Hi girl!" I give her a fuss.

Unbelievable – Mum's gone and locked me out! Crap. She said she would meet me off the bus, thank God she didn't though, she looks like shit! "What we gonna do, hey Brony – shall we call her?" But when did Mum ever have her phone on? I try anyway. "Come on – answer! See told you, Brony, useless."

I bang on the door in case she's asleep or something. "Mum! Mum – open the door!" Nothin', so what do I do now? I give her one last chance... "Come on, Mum, answer!" I'm starving. I talk to Red, take my mind off it.

"Hi boy." He wants apples, he show his teeth, like grinnin' – nope no apples today. Hey fancy a go round the paddock? I could check with Dad – say how careful I'll be. He might say yes. Typical, no answer. And I'm thinkin' last chance Dad...

"Hello."

Crap, Aunty Caro answers. "Can I talk to Dad?"

"Hello, Finn is that you?" I don't like talkin' to her – she's smarmy – asks tonnes of questions, like she's interested in you.

"Yeah, can I talk to Dad?"

"How are you? I bet you're enjoying the new school. Are you learning Welsh and playing rugby? We'll be

186

watching you at Twickers!" She does this laugh that sounds like Red neighing. "Is everything all right?" She doesn't give up.

"Yeah, can I talk to Dad?"

"Finn, your father's really busy at the moment, can I help?" Like she would know how to tack a horse. I don't think so.

"No, I need to talk to Dad.'

"Is it anything urgent Finn because...?"

I get cross, "Yeah it's really urgent, can I talk to him ... now?" There's rustlin'.

"Finn, hi, hey how are you, sunshine? Everything OK?" Why do grown-ups always think there's something wrong when you call them, and then never let you speak?

"Dad..."

"How's school going? Did you win the rugger match? And how's Mum?"

"Ok s'pose..."

"Which – Mum or school?"

Too many questions. If he just shut up then I could ask him about riding.

"Both I guess." And I really didn't mean to say, "'Cept Mum wasn't at the bus and the house is locked, but Dad..." Cos I knew he'd go ape.

"So who's there with you?"

"Brony, but Dad..."

"Brony? Who's Brony? Where's Mum, Finn?" Like, how should I know?'

It's all goin' wrong. I wish I'd never phoned. "Brony's the

187

dog, remember, and I don't know where Mum is. Listen, Dad, can I ride Red, just round the paddock, no jumping."

"Finn, no! Absolutely not. Bloody hell, Evelyn... Sorry – I mean, how long have you been there on your own? Is her car there?"

"Yeah, car's here, but why can't I ride, I'll be really careful."

"No, Finn, not on your own. Are you sure Mum didn't say she was going somewhere?"

"No. I said. She's been a bit ... well a bit weird, then today she was OK again, 'cept now she's not here, anyway, Dad, I'll be really, really careful pleaseeee let me ride."

"Hang on a minute – weird what do you mean weird? Why didn't you call me, Finn?" Why doesn't he listen when I say she's OK?

"Cos you said it had to be an emergency." That's what he always says, he's so busy, blah, blah, and it wasn't an emergency, was it?

"OK, OK, so what kind of weird, Finn?"

"Usual, bit like before."

"Like before – in what way? Help me out here, Finn."

"Just the same stuff, stays up, doesn't sleep – made loads of cakes then smashed them all up, doesn't get dressed. But, Dad, please, I promise I'll be careful..."

"Is she drinking again, Finn, can you tell?"

"Maybe ... umm, not sure." Now there's gonna be trouble – I'll get the blame.

"Oh God, I thought she'd be OK this time, new place – things to keep her busy. I shouldn't have listened to the counsellor." I think he's talking to himself now. "Look, sit tight, Finn. Don't touch the horse. I'm going to make some calls – give Grandma a shout. It's going to be OK, Finn, just promise me you'll wait there at Pengarrow. Sorry, old chap, I really thought some time without us all fussing over her might do Mum some good – help her, you know? Look, I'll find someone who can let you in OK? I'm going now but I'm going to call you again in ten minutes, and I'm on my way home – leaving right now. All right, Finn?"

"Yeah, all right." Crap – I only wanted to ride and now it's gone crazy. Mum's gonna be soooo mad if Grandma shows up. All he needed to do was say, "Yes Finn you can ride," not come home and bring Grandma.

I'm so hungry, lunch was mingin' again today. Shit.

"This is all your fault, Jesse! I'm stuck here looking after Mum, and if you'd never been with Jazzy, we'd all still be in our old house doin' normal stuff and Mum might be normal too."

Then from nowhere someone says... "Who you shouting at now then lad?"

It's the Jesse clone, he twitches, and hunches down, looks scared. "No one," I tell him.

"Funny thing to do then."

"So, what d'you care?" He goes to leave, looks like he's about to run.

"I don't."

"Hey, wait." He looks so like my brother – maybe shorter, bonier. His eyes look purple – like he's been punched. "Who are you anyway?"

"Why d'you want to know?"

"No reason." He looks like he's gonna run again and I want him to stay, don't want to wait on my own. He thinks for a bit, then says – like he's telling me some great big secret – "Nye, I'm Nye Morgan." I know that name! He's the one what wrote the letter about going to war, about the stuff Mr Evans is teaching us! But that's too weird. That's like a million years ago. I'm scared, he's starin' at me. I mean he's there right in front of me, like not a ghost at all, really real. Shit ... am I going crazy like Mum? After ages I tell him: "I'm Finn ... d'you know that Alys?" I don't look at him now. I kinda hope that he goes, I think it's better if I'm on my own cos my head just can't sort this.

"Aye, that's me mam." Then there's another long quiet, I think he's gonna go cos he keeps checkin' over his shoulder and lookin' around, but then he says, "You waitin' for someone?"

"Yeah, me Mum, I'm locked out."

"Mam's got a key. Come on, she'll make you something to eat, too, it's not far." He looks in a hurry, still checking over his shoulder. I don't want to go with him, I mean if he just disappears in the woods and I'm stuck there – I'm not scared – but ... I wish Mum would get back, like, now.

"You lookin' for someone?" He frowns at me, shakin' his head, and off he goes towards the woods. So I go. I mean Mum could be forever, and I'm starvin'. I stop thinkin' stuff and follow him. I have to run to even keep up but first I tell him...

"Hey hang on, I need to text Mum and Dad."

"Do what?"

"Text." *Gone to nyes.backsoon f*

Doo Jel. about £50.000
pounds. Gill
A Slater 1.0.9ᵈ — 2b.

Chapter twenty-three

I heard Finn. I did. I banged on the bathroom window, calling out to him. He didn't wait. I wanted to tell him that I was trapped up here by Amelia, her constant calling, her piercing voice was making a breaking pain in my head. I watched Finn head off into Hollow's Wood with Alys's boy. Nye is so like Jess it makes breathing hurt, but at least he's still home in Wales, not on some awful boat back to the Front in France. I ran from the safety of the airing cupboard where I'd spent most of the day hiding after trying to escape in Jesse's room, ramming my hand over my ears, crashing two at a time down the stairs, shouting Finn's name over the sound of Amelia Wolfe, over her ringing, her messaging.

All day it had been the same: first Caroline, cold, curt Caroline. "Message from Andrew: he hopes you have a great weekend, he has to stay in London to brief the Minister before the European Conference on Monday. He will be out to dinner this evening and back late so no time for a call…" I shut her out, hating Andrew for his cruelty in using her to leave his messages. Then Amelia was back. I pushed the delete button on the answer machine and missed, catching some other replay instead.

"Evelyn stop being so difficult. Are you ill again? You're behaving just like your mother, don't you think? We're beginning to worry you're a danger—"

"I'm nothing like my mother!" I shouted at her message.

"You have six minutes recording time left," the answer machine robotically reminded me. I stabbed the "delete all messages" button over and over, never wanting to hear that hateful woman again. Without waiting for a ring and as if

sitting in judgment the machine clicked again into life: …
not at home please leave a message…

"I know you're there Evelyn. You can't hide. Who's
looking after Finn? Are you up to it Evelyn? Evelyn. Evelyn?"

I snatched the machine ripping the power cable from the
back and threw it to the floor, small bites of plastic spun
across the slates.

"Evelyn?" It still nagged until I brought my foot down
hard, stamping. My heart banged in my head, I grabbed
Alys's book as a thing of comfort and ran up the stairs. I
tried Jesse's room first but Amelia's voice still eased through
the floorboards, so I fled to the bathroom, throwing open
the airing cupboard door, letting the dark, dry warm space
swallow me whole. Here it felt safe.

"There, there now girl, hush." I conjured Nana to be in
here waiting for me with the dark. I lay my head down on
her lap gripping Alys's book to my chest, hugging my knees
in tight. "Lady la-di-da can't harm us in here," she reassured
me.

"She wants Finn, Nana. I know she's gonna take him."

"No one's taking Finn, dear, no one."

"But she's coming, you heard. They don't trust me on
my own."

"Shhhh. Stop getting yourself in such a stew." Her hand
brushed over my forehead sweeping away the chewed-off
hair. "There now, forty winks and you'll feel ready to face
the world again." Her hand swept across my skin again.

"Nana, please tell me I'm not like Ma."

She chuckled. "You have her eyes, Evie." I had wanted

to argue but she started to sing, "*Keep smiling through, just like you always do...*" Soon I was heavy with sleep and dreamt of the past, of the wars I'd had with Amelia and the endless waits for Ma.

And that's when Finn's calling and door banging finally woke me.

I snatch a coat and someone's boots, throwing open the door, yelling after Finn and Nye. The boys have vanished through the branches before I'm across the front yard. Fixing my eyes on the point of their disappearance I clumsily chase after them. Hollow's Wood has grown straight from Tolkien's pages, riddled with mischief, trickery dripping from every twig. Trees and bushes close behind me, every colour of green arcs above, a buzzard shrieks a warning that an intruder is on her way. The bent and tumbled trunks hide rustlers and twig crackers, something to the left rushes home to tell the news to the rest of the warren. The ground is padded with a hundred autumns' worth of leaves, my footsteps snap and everything is covered in a deep green velvet moss. Blades of light stab through the leaf canopy piercing the ground, spilling puddles of sunshine here and there. The air is thick, layered with fresh citrus sap, bluebells, wild garlic and deep decay; I can taste it.

I scramble up a burrowed slope to what looks like an old track worn through the trees. The two boys have vanished, swallowed by the woods. My desperation to catch Finn relaxes a little, the trees give off calm and protection. I feel that he is safe, the same sensation that Alys brought last week as I waited for Finn to come home from his school escape. The old lane turns and wiggles down a steep hill. There's a huge oak thrown across the track by a gale many winters ago, I scrabble over it, breaking off rotted chunks with my cumbersome boots; shiny, wet-looking beetles scuttle for cover deeper in its trunk.

I get a sudden taste of wood smoke.

I'm sure I hear voices.

The lane levels and sweeps roundand off out of sight. A flicker of nerves ignite, my breathing tightens – there's nothing to be scared about, I remind myself. Finn's laugh reaches me through the branches.

The track bends, finishing suddenly at a small stream; a huge piece of slate resting on two rocks either side of the water makes a slippery bridge. And popped up on the opposite bank is a tiny little house cut into the hill, almost camouflaged by the overhanging trees. In fact, its entire roof is a thatch of ferns and moss.

"Prynhawn da a croeso. Won't you come in?" Alys's voice breaks into my astonished stare. I look up and there she stands in her doorway.

"Mum!" Finn shouts as he runs down the riverbank, "Come on over." I cross the slate bridge and scramble up, my boots crushing the wild garlic, filling the air with Indian take-away. A narrow wooden gate, greened over, is set into a dry slate wall that surrounds a handkerchief of garden in front of the little house. A glistening path jigsawed together from chunks of slate leads to the door.

"So, you found us then?" she laughs at me, raising her

eyebrows at my gnawed-off hair then turns her back and heads into her home.

Heaving the boots off I step into Alys's world. The whole house seems to be made up of one warm dark room. I have been here before; this is almost a replica of Nana's kitchen. The cluttered dresser at one end, a home for everything and anything that might be useful, the table scrubbed to driftwood grey surrounded by a mix-up of chairs, all copied from my childhood. Something steams on the blackened range, a brown mixing bowl straight from one of Nana's cupboards waits on the wooden draining board, dough rising in a dome. Jars, short, fat, tall and wide, filled with things fermenting and pickling, line up along the windowsill creating stained-glass window lights across the kitchen floor.

Nye and Finn follow us, clattering in through the door, their muddy footprints glistening in the sun that beams in. Chairs scrape as they throw themselves down, dragging with them the smell of earth. Finn is modelling every kind of mud from cheek to feet. He glances at me – he's annoyed.

"Didn't you hear me, I called and called you," he snaps.

"I did, I just wasn't quick enough … sorry." I mumble, embarrassed to be bringing a scene to Alys's table. She puts a plate towering with flat scone-like things in front of me; Welsh cakes she calls them – they're warm and delicious – Willow would like these for her café. The food acts as a barrier to Finn's anger. The boys devour them. I try to tear my gaze away from Nye, unsuccessfully. I make him fidget uncomfortably. He's a copy of Jesse, his hair is shorter, sharper, but the colour, the warm gold that glows in any light is identical. The curve of his cheek has the same down, like his top lip – bleached white thistledown, itching to turn to whiskers. Nye's hands are rough, red scrubbed and black nailed. Jesse's were finer, the only stains on them from misbehaving pens. The boy can avoid my gaze no longer and turns, staring hard back at me, but he's nervy, twitchy.

"You look so like my Jesse." I try to explain away my scrutiny.

"Who's Jesse?" He asks with an accent that sings two hundred miles west of Jesse's.

"My brother, he got—"

"The lad who watches you ride that pony of yours?" Nye snorts trying to smile but fails, his face shrinks back to scared.

"Yep, that'll be Jesse."

Quiet falls over us, allowing the sound of voices in through the open door. Nye catches my eye as he tenses and slides from his chair to crouch in the far dark corner of the room. The voices carry on past the gate and up the lane that climbs the hill behind Alys's house. Nye shoots from his hiding place and scrambles up a ladder I hadn't noticed that clambers through a hole in the kitchen ceiling. We sit and listen to his movements above us and within seconds his head pops through the opening.

"Just Elfyn Thomas and his boy," he announces, his face pale and scared. Panic is clearly gnawing at this boy – he looks hunted down by his fears.

"There we are then," Alys mutters, seemingly unmoved, incurious, resuming her sewing. Nye's head disappears again.

"Not been the same since he came back – says he hears the shells going off, screams at night so he does. Says they'll be comin' for 'im. But who, he's still just a boy, they can't make a boy fight, can they?" I shake my head. "I need some water, lad," she says to the room. Nye stays hidden so Finn picks up the bucket by the stove.

"Tatws," Alys nods at the mud pile. "Knife's on the draining board." She pushes her needle back into the white linen, intent on her stitching. Poking at the mud I reveal potatoes; I hate peeling spuds but sense Alys is not interested in the effect potatoes have on my city-soft hands. I scrape and scrub; she sews. Her presence is companionable but her silence is a road block to all I want to find out. Top of the list, apart from the obvious questions about Nye, is Auden, because they seem very alone, Nye and Alys in this little world of theirs. One question knocks into another, I puzzle on how to start.

"You must be so relieved to have Nye back home again with you."

"Aye."

"He won't have to go back to the front will he?"

"No." Not once does she raise her head.

"Is he OK? He looks… It must have been horrific," I add, lamely.

"He'll do fine Dr Rees said, just needs time."

"And the other boys from the village, are they all safe?"

"No news as yet."

I try a different tack: "What are you sewing?"

"Just mending shirts." I don't know why she doesn't just

say shut up, be quiet. But I can't help myself, I'm now curious – those shirts won't fit Nye.

"Whose shirts?" I sound nosy.

"Those tatws should be boiling by now."

"Sorry."

"Well pop them in that pot, make sure the lid's back on tight now mind."

Asking the same question a third time seems rude; things have ground to a full stop. Finn returns with water, camouflaged in more dirt. He's dispatched back to the stream to clean up before supper. The meal we eventually share together is rough, simple and comfortable. Finn babbles on like the stream outside, Alys nods and smiles, saying little. To me Nye looks haunted, constantly glancing at the doorway, stopping mid-mouthful, listening to the evening. He's almost too fragile to speak to, so I smile at him as kindly as I can and let Finn's rubbish wash over us all. The food is finished too fast; dessert is the dark walk back to the house of Amelia Wolfe's calls. Neither of us is in any hurry to return.

"Night cap before you set off?" Alys suggests making sure we know time is running out.

"Yes please, that would be lovely." She nods to the dresser where a bottle with a ruby glow waits. Nye grabs four muddled glasses, half-filling each one. Finn, expecting Ribena, gulps his, instantly exploding in coughs and splutters, spraying liquid everywhere.

"Steady lad!" Alys thumps him on the back.

The sloe gin slips down warmly, wrapping us up for the

walk home. As we reluctantly make to leave Alys passes me a basket: loaves, a pie and a jar of jam nestle inside. "Need to keep eating," she adds.

"Thanks. See you soon?"

"We'll see," she says eyebrows still raised. "You need to be getting back to those visitors of yours."

"Visitors? What vis—" She cuts me off.

"*Nos da*, you've got just enough light to be getting home by." Time's up, conversation's finished.

"Thank you," I say again. "It's been … lovely."

"Hywl, hurry now they're waiting for you."

Chapter twenty-four

Nye is weird – it's like he's being chased or something, always checkin' over his shoulder; he's so jumpy. I had to run to keep up with him and that's hard in woods cos there's branches and stuff to trip on. And man, if you trod on a twig and made it snap he's like a bomb's gone off or something, hands over his ears, shakin' on the ground – but I guess we all go weird sometimes. I mean my mate Luke in London, he's totally freaked out by spiders, no way could he sleep in the den at Pengarrow, he'd freak with all the webs there, would think one's gonna land on him when he's asleep. I sleep with Jesse's phone, that's not weird, it makes me feel he's around. I can listen to his answerphone message – hear his voice. And then like sometimes, there's these random texts come through, just :) They always come on bad days, like when school's crap, or Mum's strange, and they make me smile. I pretend it's Jess. So what, we all do stuff. But Nye is weird – mental weird.

Jesse doesn't like him; I can see him just at the side of my eyes pretendin' he's not there, but I see him looking. I stopped and said, "You joinin' in?" But he disappeared into the trees. I tried talkin' to Nye. Jess can sulk – I don't care.

Nye doesn't say much, just does stuff. Like gettin' wood, gettin' water and gettin' all freaked out. I think he's ill, I think Alys should take him to the doctor's. It's so spooky how much he looks like Jesse – exactly like. It's weird. Mum sees it too – she can't stop starin'. I asked him why he wanted to be a soldier – I mean I know it's cool being in the army, but all the other stuff ... he went white, shiny and white. His mouth went sort of purple.

"Cool?" He said but his teeth were shut tight, "Cool? What's that?" He shouted right in my face. I was gonna say OK, OK keep your hair on, but I thought he might hit me. Then he sat down, covered his head with his arms, I think he was crying, his voice went all jaggedy. "It was the thing to do. Them posters. WE NEED YOU. An' Idris an' Evan going, would you 'ave stayed?" He looks at me his eyes pink like the mouse I had. "I didn't want to wait around like a mami's boy, I wanted to be part of it. And the girls they thought we were heroes, throwin' themselves at ya they was, throwin themselves, even Meredith Roberts." He goes quiet, we both watch his tears fall in the mud. "Heroes they said. Heroes..." He goes quiet again, his shoulders shaking up and down. "I stood there up to my knees, right here," he points to his leg, "in mud. Covered I was, and waited and waited for zero hour. Our COs callin' us gentlemen... Gentlemen don't grovel in mud. And then they blew that bloody whistle an' up they all went. And I was scared, I was, I couldn't move, and then back they all came blown through with bullets before they'd even got themselves out the trenches. Dai Howells fell at my feet, his face gone; Ellis Hughes hung on to the ladder blocking everyone, screaming like, with his arm blown off to a bloody stump... All of them just a pile of meat. All them boys gone... No boys left in the village now, just me, Nye, the coward..."

I wanted to say sorry, but it sounded stupid. Part of me wanted to touch him, not pervy, but like Mum or Dad do when stuff goes wrong, but I couldn't. I stood there. I watched him and I felt bad, and I felt embarrassed and I wanted to walk away and not see him but I knew I had to stay.

Jesse stayed watching from the trees, stayed sulking, he wanted me to go with him. I wanted to but I knew I had to stay with Nye, didn't matter how long – I had to stay. Nye stayed with me, he didn't leave me there waitin' for Mum, I mean I'd been there for hours and Mum still hadn't shown up. In the end I went an' got Alys and that's when Mum finally got here.

We stayed quite a while, Nye didn't say any more. He hid upstairs when people walked passed, kept mutterin' they were coming for him, but never said who or why.

Alys never said much, just made us food, and I felt sorry for Nye, his dad isn't around, well I didn't see him an' they don't talk about him, and he hasn't got any brothers, he's like me, on his own. That's hard cos you don't always want talk to your mum about stuff. I mean Mum doesn't understand most of it anyway, specially sport, and cars and computers, and I don't think Alys understands Nye cos no one's helpin' him. And like all his mates sound like they've been killed.

Didn't fancy walking home. Mum didn't either, I could tell; she kept talkin' about stuff. Walkin' home in the dark in the woods is scary. I don't mind that stuff if Dad's there with torches, but with Mum, who's a wimp, it was spooky. Everythin' makes you jump 'specially the owl – that totally freaked me out. Then the Shadow Man showed up...

Chapter twenty-five

I couldn't believe the sound an owl could make! Nearly jumped out of my skin! Poor Finn – I'm supposed to be the adult and there I was clinging to him. We slipped and slid down the bank and across the stream from Alys's house, and with each step the evening darkened. The oil lamp in her window called us back and I slowed in the hope that she might shout for us to return, maybe sit the night out by her fireside. Pengarrow would be dark, damp and empty when we got back; the Rayburn probably sulking, the hot water gone off for the night. Alys's basket of goodies happily chinked at the crook of my arm and I couldn't stop thinking about who she thought might be visiting us.

The track was harder to follow in the twilight. Something with glowing yellow eyes froze in front of us, hoping its stillness would make it invisible.

"What's that?" Finn asked pinching into my upper arm.

"Not sure, fox I hope." Our voices frightened the creature, rocketing it into nearby trees; we listened as it snapped across dead twigs. Again the owl swooped close by, calling to a mate. My heart hammered. How much further did we have to go? It would be easier just to head back. Finn tuned in to my thoughts.

"Can't we go back to Nye's house, Mum, this is giving me the creeps."

"Not much further." I stumbled down a rabbit hole, a bramble clawed at my coat. "We should try to remember torches when we go out next time." I sounded like Brown Owl preaching to her brownie pack.

"But it was light."

"Even so, it's good to be prepared." Finn gave me a scout salute in the dark. "So what did you get up to with Nye? Did he talk much?"

"He said he didn't want to talk about the war, but then he wouldn't stop. On and on he went, it was gross, said his mates got killed right in front of him, people having their arms blown off, totally gross. Wish I hadn't asked. I really upset him, I didn't mean to. Guess I shouldn't have said anything."

"War does awful things to people, you'll just have to be very patient with him. Maybe wait for him to talk. Did he scare you?"

"Bit."

"You're OK now though?"

"Yeah, it's just – well – when he was going on about this guy who's arm got blown off and all the blood and stuff, well, it made me think of Jesse. I wanted to tell him to stop, you know, that I know what it's like, well sort of, but I couldn't. And now I keep seeing Jess as he was. D'you remember?"

"Oh Finn, I think about it almost every day, kneeling in that gateway holding on to him, everyone trying to get in and out. No room for the paramedics, and Jesse…" I stopped, grabbing Finn to me in the dark, we sobbed in time with each other. "It's OK sweetheart – just got to think about new things, you know like Red, and…" I can't conjure up any other gems to focus on. "Here." I passed him an ancient piece of tissue from my coat pocket; it had been used for tears before. We slumped to the ground still holding on to each other. I was sure we couldn't be that far from home, the fallen oak tree that blocked the path made an excellent back rest. I leant my head back trying to stare up through the leaves to the sky beyond but the overhead branches were too dense here to catch even a glimpse of the stars. I focused on the beetles that must be crawling just under the rotting tree's bark, imagined how they would feel scuttling into my hair.

"It'll never be over, though, will it?" Finn asked, his head resting on my chest, my arms wrapped around him. "You think it's all OK, then someone asks about him, or it's his birthday, or mine and he's just not there when you need him…"

"It's got to get easier, the more time that passes, it just has to Finn, that's my hope anyway."

Something screeched deep in the dark.

"What was that?" Finn's face is white scared.

"Just another fox. Won't hurt us. Come on, let's get home and get warm, eh?" But when I stood up the dark disorientated me, I couldn't fix on the path home. I made a quick guess-decision, not wanting to alarm Finn any further. He suddenly seemed very young, my little boy again. "This way. Follow me!" We walked for what seemed like too long until we came to the fallen oak across our path again. Hoping Finn didn't realise I headed in the opposite direction. This time the trees thinned a little before brambles knitted them together making the path impassable.

"We're lost aren't we?"

"Umm, no no, this was just a short cut, if we cross here

we're back on the path I came in on." I tried to make our about turn more of a loop to back up my fib. And was relieved at the clear track we begun to pick up until the route ahead is blocked by the fallen oak.

"We're lost." The words were out of my mouth before I could shape them into something more encouraging. Finn's hold on my arm tightens. Even the way back to Alys's was a mystery, we've already tried every possibility. "I tell you what let's have a bit of a rest. Here have one of these." I pass him a Welsh cake from the stash of Alys's goodies in the basket. "In a while the moon will be up and then we'll be able to see the path better." It begins to gently rain.

We half slip, dune-walking, down a slope padded with dry dead leaves. A giant tree grows at the bottom with branches that reach out into the banks around, gripping into the earth for stability. A yew I think. We creep under its canopy, slumping against the trunk. The wood is at peace under the great tree, its leaves pine-like and so dense not even the rain can wheedle its way through to us.

"This is just like camping, you know, one of dad's night hikes."

Finn snorts into my shoulder. "Except Dad always had a map and the sat-nav and a compass and a torch and Mars bars…"

"Mars bars?"

"Always."

"Well I think these Welsh cakes are better, want another?"

"Does the moon come out when it rains?"

"Yeah always, after."

"So this is short rain then?"

"Definitely." I'm thankful for the huge coat I borrowed, wrapping it around the pair of us, squeezing Finn to me, his warmth slowly creeping into my side. "Not long now." I whisper to the top of his head rubbing my face in his hair. The rain hushed wood waits out the shower with us; the shriekers and screechers have hurried for cover. After a short time Finn's breathing becomes rhythmical, I feel myself joining in with his rise and fall, the sound of the rain dripping all around us slips away as the dust of memories that Finn has kicked around form themselves into my dreams…

I'm back in the semi-silence of that hospital room designed for bad news. I am sitting alone, waiting, with hands sticky and drying – they feel like they are cracking as I flex my fingers. Silhouettes behind the frosted glass windows pass back and forth in the corridor outside. I hear his footsteps when they are only a far, far-off patter. Their volume, their beat, increases to a deafening crash as the door explodes inwards, Andrew hangs from the frame, his colour already drained. His aching eyes plead with mine and all I can do is slowly, so slowly shake my head. The moan that comes from the base of his throat stretches out his neck, he faces the ceiling and his animal wail fills the room. He collapses to his knees there in the doorway, a porter walks round his feet as they hang out into the corridor.

My dream switches to the here and now, all the characters from the memory assemble in a ring around Finn and me, sheltering too under the giant yew's branches. Ma stands beside Amelia Wolfe and Rufus hangs behind, "If only you had listened to Andrew, children don't get shot at private schools…"

"He'll be safe, Evie…" Andrew pleads. Across from them stands Jess with his arm round Jazzy. "Don't let Dad send me away, I won't go … I won't go." Someone is humming Jesse's rap song, 'Soldier boy', they repeat…

It was the kick to my foot that jolted me awake. I must have slumped to the side because Finn lands in a heap across my legs. The metal clunk of a shotgun snapping shut, springs my eyes open.

"Up!" A huge black shadow orders from behind the two barrels. I scrabble to my feet hauling Finn by some part of his clothing, never taking my eyes from the end of the gun. "This is private land. Can't ya read?" I hadn't seen anything to read. Finn stumbles back catching the basket, jam jars chink. "What you got in there?" I'm not sure which "there" he means – I'm too scared – I can't make a sound, the words are stuck at the base of my throat. "You," the barrels swing to Finn. "What's in the basket?"

"Um, errr, Welsh cakes, jam, wine, stuff … and, and I don't know…" Finn stutters. The sound of Finn is enough to free my speech – give my terror a voice.

"Leave him alone. Take it – just take it." The muscles above my kneecaps twitch making it hard to stand.

"I don't want your rubbish – I wants ya off my land, ya 'ear?" We prosecute poachers round 'ere. Now off with ya!"

"We're not poaching…" Finn tries to argue. I grab him to me trying to squash his words.

"Don't get lippy with me lad, I said off with ya, now get gone!" The shadow-man shouts, jabbing the gun barrels at me again. "I said move!" I want to move – run – but which way? Finn grabs my sleeve pulling me back from the two black holes; we stumble. "Hey where'd you think ya going?"

His bellow further tangles our feet. I sprawl over Finn, landing in the dirt. Shadow-man pounces over us, the gun pushes into my ribs. The pain is enough to ignite me, whether it's adrenalin or madness-fuelled the fight reflex punches me in the belly. I will not hold onto another son while his life runs away through my fingers. I lash out at the gun barrel, my forearm colliding with metal, the impact throws shadow-man off balance. Scrambling upright, I claw at Finn dragging us both to our feet. "Run!" I hiss crashing forwards, lurching off tree trunks, tripping on roots. We run on and on, arm outstretched in front of me scything undergrowth away. Brambles catch at my palms, laddering my skin but on we go. Never once do I release my vice grip on Finn's coat, I tug him faster forwards. My breath pounds in my head, my lungs scream for fuel. On we run, faster Finn faster.

The trees thin.

The silhouette of Pengarrow stands in the distance waiting for us.

A last sneaky root hooks from the earth snatching me down to the ground. My fall is hard, I bite dirt and leaves, Finn catches his balance and runs on. "C'mom Mum, we've made it!" he shouts back to me. I am spent. I can't even lift my head from the cold soil, my heart pounding through my bones and deep into the earth. I strain to hear shadow-man smashing through the branches behind but there's nothing, only muffled voices – lots of them, and radios crackling in front of us. With a left-over drop of energy I lift my head and try to push myself up from the leaves. Blue lights flash, their colour bouncing up and off the walls of the house, black cut-out people swarm in the front yard, I can't understand what I see. Several dogs bark. A helicopter hangs overhead sweeping the woods with a white beam brush.

"There!" A familiar voice shouts, carrying high and shrill over the buzz of noise, a new and greater panic washes through my veins.

Chapter twenty-six

1½ cup. Flour S.R.   DUMPLINGS

¾ .. Suet

Pinch Salt

mix dry then add water gradually, until dough.

I'm sorry – I said it again and again. Sorry, Mum – Mum, I mean it – I'm sorry. But no one listened. All I wanted was to ride, I didn't want Dad to send Grandma, I didn't ask him that and I didn't call the police – honest.

From nowhere, Grandma grabs me – so embarassing. No chance to tell Mum everything. Mum still had her arm round me but Grandma just grabbed me.

"I thought she'd taken you. Oh my poor darling, darling boy. I thought we'd lost you too."

Then she started on Mum, before I could even tell her about the man – the Shadow Man with his gun.

"What kind of lunatic are you, Evelyn? You'll never pull another stunt like this again. Never, do you hear? Evelyn? Do you hear me?"

Then she was back to...

"Oh my darling boy. Are you hurt? Let's take you to the lovely ambulance men, let's check you are all OK." She talks like I'm five or something. She didn't give Mum a chance – Mum just froze.

"But Grandma..." I tried to tell her. "There's a man – in the woods, he chased us – he's got a gun! Grandma!" I shouted at her. "He had a gun!" I tried to get away from her but she squeezed me tight. She always does that – makes you think you won't be able to breathe.

Mum just stood there, on her own. No one hugged her.

"Mum!" I called her, but Grandma pulled me away, to the ambulance. It's soooo cool in the back of those things. All these machines in case you die, wires and screens and stuff. The ambulance guys were really nice except I kept saying they needed to see Mum but nobody listened, cos no one went to get her. And they gave me this space blanket – like tin foil, you know like they get at the end of marathons and stuff – didn't need it, I was fine – I told them – I'm fine. I told the ambulance guys about the Shadow Man, about his gun and him chasin' us, but he said, tell the police.

No one cares there's a mad man in those woods.

Grandma fussed so much the ambulance men sent her away. She kept talking when they wanted me to answer, but it was nice of her to make us hot chocolate. Mine had marshmallows.

At last that policeman Craig Jones shows up again. The same one that came when I bunked off school. He's massive, like mega tall. He bends down to talk, which must piss him off. Anyway, he asked loads of questions but he wasn't interested in the Shadow Man, can you believe it? I told him again and again that he chased us. "He's got a gun!" I shouted at him. "What if he comes back," I said. "What if he's watching the house and murders us?" It was like he thought I was making it up or something. Only interested in Mum – in her state of mind. She was scared, I told him, like me – well wouldn't you be if some nutter chased you with a GUN?

And he's still in the woods, waiting for us.

"There!" That one word causes fear to claw at the pit of my stomach. Surely not?

It couldn't possibly be…

Torch beams swing in our direction, slicing the dark, searching us out from the trees. Finn stumbles back, throwing himself down beside me. The helicopter loops around overhead its light brushing away the night between us and them.

"How did they know about the gunman already?" I ask Finn. "We'd better go give them a description or something." I tug his arm but it won't come with me. "Come on Finn, don't be scared, it's OK now. They're here to help us." I move forward again but he stays rooted. "What's the matter? What is it?" Silently he stares wide-eyed at the circus in our front yard.

"Shit," he hisses.

"What d'you mean, Finn – Finn?" He won't look at me.

"I only called him cos I wanted to ride Red," he whispers.

"What…Called who? Who did you call, Finn?"

"Dad."

"When?"

"When you wouldn't answer the door. I called you – but you didn't answer." His face is white – fear bleached. The helicopter makes another pass over the house spotlighting it. I watch in horror as into the bright pool *she* steps. Even from this distance Amelia Wolfe is instantly recognisable, her voice pierces through the night.

"There!"

"Oh my God! What's she doing here?" I grab Finn,

hunkering down in a foolish attempt to conceal us. What the hell is she doing here? Urgently I question Finn. "So you phoned Dad, asked to ride then what?"

"Well … nothing honest, well sort of…"

"Sort of Finn, what kind of 'sort of'?" I'm beginning to panic.

"Well I told him that you wouldn't let me in, or – or that you weren't there… But then Dad started asking questions, and I didn't know what to tell him. I wasn't trying to make trouble I wasn't…" His words rush and tumble out of him in a hurry to be gone.

"So what was he asking, tell me Finn."

"Well you know, just stuff."

"No I don't know, help me out here."

"Just stuff like, you know… like were you drinking again, I told him I didn't know – said maybe – I don't know, Mum. What was I s'posed to say? I just said you were a bit weird, which you have been, and your hair…" A tear runs down his white cheek, I grab him hard to me, burying my face in his earth-smelling head.

"It's OK Finn, it's OK. You did the right thing, honey." I make myself say it. I think he mumbles, "Sorry" into my chest but I'm holding him too tight to hear. "Did you call *her* as well?" He shakes his head violently. I count to ten and then thirty, finally I make myself stand, pulling Finn up with me. "Maybe keep Alys and Nye out of this one. Let's just stick to the man with the gun." I whisper in his ear, he nods his understanding. Like cornered fugitives, we walk into the light.

221

And she flies from nowhere launching into my face. Dignity thrown aside, poise trampled: "What kind of lunatic are you, Evelyn? You'll never pull another stunt like this again. Never, do you hear?" Her words bite into me. I can't focus on her; our noses are an inch apart. Her spit cools on my cheek. With great bat wings she swoops Finn off, and in an instant she's flown him away to the disco of lights and people.

"Finn!" I call him, he turns to answer but she pulls him to her, stealing him. My feet root down into the ground, the twitching above my knee begins again at an impossible speed. I give in, crumpling to the floor. I cover my eyes pushing my fingertips hard into the bridge of my nose trying to stop the replay that's re-running in my mind...

Amelia Wolfe had soared through the hospital in the same way. The day after Jesse was born. I'd tried hard to avoid Andrew's parents since the polo encounter. In fact I had barely been in touch with Andrew; if it hadn't been for Nana's "children need their fathers" crusade he would have missed Jesse's arrival altogether. And that was my plan. We didn't need him: as far as life had shown me, a father appeared to be an optional extra. I'd managed, granted I had Papa, but in my argument, that was different. I ran back to Nana's that polo day, and slid a bolt across my life. Willow and her café kept me company. I happily baked away my waiting time, hidden, nesting in her kitchen.

Andrew had changed, so he said, as he laid down his promises with the flowers and teddies on the end of my hospital bed. I forgave him, I knew how badly behaved parents complicate life, so I re-arranged all the things I thought were needed to play happy families in my mind: Mummy, Daddy, Baby. The list was small but it seemed perfect to me. I imagined Nana bouncing our little son on her knee, wishing Papa had lived long enough to join in. And wept with relief that Ma would never be able muddy his life with let downs and disappointment. That was it. No other players invited.

But the Wolfes don't play by the rules.

I was laughing, Andrew had just suggested some ridiculous name, "You have to be joking," I told him, then the door to the room flew open, in she swooped.

"Andrew! Where is he, the little darling?" They embraced; she kissed the air beside each of his ears. Together they pored over the clear fish tank thing the midwives had put my son in. Her squawking awoke him.

"Oh hush, hush, Grandma's here." She scooped him up, he screamed in her face.

"There, there, we'll soon have you home to Nanny James. She'll have you ship-shape in no time at all." She shouted over the wailing to Andrew, setting out a childhood of plans, routines and staff that I had never heard of, never discussed. Andrew quivered, squirming in discomfort, his treachery exposed for all to hear. She returned her attention to my furious son. "Now then my little George Rufus Wolfe." She turned to Andrew, "You're right that does sound grand! George after your great grandfather, how thrilled he would be!"

I was so stunned I tried to leap out of bed, everything

223

stung and ached deeply, but that did not stop me. I shuffled as determinedly as I could to face the witch. I confused her momentarily.

"My son please, and he's called…" Quickly I scanned my brain for boys' names, but only Andrew's last suggestion remained, "…Jesse – that's right after the cowboy!" Her jaw dropped. I pulled my angry bundle from her and winced back to the bed. Amelia Wolfe boiled, her face colouring the same shade as Jesse's. Choosing embarrassment as my weapon of defence, I quickly unbuttoned my pyjamas and forced an enormous blue-veined breast into my son's tiny rosebud mouth. He was greedily grateful. Ignoring the red-hot poker pain he caused with his rough-cat-tongue, I glared at the pair them. Andrew and Amelia melted from the room. He paused briefly by the door. "See you later," he mouthed. "No," I answered with a shake of my head.

So we escaped. Like something from a poor spy movie, I huddled Jesse in a stolen hospital blanket and nestled him in the basket Willow sent me in with. It was still full of things to "keep me going"; cheese and jam sandwiches (my favourite), a flask of tea, hummus, cucumber all sliced in regimental sticks and chocolate in the form of cake, biscuits, buttons, dip and fingers. Maternity wards are fiendishly hard to get into and out of, but I slipstreamed a porter asking him for directions to the infectious disease unit. He held the door wide for me pointing down the corridor, letting me have the lift, saying he'd catch the next one.

Willow welcomed us in. She put us up in the back room; we used a large cardboard box cosied with towels for Jesse.

She said his name was cool. Like me she shared an allergy to routines. Neither of us had a clue what to do, so we poured large glasses of wine, put on the *Grease* video and waited for Jesse to make a suggestion.

Andrew went straight to Nana's – I knew he would. That's why we stayed with Willow…

…"She's clearly insane!" Her voice rips me from my memories back to my knees in the front yard of Pengarrow. Amelia shouts into the face of a police officer, even in the dark he seems familiar. The man gives up trying to placate her and trudges over in my direction.

"Mrs Wolfe?" He peers down at me from his great height.

"Inspector Jones." I reply from the ground. "I didn't think we'd meet again so soon." He tilts his head slightly and his eyebrows disappear upwards into his police hat. "Is there any point in me telling you there's a madman with a gun running around those woods." I gesture behind me.

"There's every point, Mrs Wolfe, but I need to clear a few things up with you first. Could you get up? Long way for me to shout, see." Amelia is still braying in the background, I can't make out quite what she's now accusing me of, and I pray that Finn can't hear either. As I get to my feet Inspector Jones gently grasps my upper arm, I thank him for his help but he fails to let go. "You need to come with me, Mrs Wolfe." I pull my arm away, but his grip tightens slightly. "This way, Mrs Wolfe." He directs me toward a flashing police car, door open ready to swallow me.

"Why? What about that maniac in the woods with a gun? I need to be with Finn." He tugs harder, I stumble a few steps toward his car. "Can't I come in the morning, first thing?"

"This way, Mrs Wolfe." His tone never changes, set on permanent calm. I'm getting scared. I imagine all the lies Amelia has fed him. What is she going to do with Finn? If I go now will he even be here when I get back?

"No! I'm not leaving Finn. I can tell you everything here." I struggle to free myself. His grip clamps tighter, I'm frightened, panic is rising. He can't take me away. I have to stop him.

"Now then Mrs Wolfe, don't make this difficult." As he talks he hauls me closer to the car until I touch it with my outstretched hands trying to brace myself against his force. I won't get in. "In the car, Mrs Wolfe," he says through gritted teeth, his calm tone slipping. A policewoman pops out from the passenger side and peels my fingers from the doorframe.

"No! I'm not leaving Finn!" I cry out. "Finn! Finn!"

"Mum?" I hear him shout back but it's too late I'm shoved headfirst into the back seat, and the door is hurriedly slammed. I bang on the window trying to catch Finn's attention, as he gets out of the ambulance he sees me, and panic sweeps his face. He runs to the car, our palms meet separated by the glass, Amelia looms behind him dragging him away. Gravel crunches, we climb the lane. I'm sure I can hear Finn still calling out to me.

I'm angry; I'm frightened, panic-stricken. Finn and I are

being torn apart, I have a deep dark terror that I won't see him again, the palms of my hands sting from banging the glass. I hurt; a hurt that will only stop when Finn is back with me in my possession, not hers. The police car seems in no hurry to get wherever it's going, Inspector Jones drives at old-man-in-a-cap speed, he's forgotten to turn off the flashing lights, they splash the verges blue. I feel sick – the sensation builds the further they drag me from Finn. Inspector Jones adjusts the lights; it gets much darker, very dark. The pain in my head threatens to crack open my skull. Faintly I can hear Nana singing ever so gently and I feel like I'm drowning. I wonder if Andrew will ever rescue me.

"...*And I will just say hello,*
To the folks that you know,
Tell them you won't be long..."

"Look after Finn for me, Nana," I ask her as she carries on singing. In the distance Inspector Jones asks the policewoman what I'm saying.

"I don't know. Mrs Wolfe? Mrs Wolfe?" I can hear her but I'm too tired to answer.

"D'you remember when I bought Jesse home, Nana?" I whisper shutting my eyes.

"How could I ever forget, dear? Wasn't he a poppet – just perfect!" She carries on humming the same tune...

...Willow's flat was big enough for a Willow and maybe someone interesting she met on a Friday night – a someone who understood clearly they needed to be gone straight after breakfast. Jesse and I made things crowded. Time to go home. Nana would be wondering where we'd got to. Her face glowed as I carried Jesse into the kitchen.

"Let me see him!" she cried impatiently. The kitchen was cold. Nothing boiled. Nothing cooled on the rack. Nana looked very old as she gently rocked in her chair. Papa's rocker opposite, sat still, empty, watching her.

"I'll get a fire going shall I, it's so cold in here?" But Nana was too engrossed humming to the bundle in her arms. We had soup for tea, and bread left over from Willow's café. We toasted Jesse's arrival with a glass or two of last summer's elderflower. I eventually managed to extract Jesse from Nana and fell into my old bed to sleep a hundred hours, broken into sixty-minute bites by Jesse. I'd never known such fatigue – like a very heavy hat squashed down hard on my head frowning my eyebrows. It must have been lunch by the time Jesse and I came down to face the world. Nana was still sleeping in her chair, last night's cocoa cold, skinned over on the table beside her. I remade the fire – moaning about the direction of the wind, and the damp wood. I made more tea and fell asleep with Jesse, curled in Papa's rocker. The house was quiet, it slept with us and the dark crept back to tuck us in.

Strong arms pulled Jesse from me tugging both of us from our deep sleep. I opened my eyes panicking. Andrew stood before me in the half-light. He'd found us. We hadn't made it that difficult. Jesse let out a long and hungry howl. Nana slept on peacefully still.

"Where's the phone, Evie?" Andrew demanded sharply. "The phone?" He repeated, shouting over Jesse. It seemed an odd thing to say as a greeting.

"Down the street – corner of Kelvin Drive and St Margaret's Road." I shouted back annoyed. Already.

"For God's sake, doesn't anything work in this place…" Andrew muttered dumping Jesse back in my arms as he ran from the room. The front door banged behind him. Nana shivered, she hummed quietly.

"I'll light the fire then. Will you hold Jesse, Nana?" But she slept on, so Jesse and I loaded logs one-handed. Nana's humming grew fainter just a dusting in the background. I was wondering if Andrew would come back as he crashed back into the kitchen. "Shh, you'll wake Nana." I scolded, he launched into a tirade I was too fuzzy to take in, trying to usher us into another room. "It's too cold," I told him but he just carried on that "they" would be here soon.

"Who Andrew? Who's coming?" But blue-flashing lights blazed out his reply. He let in men and held me back as I fought to stop them taking Nana.

"*Keep smiling through, just like you always do…*" I heard her faintly sing as the paramedics rushed her stretcher out of the front door to the waiting ambulance.

Chapter twenty-seven

"He's taken her! Grandma he's takin' Mum," I shouted. "STOP THEM!"

She acts deaf.

I ran after the police car, Jesse ran faster, (only cos he's older), even he couldn't catch them – make 'em stop. "STOP– MUM! We didn't do anything! Mum did nuffin' wrong! Nuffin'! Why aren't they looking for the nutter with the gun?"

But they drove off. Didn't even slow down.

All the dust went in my face – my teeth crunched, Jesse walked back with me, he would've put his arm around me if he could. But he can't stand Grandma so I knew he had to go.

Mum didn't come back. I waited – ignored Grandma when she said to come in. Waved goodbye to the ambulance guys and the police dogs and waited some more.

Mum was still not back when Grandma said it was time for bed. Where was Mum going to sleep? Grandma didn't know. And now she's mucked up all the sleeping stuff, Mum and I had this sort of camping thing going on, I think Mum's a bit scared to sleep on her own when Dad's away. I made her sleep in the den. (I told her there's no ghosts, just Jesse sometimes creaking about.) It's real comfy.

Grandma says you have to sleep in beds; only peasants sleep on the floor. And campers I told her, and soldiers, and when you go to Glastonbury (which I am when I'm 16). She's stopped listening again, so beds it is, even though I said I wanted to say up till Mum came back.

I want Dad.

He fixes stuff. Maybe he's taken Mum her things. He should call though, he should tell me. Has Dad called I asked Grandma. Deafy I'm gonna call her from now on, cos she just told me to go to bed. I mean who's gonna sleep after all this? There's a man with a gun in our woods and Mum's been taken! Jesse stayed with me, we pulled my mattress back up to the den by Mum's and we talked till it got light. We miss her, we're gonna get her back. Jesse has this plan; he won't take any of Grandma's shit. I used Mum's duvet, it smells of her soap. We bought it for Mother's Day. Dad said it was her favourite. Somethin' like flowers, like roses maybe, I'm not sure.

Grandma doesn't do breakfast.

So me and Jesse got up early. Alys hadn't come – no bread. Mum still wasn't back. That means she'd been gone all night. How many questions have the police gotta ask her? I didn't think Grandma'd mind if I finished the marshmallows but I had a banana as well. Decided to call Dad. Couldn't find my phone though. It better not've been Grandma'd, she says they're not good for you, like she would know. It's gone, and it's got all my contacts on, only one I do actually know is Mum's so I use the phone in the library – kitchen one's broken – I get nothing, not even the answer phone.

I decide to do Jesse's plan, go find Mum on my own. Can't wait for Grandma to faff around any more. The Police station's gotta be in Arborth and there's buses that go there.

Crap. Grandma's decided to have X-ray hearing today.

"Morning sweetheart." She's all kissy, yuck. "You're up early!"

"Where's Mum, Grandma? Where is she?" It's like she doesn't see that Mum's been gone all night. "I want to see her. Please."

"Soon." She says. "Let's make some coffee."

"But when?"

"It's complicated, Finn, darling. Your mother's..." She starts makin' tea cos she can't find coffee.

"Mum's what?"

"Um where's the milk gone? Ah here it is...Your mother's ... not well. She needs quiet, Finn."

"Why?"

"She just does, darling. We need to help her. Let her have some quiet then everything will be back to normal, OK?"

"NO, it's not OK. What's wrong with her?" She'll want to see me – I know. When Mum is "ill" she says I make her smile, and I tell this to Grandma, but she doesn't get it. "Let me go, I want to see her!" I shouted, even though you can't do that to grandparents, but she was being so stupid. I want to see my mum. "I want to see her NOW."

Then just like that, off goes her hearing again.

"I think we should have a little jaunt today, take our mind off things, and I know just the place!"

Arrrggh, I shouted right at her and kicked a chair, my foot caned, but I ran out anyway.

A picnic? That's what Grandma thinks will fix everything! She's having a laugh. Her picnics are crap

234

anyway. Mum-type ones are the only fun ones. She doesn't plan hers, they just come into her head like all of a sudden, and she's like – let's go somewhere – and she means it, like right then. She did night picnics as well, woke you up, 'specially if Dad was away. If it was frosty, or it had snowed or the moon was big then we'd go to Marble Hill Park 'n' take our blankets. Mum knew this place at the back of an old house. There's a den, Mum calls it a bomb shelter, she played in it or something when she was little and it's best not to tell Dad as he's not keen on that type of stuff. One day she said it would be mine and Jesse's, but I don't know if she just meant the den or the old house as well... Anyway we'd go in there and drink hot chocolate, although sometimes she forgot and the flask just had cold water, and then you had to pretend it was hot chocolate.

Grandma wastes the whole day when we could be getting Mum. Surprise, surprise we go to some old house – Scolton Manor, I think. Then Grandma complained about lunch, no salad, how embarrassing. It took ages. Grandma is so slow at driving. "Make sure your trousers aren't dirty," she goes, and, "Take your shoes off," just to be in her car, can you believe it?

We get back – still no Mum.

I've had it.

So maybe I was a bit babyish, but like if someone took your mum away, and your dad doesn't show up and you're stuck with Grandma and she says Granddad is turning up as well, you would lose it.

I didn't want her hugs. I want Mum, and I shouted at her.

At least I finally got to talk to Dad. I told him all the stuff, Mum's gone, you know and the man in the woods, the police, Grandma saying Mum was ill. Get this, he knew already! I was like, well why aren't you here, Dad! I need help, we've gotta get Mum back. And d'you know what he said? He'd be there as soon as he could, definitely by the weekend. Arrrrggh. Not quick enough, Dad. Don't leave me with Grandma.

He had to go. Work as always.

"How about a quick game of backgammon, darling?" Grandma said.

"Fuck off!" I told her. I'm so in trouble now. I ran out the house and the only place I could think of escaping to was the stables. I wasn't going back to the woods with that Shadow Man shooting things.

Red was pleased to see me, though. I brushed him like Alys showed me. Told him about Mum. Decided to ride, got stuck with the saddle though, couldn't pull the girth thing tight enough.

"You're doin' that all wrong, lad. Ya want some help?" Nye! He still looked totally weird. Looked over his shoulder every five minutes. But he listened. He listened about Mum. And when I just couldn't tell him any more, when... Well he gave me his stinky hankie, and we sat in the hay, not weird or anything, I don't like hugging boys or nothing, errr...

"None of them care," I told him. "They've just left me on my own, what if she never comes back? What if Dad never finishes his work?"

Chapter twenty-eight

I am disorientated. Digging around in my brain, I've got bits of a journey in a police car, helicopters, Finn screaming and Amelia Wolfe taking him away and then there's danger, I can't see it or hear it, I just know it's chasing me, hunting me down, but I'm so tired I can't run away. And then these images come round again as if stuck to a carousel, circling constantly, making me dizzy and sick. I can't find the beginning or the end of them so that I can unpick them and make them stop. These things, this fear, weigh me down to the bed that I lie in, my limbs, my head, too heavy to lift. I feel I've been spirited away to a white place – tucked in where they take people to be forgotten about. It must be Amelia, she's told them I'm mad, so they've hidden me here to sleep the rest of my life away.

My head hurts so much that I can hardly bear to open my eyes, I worry movement may split my skull in two. Thinking is pain and memories have gone missing in this white place along with my Finn and Andrew. I tried to look for them, got as far as the door to this room, but the floor here bucks and rolls in a stormy sea, someone got me up off the floor, a nurse I'm sure, but she couldn't tell me where they were. I fight panic, but it's a huge ball that I can't quite push to the bottom of this murky pool I'm floating in – just as I go to sit on it, squash it down, up it explodes through the surface showering everything in fear.

"Tell me they're OK. Tell me they're coming." I ask the starched white ladies when I wake. "Shh," they swish as they pass. "Everyone's OK." they lie, so I go back to this list I've made, in my head of course, pens, paper, items written

238

down, all missing along with colour in the white place I now sleep. My list, my safety net that keeps me breathing in–one-two, out-one-two goes: Finn and I in the woods, I remember this now, it's a crisp clear picture I hold onto, then Finn and I are lost in the woods, but a mussy image of a maniac with a gun, and running, and Amelia all come after … then the lights and uniforms all get tangled and I can't place them in any order. My breathing forgets to count in-out-in-out and back to the beginning I go, Finn and I in the woods… My head hurts.

So I shut my eyes. At least now Nana comes, not just that deep blackness, she brushes the hair from my forehead – her palm is cool and coarse, picked at by years of vegetables, it scratches gently with each sweep. The rhythm of her hand matches my breathing we're in time with her humming. *I'll not forget you sweetheart…* her tune says.

And when I ask them, the nurses in white uniforms whose shoes squeak across the glass shiny lino: why am I here, can't I go. They tut, "There, there, nothing to worry about now, dear." They pat the back of my hand and it fills with ice. And I fall back into that darkness, worrying even more.

I've spent so long in the darkness that Ma has found me, she's walked back all the way from the past and sits there. I've managed all these years to make her stand on the edge of my dreams. I've told her to get out, let me sleep in peace. But Ma didn't want to be forgotten, buried. So years ago we agreed, my anxiety and I, that she could stand in the corner of my sleep – watch, that's all, nothing else. But she's there in my bad dreams standing beside Amelia, smiling. She's helping Amelia pack up Finn's things so they can take him away. I even saw her walking in Hollow's Wood with the shadow-man, his gun broken, draped over his arm, hers looped through his other.

And I know Ma stands out in the corridor of this white place, where the shoes squeak up and down, up and down. I hear her. "What a mess, Evie," she laughs in a breathy whisper, "Nothing you can do." This I do remember! I struggle to piece together how I got here, but I can pull this memory of Ma standing in Nana's house jeering. "There's nothing you can do about it…" Nana and I had just come home; Nana had been in hospital for weeks with pneumonia, I thought she was going to die. I was thinking about the man I'd met in the canteen there, his dark hair so black it was almost blue, his pale white skin and dark sharp stubble, Andrew Wolfe he'd said his name was. Nana stumbled as we reached the front door she put out her hand to save herself and the door swung open – unlocked, not how I'd left it.

I thought the house was empty but Ma was waiting; she'd brought in some builders, I'd only been gone a day or two – maybe three. The kitchen wall was already rubble, part of the floor had gone, a trench like an open grave bitten into it. "Sorry started without you!" she laughed, drunk maybe, high possibly? Nana gasped and slumped against my arm, no weight to her at all. "You belong in that home – you need looking after – look at you!" Ma jeered. "You can't live here now!" I eased Nana into the rocker by what was left of the stove, her hand printed in the dust on the arm and sent clouds of it into the air; even now I remember the taste, its chalkiness. Nana started to cough, choke. What made me lunge at Ma I can't decide, anger, hurt, betrayal; anger I think, mainly anger. I wanted to shake her. I know I wanted more than anything to hurt her. She staggered back as I moved, her ridiculous million-pound heels caught in something, the feathery collar of her sweater rushed up to tickle her face she crashed backwards, downwards, her head cracking on the edge of the trench her builders had made. She gargled, the sound that she made at the mirror in the bathroom when she cleaned her teeth. I looked down at her, at the single feather in my hand, trying desperately to remember – did I touch her – push her or did she fall?

Chapter twenty-nine

Man, there are people everywhere! "Team Grandma" she calls it – and Granddad's on his way. Great. He's OK and everythin' but there's sooooo many rules when he's around:

Be quiet

Speak up

No telly

No chips (common people eat chips)

No chewing (gum)

No stayin' up

Definitely no swearing

No football (common people again, although he can't've seen how much Rooney gets a week)

Can't just use only your fork for eating

Obviously sitting up straight

No mutterin'

No trainers

Not keen on jeans

Perfect school report

Wants to know what you're reading. Reading – he's havin' a laugh!

Blah

Blah

Blah

And he's obsessed about people takin' our photo – like who's gonna care – oh yeah, Granddad, cos he thinks he's famous. Not.

Sometimes he goes on telly – no big deal – just late night news stuff that no one watches apart from Dad.

People ask him questions which he doesn't answer, I watched once. Hope Dad gets here before him.

But no one's mentioned school – weird.

So there's a guy on Dad's mower – another diggin' stuff in the back garden, and his mate is hackin' hedges. Then there's a lady in the kitchen, not Alys, she's disappeared. Typical. This one's Mrs George, her smile doesn't work. Mrs George and Grandma are movin' stuff, throwin' things away. I rescued Mum's old radio from the chuck-out pile in the garage, she'd be gutted if it got binned. I've put it up in the den, luckily it's not broken, it still plays the song Mum hums when she goes to sleep, but I can't turn it off, it kinda does its own thing. I need to keep an eye on Grandma, she's going through all our stuff, all Mum's things, things she's had ages, plates she likes, pictures Jess and I did, they're crap but Mum likes them. My rescue pile in the den is gettin' massive!

I'm gonna ask Dad about school. I guess there's no way they're gonna let me stay home for good.

Mrs George makes quiche. It's disgusting. I'd rather eat eyeballs.

She doesn't talk much either, like you ask her if it's OK to get a drink, cos she's kinda moved in and taken over the kitchen, she looks over her glasses until you go. Maybe she doesn't understand, maybe she only speaks Welsh. But she talks to Grandma, I heard her. Everything she makes and cleans smells bleachy. Not like Alys, not like Mum, you wanna eat the stuff they make, you know it's gonna be good. The Ribena's gone, there's only water and someone's drunk the coke and lemonade.

"Don't want to rot your teeth now do we?" I'm like what d'you think toothpaste's for? But apparently that's being rude. You can tell Mrs George won't make chips, I don't think she likes food. People who like food are round, like Willow and Mum, 'cept Mum's not that round any more, shes gone a bit like Mrs George, not that old but definitely spiky, but Alys is roundish.

Mrs George found the old book, the one Mum had and she was gonna chuck it, don't I told her, it's Mum's. "It's clutter," she said, so I took it, it's goin' on the rescue pile. The book is actually quite cool, I know it sounds weird, but it was Alys's once, her name's in the front. There's loads of stuff in it, even stuff Nye wrote, things like when he was fighting. The paper is so old it cracks when you turn the pages. And it smells. There's even an old wedding invite from before the First World War, that's mega old! And at the back Mum has been writing, carryin' on from Alys. I'm sure she won't mind me reading what she wrote. It make's it like she's here when I read her words.

I miss her, really, a lot.

I liked this bit Mum wrote.

May 23rd 2010
Haven't seen Alys for a day or two. Hope she's all right. She must be so worried about her boy. I can't imagine how I would feel if Finn disappeared like that off to some crazy war in Afganistan or somewhere. In fact I

246

don't even want to imagine him grown up. I want to keep him with me safe always. Let's face it he's the only person who keeps me going these days. Still maybe one day I'll win the lottery then we can escape in that campervan I've always dreamed of, drive across the world and find out new things. I think he'd love that.

I found a pen only it was green. Mum and Alys won't mind. And I wrote in at the bottom – *great idea Mum, I would love that.*

I copied them, I put:

June 13th
Two days ago, the police took my mum but we'd done nothing wrong. We went to Nye's for tea then a man with a gun chased me and Mum all the way back to home. We did get lost as well. Now Grandma has come and she is changing everything. And we have Mrs George to cook. She can't cook. Granddad is coming. Dad promised to be here for the weekend. I'm going to ride my horse Red. I can now do the girth on the saddle Nye showed me how. I hope you come home tomorrow Mum I miss you.

(That did sound wet – but Mum will like it when she reads it – and I do, I miss her.)

Chapter thirty

I was right, this is a dumping ground, oh not your desolate NHS kind, someone is paying a king's ransom to keep me hostage here. It's a pristine white calm palace with corridors of pigeonholes for the broken down and addicted, the word hospital unmentionable, a banned obscenity. No, this is a place of recuperation, restraint and attempted recovery – a place to stick you out of the way so you don't cause any more embarrassment. The very air is laced with sedation, to breathe here is to sleep, endless blank hours that match the white un-disturbing walls. Everything is under control.

Today their pattern has changed. I'm allowed to thaw out for a while, be in charge of my own mind instead of some drug holding my brain submerged whilst it drowns. But as the meltwater of feelings and emotions trickle back in I struggle with the panic and sheer desperation of getting to Finn. I need to see him, touch his face, drink in his musky smell. It takes all my energy not to run. I'm allowed out of bed, I stop my feet, make them still, hoping nobody notices their anxious-to-be-away dancing. I'm allowed to sit, and tuck my hands underneath me to hold me down onto the chair. I meet a consultant who wears a grey and serious face. He's here to bully me, help me follow his commands, all of which are slow: a slow recovery, a slow reintroduction. I want to roar at him that I'm in a hurry, that I need my child, that I'm no more ill than he is, but I know this will only bring back that leaden sedation. I want to yell at him, "My son died, this is how people are when they grieve – they fray a bit." He doesn't want to listen, he wants to explain and discharge me from his very long list. He leaves, his lecturing complete, his nurses scuttle after him like white beetles. I tell them how tired I am and that all the pain has now gone, could I try to sleep on my own no drug pillow to suffocate into, I promise to call if I have any trouble. I want to dream of Finn, I want to come up with a plan so that I can be with him, saving him from them.

Jesse comes. He sits on the end of the bed staring at the ground. He wears angry, it falls off him, hangs in the air, the same mood he was in the week before he died.

Why doesn't life, or God, or fate – whoever's in bloody control – let you know; this is your last few days together, party hard, make the most of it? But nobody told us, so we squandered our last grains of time with him.

Jesse spent that week storming in and out, leaving clouds of rage for us all to walk around. "Why is no one talking?" Finn asked me as he followed me from room to room on clean-up day. Where did I start with an answer? More trouble, I guess – trouble and Jesse, two best mates who should never have been introduced. It was like he had a sixth sense for it. He was drawn, right from nursery, to the kid that was going to blow the whole thing apart, then he became that kid, the one the other school-gate mums pleaded with their children to avoid.

Why, we asked him? We spent all of the teenage years Jesse had asking, pleading, demanding, why? Why would you do that, why *didn't* you do that, why would you say that, think that, be that? And he'd grunt, shrug his shoulders and disappear to his room sending his angry rap music shouting back down the stairs. Being a general pain-in-the-arse was tedious but manageable. Once a month Andrew and I were summoned to the Head's office, everyone apologised to everyone, promises were made, which by the time Jesse came home that evening he'd snapped in two. But it changed when Jazzy showed up. At that point Jesse took a real wrong turn and he tumbled downhill. So Jazzy was black: that didn't make her bad; Jazzy was sixteen going on twenty-five: not a problem. But Jazzy had three step-brothers all of them whiter than snow, and that *was* a problem. They were older, uglier and dangerous. How could Jesse possibly resist?

The more we ranted the more he raved; disappearing for entire weekends, re-appearing on the doormat Monday mornings like a badly wrapped parcel, unsure of which way up his week was. Drugs? Possibly. Drink? Absolutely – he was doing a good impersonation of my ma. I wanted my boy back, that little plump golden child that crunched snails and loved a rainbow; of course I blamed Jazzy, I felt she had stolen him – shown him a cave of delights he couldn't resist. She'd taken the child in him and folded him into an angry young man.

Andrew tried to ban Jess from seeing Jazzy. He introduced curfews, which of course were ignored, so he cut off his allowance and Jesse just stole what he thought he was owed. Andrew spoke to the school; he spoke to private counsellors, but worst of all he spoke to his father. Rufus Wolfe poured petrol on the whole situation, stood back and threw in an ignited match: he enrolled Jesse at Eton, to board. No consultation, just a kit list through the post on Jesse's last Tuesday.

"No-fucking-way!" was used a lot, and not just by Jesse.

"How dare you!" I shouted in Andrew's face; that was when Andrew confessed that he had already gone to the police with his suspicions about Jazzy's brothers and the drug dealing at the school gates. He said he wanted to protect Jesse but that's because he knew Jesse was no longer safe. He might as well have pinned a target to Jesse's heart.

On Jesse's last Wednesday, Jazzy showed up to help him pack; they'd decided he'd be better boarding with her than a bunch of toffs who couldn't get their facts straight. I invited her in, offered her tea. Chewing, she tilted her head to one side and made her face into, "You have to be joking right?" I begged, it wasn't pretty but they stayed, in fact she stayed that night, her in Jesse's room, him on the sofa, at least until I fell asleep. Andrew's ministers were behaving badly and Caroline had stepped in yet again to help him through a "busy" night. It helped, him not being there. The next morning we had breakfast together, two meals no shouting; awkward silences, but no name-calling. She drank coke and ate the crisps meant for Jesse's packed lunch – I suppose that's almost a meal if you're a sixteen-year-old girl.

Andrew appearing through the front door silenced us all, his footsteps along the polished hall floorboards, eight paces from door to dining room pounded in on us. He stood in the doorway. As a breath he hissed: "Get out!" and as one they scraped chairs and slammed out the door. I shouted after Jesse about his tie, the front door bounced back open. He never did come back to shut it even though I yelled.

Finn wriggled round me to his school bag weaving in and

out past Andrew who was still standing in the same spot, and silently flew away to school too. In my mind the sirens started then, the moment Finn left, but they can't have done…

For the first time in the thousand times that I have run these events through my dreams, I know with scalpel-sharp clarity I want to blame Andrew. There it is. I want him to carry all this. I take Jesse's death and I lay it at his feet. If he hadn't spoken to the police … of course it's all his fault. And I want to scream this in his face over and over. You killed Jesse long before Jazzy's brother put his finger on the trigger. For too long grief has obscured this black-and-white fact, greying out what Andrew did. Allowing Andrew to offload his guilt: blame me for not "moving on", tuck me away here and pretend I'm going mad, having a break down. Bury himself and evade the pain of what he's wrought in the world of Westminster that he shares with Caroline and his father.

When I wake Andrew is sitting in Jesse's space on the end of my bed, wearing the same stance, dejected, sullen. For an instant I have to concentrate on his realness. I sit bolt upright, the screams and accusations barely held back by my clenched teeth. He knows what's coming. He knows I know. Guilt gives him a bile-coloured aura. He's nervous but he's chosen his position well, any outburst from me now will be witnessed by those he's convinced that I'm mad. I shut my eyes, swallowing and choking on my fury. It can wait, but it will come.

His profile is tired, he stares into a space that's gloomy and I don't care. He tries to arrange his face into something pleasant and welcoming but he can't find the expression he's looking for. He takes both my hands in his and looks deep into my soul, I pull away but he holds on tight. Eventually the moment is swept away by a busy nurse, watch-checking and form-filling. He springs from the bed to talk to her. They move to the door, talking about me not with me, no one invites me to join the conversation. Clearly, without my involvement, they make decisions, a deal is struck, Andrew shakes her hand and off she hurries.

"You can come home!" He gives me the statement instead of flowers or grapes, as a present, something I'm supposed to say thank you for. I have no words for him other than those burning at the base of my throat. He babbles about Finn and school, the pony, how everything is under control, how his mother has everything under control.

"Why is she at the house still?" I imagine her sweeping through Pengarrow bleaching the life and family out of it, replacing it with her idea of home and how it should be. Inviting in people to cook, clean, garden, iron, pick up and put down – staff, as she likes to call them.

"Because," he's angry, "Finn needs someone to take care of him. And Mother is doing a splendid job. Everything's unpacked, sorted and … and…" his face flushes again with guilt, more of his underhand plans escaping him, "she's even made a start on some of the renovations."

"What renovations?"

"Evelyn if you're trying to pick a fight…" his words hang, his tone is weak as he gets busy packing things that aren't really there to be packed. He conjures clothes for me, all new, labels swinging, a size too large in an unwearable style. He produces a baseball cap and looks toward my hair. Involuntarily I touch my scalp having forgotten the shearing incident, for a moment I want to tell him it was a practicality not a statement of madness; his obvious embarrassment angers me, I stay silent. I look like a pensioner when I'm dressed and I throw the cap back on the bed, let him be embarrassed, ashamed.

Forms are signed, nobody really meets my eye, and Andrew is handed a party bag of pills, no balloon or cake. We shuffle out of corridors and back into the real world, which is gently raining. In the car the windscreen wipers helpfully fill the mounting silence. Motorway miles pass in grey drizzle.

"What happened, Evie?" He's bypassed the road home and driven down to a wild grey stretch of coast where he thinks we can talk out to sea and not look at each other. "You put Finn in real danger…" He has to stop himself before his anger runs away with his control. I-put-Finn-in-danger, I roll each word around my brain tasting their irony.

"How dare you!" I turn to look at him; he stares harder at the sea. "I wasn't the one running away back to London and Caroline."

"Caroline? What the hell has she got to do with it? You locked Finn out!"

"I didn't lock him out! I called you and every time *she* answered." This isn't what I want to discuss. Andrew once again is manipulating the situation in his favour. But now I can't help myself, it's tumbling out wrong and muddled. "I want to know what's really going on."

"Nothing! For God's sake, I told you the other week. She's a colleague, and actually, damn it, a very good colleague. You're being paranoid."

"*Paranoid!*" I shout.

He throws his hands up and bangs them on the steering wheel.

I shout the words out. "This... All this mess ... you made it – made me like this. I can't live without Jess. You took him away – you went to the bloody police..."

"For Christ sake! I don't want to live without him either, but I've got to, I can't just give up like you're doing... And what d'you mean I went to the police? What are you saying? What, that I killed Jesse because I reported those evil bastards? Is that it? Do you really think that of me? Jesus Evelyn, you're sick ... sick to even think that!" Andrew yanks open the car door and slams it behind him turning his back but I know he's swiping at tears. I get out of the car too. It's windy which is good because I have to roar and that's what I want to do.

"I'm not sick. I'm grieving for our son who got killed after you went to the police and made him a target. After you got your father to send him away... You had to send him away cos you knew ... knew they'd come looking for him because of what you'd done!"

"What, so you think that it was OK to let those thugs supply Jesse with drugs, get him dealing for them, maybe even selling to Finn... You think that I should have ... what? Just sat there and said nice one Jesse, hope you're making a tidy profit. Is that it, is that what you think?"

"No. Jesse wasn't dealing… He wouldn't… How dare you say that."

"Oh wake up, Evelyn, how naive do you want to be? I found the stuff in his room…"

"You're lying."

"Why would I go to the police if I didn't have proof? I wasn't telling tales, Evelyn. Our son was putting people's lives at risk … Finn's life at risk – what kind of parent would I be to ignore that?"

"So you stood him out on his own and let them kill him instead…"

"How can you say that? How can you blame me?" He yells at me into the wind, a line of spittle foams across his cheek. He swipes at his face, "I had to do something … I had to protect Finn, if he'd just gone to that school… He would have been safe… He would…" Andrew is spent. I'm waiting for him to blame me for not letting Jesse go to Eton, for letting Jazzy back into our home, I'm waiting. He buries his face in his hands sobbing. He'd never said that Jesse was dealing. Jesse wouldn't do such a thing. Andrew has to be lying. It has to be an excuse to cover his guilt. Jesse couldn't do that. Dealing drugs … he couldn't. In my cold heart I know that all he's just said are learned lines from Rufus Wolfe. Andrew has to take the blame; he knows and now so do I.

We've reached stalemate on opposite sides of the car. The wind races around us ready to steal any of our words and I have no idea where we go from here. I want to get back to Pengarrow, I want to get Finn and then I'm stuck, then what? Do I want to leave? Or stay and watch Andrew leave?

The bay of Newgale sweeps in front of us, the sand as grey as the sky, a purple sea thrashes angrily against the beach. I could run down the pebble bank now and crash into those cold waters, let the Irish Sea wash me away. Imagine never having to get up another morning to face another day, never having to be without Jesse again, or fight Andrew, or obsess over Caroline or his family, never having to dream Nana or run away from nightmares of Ma. I walk away from the car and sink my heel into the stones. I rattle a foot down the bank and dig in my other foot and traveling lower, in six rolling strides I'm onto the wet sand. I think I hear Andrew calling out my name. Down here the sea spray swipes at my face and the waves roar at me to come closer, their tug and pull irresistible. Ice water seeps into my shoes, the air is laced with salt I can taste on my tongue, my lip. The tide draws me closer, my eyes fix on the horizon where a curtain of rain sweeps in towards the shore. The first wave that froths up to my knees throws the air from my lungs, the water grabs around my ankles pulling me out, I wade in another stride, I push my foot through the waters to take another step and am snatched from the sea's spell by a hard sharp grasp of my arm.

"Evie!" Andrew shouts against the wind and sea. He drags me back and we fall tangled in our limbs and the waves. "I'm so sorry, so sorry… I tried to save him … I'm sorry." He sobs into my hair.

*

259

This is weird. After that night – the bad one when they took Mum, I hate even thinkin' about it, I see her face sometimes just when I go to go to sleep, it scares me. Anyway, by the morning Dad's come back! (I wish I could get both parents at one time.) And grown-ups, right, when they feel bad, or like they have cocked up over somethin' it's kinda good cos they start giving you stuff, and being with you, checkin' you're ok and stuff.

I still hate Mum being gone. I mean I miss her. But she's gone to get better Dad said, very better, and she's very tired so no point in going to the hospital just to watch her sleeping that is boring. To start with I thought Grandma had sent her away to prison, cos the police took her. But Dad said she got ill in the police car – I think more than car sick, really sick, so they took her to hospital and that's where Dad said she's sleeping. She's been asleep for like over a week...

Dad goes to see her every day. It's miles away. He takes her new flowers every time, and when he gets back I ask him how she is, can I see her and stuff but he just says she's tired, she doesn't even know he's there! Poor Dad, drives all that way then has to sit on his own while Mum sleeps. Grandma doesn't go, I told her that I was OK here on my own. I know how to look after myself. But she says she'll wait till Mum comes home. I hope that's soon cos Grandma doesn't know all the things I like, not like Mum does.

Tomorrow Dad and I are going riding on the beach. We've been goin' to this place called Marros, you can learn to ride there, they have horses so you don't have to bring your own, which is nice for poor people (not s'posed to say stuff about poor people it means you're spoilt). I'm not showing off; it's just poor people can't buy horses they have to spend all their money on food. Anyway the Marros stable people can take you on your horse right down to the beach. That's called hacking. And me and Dad are doing that after school, cos the tide will be out – you can't ride when it's in, no sand see. I wrote it down for Mum so she would know all the things I've done, like I'm telling her really as if she was here. I wrote it all in Alys's book.

June 20th
Went riding today on a beach. We borrowed their horses this time. My horse was called Bryn, he was like Red but fatter and slower. Dad had a massive horse called Harvey. A lady called Heather came with us and showed us how to ride to the beach. Then we did a race. Heather and her horse won. It was awesome. We got really wet. I want to ride on the beach again.

I think Mum would love it. I hope Dad takes me again when she's back so I can race her too.

And there's this other weird thing going on. Every Tuesday, I have to go to the doctor's in Arborth, not cos I'm ill, no. I have to see this man and have a chat – *every* Tuesday. Maybe he doesn't know anyone, who knows, but you'd think he'd want to talk to grown-ups not kids. Anyway he really likes me – asks millions of questions, wants to know who my friends are, all about Jesse, and Mum and Dad, and Grandma and Granddad. I said to Dad we should ask him to tea then he'd know what I was talking about and wouldn't have to ask so much. This man says I can call him Mac. I said he could call me Finn.

I told Mac about Mum's hair, I hope it's grown back, I don't like it all cut off, she looks strange. Jesse said not to talk about it, said she might cry about it or something, he said girls get upset about hair – even mums, sometimes. I hope she wakes up and comes home soon.

Crap, two days and Granddad turns up. Hope he's chilled out. Maybe he can calm Grandma down – she's changing everythin', movin' things, unpacking everything. AND, she's put away Jesse's room, he's really pissed off and Mum is gonna go ape. She's put his things in big trunks in the den and I've had to move out of there into a "proper bedroom" as she calls it. I don't know who's put her in charge. Mum's gonna have to go back in with Dad which I don't think she's gonna like.

I hope Mum and Grandma aren't gonna end up shouting. They usually do. And Dad has to say sorry to everyone and then Mum won't talk to him for days sometimes. Then Dad has to take Mum home. But this *is* Mum's home so I don't know where he'll take Mum, if they fall out, just so long as it's not back to the hospital. I think Dad just wants everyone to get on.

Anyway – sports day tomorrow. Obviously, I'm gonna win the sprint, they're all so slow here – Luke was fastest at my old school, then me. I'm gonna cane 'em! Wish Mum could watch, I mean it's good Dad will be there, he's never been to my sports day before cos he always has to work; he's really excited. I asked him not to bring Grandma, she's sooo loud, well embarrassing.

Wish Mum would come home soon.

Chapter thirty-one

I push myself up from the knot of Andrew. Waves rhythmically break over our legs. I sit to face him; the sea, the spray, the wind beating against us, we both shake with cold. He's staring into my face and his appearance is new to me. So much has washed away, all the hard lines that had set in, erased, his eyes have gone beyond pain; his expression is broken. "I wanted to save him," he's still whispering. And I can't tell tears from seawater. I put my hands on his cheeks, his skin is blue and I pull him into me holding his skull under my chin. I can't say, "It's OK." Or promise any move forward from here – from this point on the beach. Is this where it stops for us? Eroded by the sea, taken out and dissolved into the oceans. Something within me opens a small door that locked shut a year ago. It leads to forgiveness, a warmer place, somewhere where I'll no longer be alone. Andrew shakes into the bones of my chest, I rest my head on top of his, looking out along the waves to the point where the shore disappears into sky.

A boy in a badly fitting school uniform strolls slowly towards us, his hands rammed into his pockets. He looks up, "I did it, Mum… I did … I sold drugs, and Dad tried to stop me …I did it Mum … I did…" From a place too deep inside me to know, a howl escapes that is matched by the wind, "No…" I cry out to my Jesse, to the little boy who baked fairy cakes with me, ran naked round the garden while I chased him with water, that golden innocent child I held till he fell asleep. "But I grew up Mum…" he whispers in my head and his voice is a pain so unbearable I cry out again. And as a final destruction the waves smash over us, and the violence of the water is right.

Chapter thirty-two

Today I found this list thing. I think it's like stuff that's none of your business. I think it's what Grandma is going to do to our house – even though it's ours – not hers.

She's got this man who follows her around in the mornings. She points to things and says they have to go, or be knocked down. He spills his tea when he walks. I don't like what he's doing, but he's ok. He's in charge. He tells all the builders who come where they have to work – what they have to do. And I follow him like he follows Grandma. He says stuff like "You checking up on me lad?" Then he laughs. He has the biggest laugh I've heard, everyone hears it and we all smile when he does it. And when he laughs you can see his four teeth, that's all he's got, they're all different colours and point out different ways. He must have real trouble chewing toffees. He's called Garth.

I think this list is Garth's. I took it. I put it in Alys's book. I don't know why. Well I do – I thought it might stop him knockin' stuff down. Yesterday he looked for it and he went out and shouted at the man who's takin' the white off the outside of Pengarrow: "Where the fuck's the schedule gone, Dai boy."

Schedule of Works: Pengarrow

Rewire entire building:	Ivor Jones & Sons.
Install new boiler Upgrade central heating system:	Matt the boiler
Install solar panels on south facing wing Install new lighting fixtures throughout:	Tomos Rees & sons
Install kitchen, in slate floor, new aga.	Arbor Stoves
utility room extension plumbing, conservatory breakfast room:	Matt the boiler
Renovate/restore lounge, expose stonework to alleviate damp in left hand corner:	Rhidian Evans
expose concealed fireplace, lay new oak flooring:	Rhidian Evans
Install shower room on ground floor:	Matt the boiler

This morning Garth didn't show up. Grandma said a new man was coming from London. "Someone who knows what they're doing." The man takin' the white off – the Dai boy – came down the scaffolding said he was going home, and so did the man pulling wires out of the wall in the lounge.

Today Pengarrow is all quiet. Grandma has gone out to find more people to tell what to do. Jesse came back. We went to see Red.

I feel a bit bad. I miss Garth's laugh.

Chapter thirty-three

MUM'S BACK!

It was weird they turned up, her and Dad, and when they got out the car they were all wet. Dad said somethin' about them going to the beach, but they were like soakin', all their clothes, everythin'. And shivering, they were both shakin' – should've taken towels, derrrr.

She doesn't look better. Her face is white. She looks scared. Her hair hasn't grown any. Her eyes ... they're ... weird.

I thought she would come back all better. That's what Dad said. I mean she was in hospital. But I think she looks worse. She's just bones, really, I thought she would be all better.

She cried when she saw the house, when she got in the kitchen and saw the big hole where the old cooker used to be, tears came out of her eyes. I don't even know if she knew she was crying cos she didn't wipe her face, she just stood there, Dad had to sit her down in the old rocker, "At least this is still here." She said like the chair was a person you could talk to.

I'm worried she's gone really mad.

Dad told me once that I had a granny – a great granny, I think, Mum's granny, Mum called her Nana (can you get great nanas or do they have to be grannys?) Anyway Nana, Mum's nana, was *actually* mad – Dad said. Mum and her nana lived in this old house – Dad said it was falling down – it wasn't far from our old house, I think it's the one mum took us to for picnics. Living in an old house

doesn't make you mad though, cos we'd all be mad livin'
here then. Maybe he thought this Nana was mad cos she
played with Mum in the old bomb shelter – they camped
there. But that's not mad neither cos we did that with Mum
in London – in the same place. But Dad doesn't play,
doesn't pretend or look out for Jesse. You're not allowed
to say that you saw him; he stops you talking about it, like
Grandma. "See, what did I tell you Andrew, she's
poisoning his mind, with all her crazy nonsense!"
Grandma shouts at Dad. I think the "she" is Mum, but I
don't know what the "crazy nonsense" is. We're not
making Jesse up; he's there. He decides when he comes
and goes, we don't.

Anyway, Dad actually found Mum's nana dead! It
happened when Jesse was born, Dad said he went round to
see her and she was *dead* in the rocking chair! It's the one
we have in the kitchen, the one that Mum likes sitting in.

So when Mum got back it was all a bit mental here with
the mess Grandma's made. We're mostly campin' out in the
old library, don't know why it's called that, loads of shelves
but no books. And Grandma says the shelves are coming
out so Dad can have a proper "Home Office". And she said
she was going to get rid of the old snooker table in the
"Billiards Room". Dad and I told her to get lost – not to her
face – we just said ,"No way," but I thought it. You'd think
this was her house. I think Dad should tell her to chill. I
quite like all the old stuff, I don't really want it all new.

Grandma didn't even come to say hi to Mum. I think
Dad went and got her. They are *so* weird, they don't do

hugging like girls do, I mean, whenever we go anywhere you have to be hugged by ladies or worse, kissed. Grandma said "Evelyn..." and Mum said "Amelia..." and then Grandma had to go off to sort something out so she said.

Dad kept asking Mum if she was tired. How could she be tired – she's been sleepin' for ages. Sometimes he can be a bit thick. I knew what she wanted though – *Jurassic Park*, hot chocolate and biscuits. It's a no-brainer, I told Dad, we always do this, when we plan to do something else and it rains or we can't go, then we get blankets watch the film and veg out. I took her to the library when she'd got changed out of her weird granny clothes. And when I shut the door and no else was there I gave her the old book back – Alys's book. I told her that I had written all the things I've been doing while she was away so that she didn't miss out. She liked that; she actually smiled. I told her that I saved it from Grandma's clearing out. I am sure she whispered, "Witch". And we curled up on the sofa. I think she was asleep for most of the film but she never let go of my hand.

I might ask to stay off school next week. I'm gonna ask Dad because someone's got to look after Mum, haven't they, and Grandma's not going to do it, that's for sure.

Chapter thirty-four

"Home at last," I thought, until I stepped out of the car, not to our home but into a building site. *She's* hijacked it. Pengarrow lies in ruins, its heart ripped out, skipped along with anything else that had a history to it. I pray Alys isn't watching. It's a final betrayal by Andrew, he's guilty and he can't meet my eye. We didn't speak the whole way home from the beach. The numbed coldness that we were both feeling spread through the car, I didn't even hear its engine. The word 'sorry' rings around my head, and I know it's not enough, because it can't change the past, can't explain it, can't and won't bring him back – leaves Jesse as the ghost that passes along the edges of my life. I listen as Nana joins in, "We're sorry dear, we are, we thought that if we left you with her she would *have* to take care of you, sober up – get organised … we never thought she would leave you alone in that flat … put her work first … what were we thinking … we're so sorry, dear… So sorry." It's so easy to say, so hard to mean it, I tell their voices. "I didn't think it through. I was so stupid Mum… I'm sorry." Oh Jesse, Jesse: if I could hold you one last time, one last time. I sink my head in my hands, pushing fingers into my ears to silence them. Andrew stares straight ahead marooned in his grief. The ragged seam joining us snaps another stitch.

And we arrive to this. I look up at Pengarrow, I think all I felt, feel, is heartbroken, for the house, its past, its memories.

Amelia, though, is in heaven – in charge, destroying and bringing things back under her control. Her greeting an icy, one word, "Evelyn". I reciprocate: "Amelia". Poor Finn stood there avoiding all the dislike, cuddling me up in the library with a bad film. I shut my eyes for a while but I could hear Amelia shouting down the phone to some errant contractor. What right did she have? Who'd given her permission? Was Andrew that weak-willed he'd just said, "Go ahead Mother, gut the place." Or had this all been part of his grand plan – his new start? Nerves jingle up my left side moving into my lungs, the closeness of Amelia alarms me. We don't spend time together, there is no relationship between us only a gulf of hate and mis-understandings; neither of us wants to build a bridge, if it were even possible. But tonight I presume she'll be sleeping somewhere under the same roof, I pray it's the room furthest from the one I'm sleeping in. Imagine if a newly evicted ghost were to sneak up in the deep dark hours and smother her with a pillow, suffocating her orders as they queued up on the tip of her tongue. Imagine.

The floorboards over our heads groan as she passes, back and forth. Back and forth the sound of her voice squeezes between the gaps of the planks; she's discussing our bathroom with a plumber. I wonder if the airing cupboard with Alys's list of linen is still standing or whether Amelia has ordered its destruction as well. The noise from the house as it gives up, its dying groan, is intolerable, the sound of eras ending, I need to be out of it and suggest to Finn we go talk to his pony.

The stables are a haven, untouched. Red the pony is exactly the same. The builders haven't ventured this far. Finn and I climb to the top of the hay bales, collectively breathing out our relief. Brony dog slinks around the corner doing her impression of invisible. The swallows loop and race in and out arguing noisily, and the sound of the pony endlessly munching hay gives the afternoon its heart beat. Finally, there's a place to rest, a space where all my tumbled half-thoughts can gather into a mass I can read through. In here, with Finn and the hay and the horse I don't feel so afraid, so out of control, and helpless. I pull Finn to me and hug him into my bones drinking in the smell of his hot damp hair. "Missed you," I tell him. "Me too," he replies. "Don't go again will you?" I shake my head. "Not without you I won't." Brony forgets to play invisible and scrambles up the bales to curl round us.

"Here, I saved this for you!" Finn thrusts a rosette into my hand. "You could stick it in Alys's book, maybe keep it safe."

"Wow – amazing … I missed sports day? I'm sorry, I've never missed…" I have to hug onto him again I need to move on from constant crying; it's not fair on him. "Ok, I'll stick it here." I open the book on a page with vivid green writing… "And you rode on the beach. And where did Dad find a cinema for goodness sake?"

"Carmarthen. It was a bit small, not like London, but not too bad."

"Nothing's like London, Finn."

"I miss it a bit, but at least we've got beaches now."

"And horses."

"And Brony dog."

We wiggle into the hay making little nooks for us both to curl into. I ask him about school, it doesn't look like much progress is being made apart from sport. I hope this will finally be the breakthrough for him. Winning the sprint has clearly given him some kudos amongst his peers. We chat on as if nothing had changed since the day we loaded the final box into the Red Dragon Removals lorry. He fills me in on all of Luke's comings and goings, how slow he is this season and how fast he, Finn, is in comparison. I wonder how they worked all this out when no one actually times them, it seems to all depend on how many people you keep beating divided by the number of times you come first. An ache is developing at the top of my cheekbones from smiling and laughing with Finn, something that I haven't done for too long.

Our peace is splintered, Andrew frantically roars my name. Brony dog hurries off sniffing the incoming trouble.

"In here!" Finn and I call back to him as he races red-faced round into the stable.

"I've been searching everywhere for you. Didn't you here me calling? You're supposed to be inside, resting." I can't tell if he's angry or anxious.

"I needed some peace. Nobody could rest with *her* shouting her head off so we came to chat with Red, that's all."

"You have to rest though. Someone needs to be with you. Keep an…"

"Someone is with me. No one needs to keep an eye on me. And the last thing I need is rest – I've been doing that for a fortnight – and who could in there, with our home being torn apart." Finn, like Brony, senses war. Quickly he hides the book and scurries down the hay making excuses he needs a drink.

"She's is *not* tearing the house apart. She's trying … trying to help while I look after you and Finn!"

"I told you, I don't need looking after. I'm here for Finn now. We don't need her.

He hunts an answer. "But everything is broken, the wiring, the heating, the boiler… Someone needs to organise…"

"But you thought it was all OK three weeks ago when you swanned back to London… If it's all such a wreck why the hell did we buy it, why not buy a new house, or stay in the house we already had?"

He sighs, shoulders slumping. "I'm not fighting… You know we couldn't stay in London…"

"We could…" I mutter.

"Well I couldn't! Not everything is about *you*. I thought we needed this place… Thought the change would … would help." He waves his arms in the direction of the house.

"But there's no change! The moment we arrive you're off back to London… Back to Caroline!"

"But I have to work for Christ's sake. I had no idea the Minister would do a major U-turn the minute my leave started." He runs his hand over his face, fingers rasping along the stubble of his jaw. "And I work with Caroline, that's all … as I tell you again and again. And if I don't work, who the hell is going to pay for all this?"

"But nobody *wants* 'all of this' Andrew. Finn and I don't want to be tucked away out of sight in the middle of fucking nowhere!"

"It isn't 'nowhere'. If you hate it so much why on earth did you agree to move in the first place?"

"I didn't."

"Yes you did."

"I was just trying to shut you up, I never wanted to come here, why would I? This is all your big bloody idea. And why, on top of everything is *she* here, tearing it apart?" I scramble off the hay to face him. "Did it not cross your mind that I might have an opinion on what I'd like our home to look like, or does my opinion not count any more?" In my head I'm shouting this at him, but in reality I don't have the strength. I want to rant and argue with him. I want Andrew to send his mother home, and I never want to hear or see her again.

"Send her home, Andrew… Make her stop…"I beg him. I hadn't seen her slinking up behind him placing her hand on his shoulder in ownership.

"I'm going nowhere, Evelyn. How dare you speak to Andrew in this manner. How ungrateful are you?" Andrew moves to stop her, she silences him with her raised hand. "You can't expect Andrew and Finn to live in this chaos whilst you decide wether or not to have yet another breakdown! You're incapable…" Gently Andrew cuts Amelia off, he turns his back on me and mumbles something quietly to her.

"OK darling." Amelia smoothes his arm, places her hand on his cheek, gazes up at him. Something in their intimacy reminds me of lovers and I'm revolted.

"Evie, will you come back inside? You have medication to take."

"I'm not taking any more pills – I need to know what's going on. I'm not a child to be ordered around. Just because I disagree with everything you're doing doesn't make me ill or mad. I don't want to live here, I don't want *her* in our house, and I'm not coming in. Just go away. Leave me alone." He moves towards me grabbing my arm. "Leave me alone!" I hiss in his face. He tightens his grip – it hurts. "Get off!" He doesn't let go. It's in self-defence I slap his face with my free hand, like that time long ago in the polo marquee. I'm surprised how much his stubble stings my palm.

BREAD

4 oz yeast
2 Table Spns Dem Sugar } Mix & put in warm place to work.
½ pt. lukewarm water }

USING DRIED YEAST

2 tablespoons BRAN.
1 bag Wholemeal Flr.
+ white flr to 6 lbs
9 small teaspns Salt
2-3 oz Lard.

Put — 50 gm Dr Yeast
in ½ Tablespn Dem Sugar
Flr. 1 PT L.W WATER
Put in closet.

add yeast when frothy plus another 2½ pts warm water
Mix with wooden spn until workable by hand.
Keep folding & pressing out until mix is smooth.
Weigh up 1½ lbs larger tins + 1 lb smaller tins — Greased
make into

Chapter thirty-five

Put in hot oven at 425° for ½ hr then change
loaves over top to bottom shelves. Leave for another ½ hr.
If tops when tapped sound hollow & cooked at bottom
turn out onto rack.

5.1 oz Flr.

Result

The shoutin's started. I knew it would. Mum is actually screaming at Dad. And Grandma is shouting at Dad for letting Mum shout, and Dad is shouting at everyone. It sounds like he kicks Brony dog – she whines and runs off.

That's what I wanted to do, run off. Tell them all to shut up.

"SHUT UP!"

I do it. I stand at the top of the front door steps and shout it so hard my throat actually stings, but they're all so loud nobody hears me.

Then they all stop, everyones watching Granddad's car turning into the yard.

Chapter thirty-six

ELDERFLOWER CHAMPAGNE

2 heads of elderflower 1 gallon water
1½ lb. white sugar 1 lemon
2 tablespoons white-wine vinegar

Pick the heads when in full bloom and put into a bowl followed
by the lemon juice, cut-up rind (no white pith), sugar and
vinegar. Add the cold water and leave twenty-four hours,

6. Elder flower
1½ lb. Sugar
3 lemons:

His voice booms as he erupts from his car, demanding instant attention.

"Andrew, my dear boy!" He bellows to the whole of Wales. "The old place doesn't look so bad!" He speaks as if he owns Pengarrow. As with everything else Rufus Wolfe speaks of, there's an intonation of ownership. I watch them from the safety of the stable. Amelia swoops off to meet him.

"Darling," they drawl, embracing and air kissing each other.

There's the sound of hollow drums as Andrew and his father back slap – it's all so self-congratulatory, I can barely watch.

"My goodness, even the old milking sheds are still standing! What's the plans for those – garaging? And the orchards – still producing are they? D'you remember the wonderful cider?

"I certainly do! Gracious we had some parties!" Amelia titters her reply cut from glass. Finn slopes down the front steps. Performing a duty, he moves to hug his grandfather.

"Finn! You've grown my boy." They collide in an uncomfortable, mistimed greeting, Rufus recoils from Finn's attempted embrace and thrusts out a hand for a cold English welcome. I watch my son as his whole body is heartily shaken from the hand backwards. Amelia gathers her flock to her and steers them off round to the back gardens. Her laughter hangs in vapour trails behind them.

I stay standing in the place for the unincluded, a tingling shock racing up through my feet, my spine, surprising the hairs on the back of my neck erect. It arrives in my brain and races round the empty space there shouting, *"They all know this house*." How? How can that be? I flick back through memories, checking the endless house details Andrew force-fed me; away-from-it-all places in Scotland, Cornwall, Devon, Northumbria and, I'm sure, Wales. Slumping into the hay pile again, I repeat myself, "I'm sure he showed me places in Wales." How else would he have known Pengarrow was on the market? I try to extract the image of the estate agent that showed us around, but dimly from my place of forgotten things, a memory of the old woman, the one that gave us tea and cake struggles into focus and now I look at that memory of her, I see how like Alys she was, but a hundred years older. And I remember how when I told the Max Boyce postman, he laughed and said the place had been empty for years. So how *did* Andrew find it, if he didn't already know about it?

Had I foolishly fallen into a trap, one of Andrew's grand schemes? I'm angry, every which way, and can't make out a target for my rage. I'm as much to blame as Andrew is, I should've stopped his crazy plans, refused to take part, to stay put. Why didn't I? Because I was – still am – a heap of mess that can't be decisive about anything. Andrew saw his opportunity and buried us in the countryside out of sight and out of mind. "Arrrrgh!" I shout at the stable rafters, scattering swallows. I slump back into the hay and wrap my arms across my eyes trying to shut out the day. I listen to my memory of Nana humming and Willow persuading me not to go.

"You will come back eventually, won't you Evie? You can always doss here if there's no where else …"

287

I think of Nana's house rotting on the edge of the park, it's still mine, what's left of it, whispering with all the ghosts from my past, and Ma… "Come back," Willow whispers.

"And I will just say hello to the folks that you know, tell them you won't be long…" Nana sings.

Avoiding a confrontation with my in-laws I drag myself from the warmth of the hay and, grasping Alys's book, hurry inside to find somewhere to hide out for a while. Inside Pengarrow has lost its smell, its identity. Emulsion and freshly sawn timber bounce off the walls. Things shine; their history polished away, all the webs of memories have been cleaned out from the corners. On the stairs I meet the man who's destroying the bathroom. He nods, staring at my hair, and leaves a trail of sawdust as he heads on out the front door. I fight the urge to bolt the door behind him, keep him and them out.

On the landing I force myself to open the bathroom door. The room as I remember it, has been removed, the bath, the walls, parts of the floor. Under the ancient boards that have carried hundreds of years of bathers, copper veins run carrying hot and cold. The only thing that remains intact is the door in the far corner of the room – the door to the airing cupboard – it even still looks dusty. I realise that I'm holding my breath as I pull it open, and unbelievably, nothing has changed. Sheets still sit here fresh from the line with razor sharp folds, everything in order, everything in its place. The space wraps arms around me in a welcome-home embrace, holding me in until I feel still again. I squeeze into the corner and open Alys for company.

June 22ⁿᵈ 1898

Mrs Ebsworth called me to her kitchens. I swore I would never enter that house again, but Mam was having none of it, says unless I'm bringing in my share I can hop it – find my own way. So first thing, she practically drags me to the big house. Mrs E was in a fine old temper I gave up listening in the end about how I didn't deserve another chance after the spectacle I had made of myself, embarrassing the Judge and his family. I was leaving only Mam had hold of my arm tight like so as I couldn't move. And all the time, the only thing I could think of was Auden, oh how I want to hate him, rip out his heart like he's done to me. But I love him, I love that man with all my heart, and it hurts more than I can bear.

I'm to have my job back in the kitchens, twice the pay, time off at Christmas and the old woodcutter's cottage in Hollow's Wood is mine for the taking if I need it! Mam and Mrs Ebsworth can't believe what they're hearing! "What you done to get such privileges, Alys bach?" Mam hissed as we left. I shouted to Mrs Ebsworth, "I'll think about it." And I heard her choking on her cuppa. "Think about it girl? You'll be in there tomorrow morning with the sunrise scrubbing them floors and thanking your lucky stars, you hear me." Mam was furious, but she didn't understand, I didn't want Auden's charity. We didn't speak for the rest of the day I went down to the river for the peace.

I can't spend the rest of my days waiting on him and her, watching them together. I'm so angry with him that he could even think that I would want to be under same roof as him! But the cottage – that would be handy, my own place for me and the babi… Mam will be throwing me out soon as she knows – shaming her house and her good name. Maybe I'll write to him, this'll be the last time though, I'll take the cottage, just till I get back on my feet mind, but I'll not wait on him and his fancy woman.

July 10th 1898
Told Mam about the babi, she belted me round the head with the broom, picked up my boots and threw 'em out the door and told me to follow 'em. Didn't even want to hear my side, but then I knew she wouldn't. I'm best off without her, can take care of myself. The cottage 'nt too bad. Someone's been in and left a few sticks of furniture, nothing grand, but it'll do. And some food and bits. But how am I going to look after myself, when this food runs out, where's the next lot going to come from and the one after that? Who's going to take me in now with a babi on the way.

I went down to the river again. Water was running high and black after the heavy rain. I thought how easy t'would be to jump in, let it carry me away out to Cardigan Bay. Standing on the bank I swear I was

about to jump when this arm grabs me from behind.
"Hey you be careful there, lass!" he shouts, pulling me
back down onto the bank. "You slip in there and that'd
be the last anyone'd see of you." Davey Morgan, miner's
son from the village across the valley, mine's not good
enough for him, went off to join the Navy, so what was
he doing mooching along riverbanks. "Shouldn't you be
at sea, Davey Morgan?" I snapped at him, shore leave
he reckoned, just my luck. He made such a fuss – insisted
he walked me back to the cottage but I wasn't letting
him in for his cuppa I made him drink it on the
doorstep…

I was so engrossed in what Alys was saying that I didn't hear
Finn calling me until he'd run past the bathroom and carried
on up the next flight of stairs. I knew what it would look
like to appear from a cupboard; I'm sane enough to see
through another person's eyes. So I wait until I hear his feet
creaking across the ceiling above and slip out on to the
landing to follow him up the next flight of stairs.

"Mum!" I surprise him in the doorway of the den. "I've
been looking for you." His expression clouds. "Granddad's
here."

"Hmm, I saw." There's an awkward silence.

"So let's have a look at all the stuff you managed to rescue
for me!"

His face relights and he pulls me over to a chaotic heap
that looks like rubbish. From the bottom Nana's radio begins
to hum a happy-to-be-found tune. "Let's get sorting, maybe

we can make this room into a sort of study for you and me to do homework in."

"But you don't do homework," Finn points out.

"Yeah I do now," I lie.

"Great." We set about dragging dumped and unwanted furniture into a sort of study looking shape. When we've finished we've found a table for the radio, which is still singing with joy at its new home. We both have a desk to work at and bookshelves for our treasures; Finn's displays three buzzard feathers, some colourful rocks and two shells he's beachcombed. Mine has Alys's book. A sunken sofa slouches across one end of the room, which we've disguised with an old blanket to make it look comfy. By the time we've finished our hands are grey grained with grime and the air in the room sparkles in a dust blizzard.

"It's perfect!" I flop on the sofa, something twangs and digs in my bottom. And the room *is* perfect. You would know the moment you walked in that this space belongs to Finn and me, and in the corner beside my desk is Jesse's space, filled with what's left of his, after Amelia's culling. Finn throws himself beside me, causing a puff of dust motes to cloud the air. I reach for Alys's book.

"So let me read what you've been up to then." I turn to the page about the horse ride on the beach.

"...And the horses just ran straight into the sea, everything got wet, our shoes, jeans, everything!" he finishes.

"Was it scary, I mean the horses must have been going so fast. I would've been terrified!"

"Yeah, that's because you're a girl."

"Thanks."

"But it's true. Girls always find stuff like that scary and it's not, it's way cool!"

I laugh and kiss the back of his head, I'm relieved that he leans back into me, I drink in his smell, which has a foreign hint of changed washing powder, different shower gel and shampoo, I want to take him down to the bathroom right now and scrub him clean of Amelia Wolfe. He squirms free, intent on showing some of his new-found treasure. He's just explaining the two new shells when: "Evelyn! Evelyn, are you up here?" The door to the den groans open. Nana's radio holds its breath. The perfect afternoon escapes and runs down the stairs.

800 Tol. about 150,000
pounds. Gild
A Slater 1.0.9^{d} = 2b.

Chapter thirty-seven

Why does Dad have to go and spoil stuff? Me and Mum were chillin'. In he comes talking to her like she's the kid – like he did with Jesse, every thing cool, and Dad comes home and starts ordering everyone around. Jesse didn't take it like Mum, he just went out. Then everyone panicked cos he hadn't come home at the right time and the rowing would start all over. Why couldn't Dad see that? Is he thick or what? What if Mum ends up like Jesse – so pissed off with Dad for moaning all the time that she goes off. Then what?

So he marches in, says nothing about our den and tells Mum to come and say hello to Granddad. Mum and Granddad don't like each other. She doesn't want to say hello, you can tell. She scrunches up when Granddad's around, and Granddad gets louder when Mum's around, sometimes Grandma tells him to stop shouting, sometimes she shouts too.

I wait in the den for Mum and Dad to go down, you could hear Granddad from right up here! "So, Evelyn..." I heard him shout at her.

Chapter thirty-eight

August

"So… Evelyn." He drawls in a predatory tone. He fills the two-letter word with too much disappointment and loathing – it stretches into a paragraph. How am I supposed to respond? "So" is not a question – a greeting, it's the start of something but he chooses only to complete it with raised eyebrows. His brogues crunch in the dust as he bounces slightly on his toes still waiting for my correct response. It would be easier if he boomed, "Explain yourself, woman!"

"Rufus." I force out the name not wanting to sound meek or scared.

"Feeling better now are we, after our little drama?" I want to say no, I'm not, but how about you. "Getting a little regular these…" He hunts for a suitably condescending term. "…tantrums aren't they?" My fuse is lit I'm about to take off as Andrew anchors me to the spot with a gagging arm grip. The atmosphere is allowed to hang there in discomfort for a minute too long, ensuring enough pain is applied. An unseen signal is registered and Amelia suggests we all sit down for dinner.

It's a thin meal produced for people at war with food; taste kept to a minimum, portions for a five-year-old. The conversation is as contrived as the dinner. It's torture. I can't help myself recalling meals around Nana's table or Willow's, or even our own. It wasn't that we ate lavishly, no, things were always simple but prepared with thought for the people who would surround the table and others who might turn up unexpectedly. We made things that you shared, large plates to be handed round, people's hands touched as you served the person beside you, maybe tried some of theirs if it looked better than yours. Eating this way – the Wolfe way – wasn't eating at all. I wonder how Andrew can just sit there and act as if all this is fine. The dour Mrs George swoops away the starter plates before anyone's really started, Finn looks relieved that he doesn't have to eat any more of it.

"You're a marvel Mrs G.," Rufus chirps, the stony Mrs G nods in agreement.

I notice the cutlery is new, the crockery new, even the table we're seated at is unfamiliar. Amelia has created a dining room from part of what we called the hall, it looks like a grown-up's room, somewhere you have to behave and whisper. This is not my home, no one lives like this – it's a hospitality suite.

"This space will work beautifully especially when Party members come down. We'll be able to sit twelve comfortably, don't you think?" Amelia's comment hangs over the table. I almost ignore it until the words drop into place.

"What 'Party members'?" I ask Andrew, turning to stare at him. His tired, pale face flushes along the top of his cheekbone. Amelia and Rufus stop talking, we're all watching Andrew.

"There will be a few visitors from Party HQ over the next couple of months." Amelia's voice has taken on an explaining-to-a-three-year-old tone. "People to help Andrew with his candidacy bid." The corner of her mouth curls in satisfaction at my confusion, victory is written all over her face.

"What candidacy, Andrew?"

"Andrew has decided…" Amelia begins.

"I asked Andrew!" I fire at her across the table without moving from my position. I notice Rufus in my peripheral vision, sitting back, arms folded across his chest, enjoying the unfolding drama. Andrew swallows, his Adam's apple bobbing several times. He fiddles with his fork.

"I've been talking with Father—"

"Poached salmon with a dill dressing, green salad and boiled new potatoes," Mrs George announces as she pushes through Andrew's half-started sentence. Damn that woman.

"Andrew?" He waits an eternity as Mrs George divides the salmon with mathematical precision. I'm about to demand an answer again when she sets the salmon on a sideboard and proceeds to do another lap of the table with the potatoes. "We can serve ourselves, thank you," I snap.

"There's no need to be rude…" Amelia hisses, but Mrs George finally recognises the atmosphere in the room as tense and storms out, tutting by the doorway and telling Amelia: "Dessert is in the fridge and I shall be going now." Her exit is theatrical.

"Well I must say—" begins Amelia.

"Andrew, I'm still waiting. What candidacy?"

Looking through me as if this is a rehearsed scene he says, "Evelyn, I've decided to become an MP." He rushes on: "The Party has accepted my application, and I plan to stand in the next election." A thousand questions swarm. I know if I speak it will be an ugly shout, so I stand resisting the urge to throw my salmon in his face, and leave the room as fast as I can without actually running.

I just can't believe that Andrew could make a decision

like this. He's spent most of his working career cajoling, teasing and extracting information and co-operation from politicians about whom he never has a good word to say. In fact, I would have gone so far as to say he loathed them. But to not even have mentioned that he fancied a go himself ... I'm stunned.

How could he?

I feel utterly betrayed. He's going to stick us out there like the goons that we are for all to see – the falling apart family with bits missing. How can he want that, how can he put us through that? At last I have sensation, and I'm surprised that it isn't anger that grips me but absolute pain, the pain of being excluded, and the pain that will come again when we're examined and turned over to the light so that the public can get a better view. I leave them to their thin green meal. One thing is pin-sharp: I will not play any part in this ridiculous plan, and neither will Finn.

Not – one – part.

I head for sanctuary, the den. I'm cursing myself for not dragging Finn with me when I escaped dinner. I wish the room had a bolt so I could shut them out and keep them out. I grab Alys's book and the scratchy blanket knitted from wire wool and hide myself on the sofa, pulling it over my head. From downstairs their murmurings creep up towards me, they laugh, carrying on as if nothing has changed. Finn's sharp clear tone rings above the others, but I can't hear what he's saying. I shut them out and open Alys's book hoping to escape from my world into hers.

July 28th 1898

The cottage is looking grand. Davey Morgan came by again this morn, fish he brings this time, fresh caught he reckons. Poaching's a crime I told him, they'll hang you out if you gets caught. No ones gonna catch him he says all cocky like. Be gone with you I tells him. I don't want him hangin' around. Yes you does Alys Thomas, I knows, you know, your mam told my mam. I want to help you. You leave me alone now I shouted at him and threw an old apple at his back as he hurried down my path. How could Mam have done that? I'll be having words with her!

Damn Auden Llewellyn. And damn you Mam, to hell and back, the pair of you.

Ha! Finn and Alys seem to be the only people in the world that actually talk sense! "How right you are," I tell her pages.

"Mum?" I hadn't heard Finn come in. "Who are you talking to? Why are you under that mingin' blanket? You know Brony dog sleeps on that when she comes up here."

I surface. "Ahh, I wondered what that smell was. Yuck. How you doing?"

"OK."

"Only OK?"

"Yeah, why?"

"Nothing, just checking, that's all." His face is full of questions he can't find the words for. He looks like Andrew did before life got hold of him. I didn't want to think about

Andrew, I was up here to forget him. Damn you to hell and back Andrew Wolfe.

"What?"

I was sure the sentence was in my head; perhaps my anger is so strong the words are leaking out of me.

"Nothing, love."

"Are you going mad, Mum?"

"Wow, that's a question."

"But are you?"

"Nope. Why, d'you think I am?"

"Well you do plenty of strange stuff."

"Like what?"

"Well you were just talking to yourself when I came in. And all that kitchen smashing, and…"

"Hang on, I told you that wasn't me."

"Yeah, but you blamed it on Alys who's … well you know."

"What?"

"Well she's… And your hair, and loads of stuff that isn't what normal mums do."

"So what do normal mums do then?"

"Normal stuff."

"Like?"

"Well like Grandma, I mean she does normal stuff." So we've got to the bottom of it at last. The witch has been weaving her lies.

"Grandma? You've got to be joking – there's nothing normal about her! I mean look what she's doing to Pengarrow, and at all our stuff she wanted to chuck out!" In agreement the radio starts up a little tune. He looks unconvinced.

"But I heard her, she said you were mad, she told Dad, she said you weren't safe. You are safe aren't you, you're not going to do anything, are you … you know like something crazy?" I get up and go over to him. I bend, but only a little because before long we'll be standing eye to eye. I kiss him on his forehead and for once he doesn't squirm away.

"I'm not going to do anything crazy Finn, I'm not mad, I'm not ill and I'm not dangerous. I'm just really cross with Dad, Grandma and Granddad over this ridiculous MP business, and I'd really like Grandma and Granddad to go home and stop changing the house, so that you, me and Dad can work out what to do next." He nods and pulls away. And even if I do do something earth-shatteringly mental, no one will notice because Andrew's hidden us away in Pengarrow, I think to myself.

"I'm going to see Red." Finn mutters. If only grown-ups had a crisis-over button like children.

Chapter thirty-nine

I slink into bed, having no desire to face Britain's next Prime Minister. I am beaten down by Andrew, by the betrayals and revelations that are raining down in hard-hitting blows. To look at him chills me. He's a stranger that I don't want to know any more. I want him to leave – go back to Caroline, go anywhere that's not here with Finn and me. I need time and ammo – calm and well thought-out, that I can hurl at him – I have to blow his idiotic ideas clean out of the water so that we can have a chance at being a family. Outside the window, behind the closed curtains, the summer evening stays up, quietly drizzling. Voices murmur from floors beneath, punctuated with loud rounds of laughter. Jesse sits on the end of the bed with nothing much to say, eventually he lies down on top of the quilt beside me, his breathing regular. I want to turn and stroke his hair and the down along the top of his cheek but I don't want to disturb him. He's like a reflection in water when he's with me, once I reach out to touch the surface his image is gone. His breathing soothes me to sleep.

Once there, Nana has much to say. She really can't understand what Andrew's playing at, she pats the back of my hand.

"There, there now dear, we'll get to the bottom of all this. You'll see, things will look so much better in the morning." I try to tell her how wrong she is but she's too busy making jam at the stove. I sleep on some more. It's dark outside – late – I turn over and now Ma is asleep on the other side of the bed; her hair is flung across her face like a tide has dragged it as it went out, the same as that last time

I gazed down at her in the trench in Nana's kitchen. Her breath is whiskied. There are so few occasions that she slept with me like this, I can remember all three times in Nana's house. And every time, when morning broke in, she'd vanished, not returning for days – once it was for over a year. I reach out to touch her hand that's thrown out across the pillow. It's icy cold and greasy, I pull away, unable to stop myself crying out.

"Evelyn? Evie, it's OK, you're just dreaming." Andrew's voice beside me is heavy with sleep. A cold hand touches my shoulder and I recoil to the edge of the bed. "It's OK, it was just a nightmare. Evie, it's me." His hand brushes my arm hunting for me. The darkness of my sleep melts into reality. I'm too angry with Andrew to bear even the slightest touch from him.

"Leave me alone." I snap. "Can't you sleep some place else?" There's confusion in his voice as if he can't grasp my hostility – like I should have forgiven him already.

"Evie, it's too late to fight, come here." He pulls my arm as if to enfold me. I yank away squirming in the covers so that my back faces him. He moves across behind me his breath hot on my neck. "Please Evie…" I throw the covers and move to get out of bed but he grabs my shoulder holding me down.

"Oww!" His grip weakens slightly.

"Stay, Evie, please stay." His voice comes from deep in the past, when it had the ability to catch my breath and soothe me. "I'm sorry… You should never have heard this way…"

"Heard? I shouldn't have *heard* in any way. You should've sat down the moment the stupid idea first popped into your head and discussed it with *me*!"

"Would you have listened?"

"Yes. And then I'd have pointed out to you how painful it is living in the public spotlight. Don't you remember all that stuff after Jesse's death, the reporters outside, on the phone, at school trying to get to Finn – they accused you of racism, remember, and of victimising Jazzy's brothers' saying they were drug dealers…"

"Jesse said they gave him the stuff to sell at school."

"You're completely missing the point. Have you thought about how all this is going to affect Finn?"

"Listen to me, please."

I pull away, lurching out of bed, I'm so angry I want to hit something or someone very hard.

"Evie wait! I'm sorry. Please, please I want to try and make you understand…"

"You're not going to *make* me understand! The idea is madness."

He continues anyway, "…Since Jesse died I've struggled, every day Evie, with the sheer waste of it all. All that life, all his potential snuffed out – gone. And I can't let his life and death *be* that, he can't end up as nothing… "

"He'll never been nothing, he's still everything!" I try not to shout.

"Or not nothing, but live on only in our memories. I want to take what happened to him, and us, and do something positive with it. I don't want any other families going through what we have been through. No other child should die at a school gate. And I want to stand up and fight for that. I want to make a difference in Jesse's name."

"So buy a bench, fundraise for a skate park or an award, or—"

"But by becoming an MP I can take my fight against gun crime and put it right at the front of everyone's attention. People will listen to me because they'll know I *understand* this issue, I'm a victim – *we're* victims of this… We have a powerful story to tell, Evie. If we can be strong – hold it together, imagine the families we could save…"

In the dim light he looks like his father ranting on, and in the pit of my stomach I feel disgust. I won't allow Finn and me to be the soapbox that he stands on to get himself elected.

"I don't want any part of this, Andrew, and I'm not allowing you to use Finn either. If you want to do 'something strong' go work for a charity." I pull the top quilt off the bed, grab Alys's book and fumble in the almost darkness for the door.

"Don't you understand anything of what I've said? Doesn't any of it hit home?"

"Not one single word." I slam the door behind me.

In the den the day is starting, a grey light seeps into the horizon, turning the room blue. I curl up on the old sofa too furious for sleep now, but I can't get comfortable, each time I move the scent of dog is overwhelming, so I stumble down to what's left of the kitchen. A space-age kettle has replaced the old iron pot that we put on the Rayburn, it glows a ridiculous purple as the water bubbles. I can't stay inside so I take my tea, Alys and the quilt out to the stable. Red snickers hello and within minutes Brony dog tick-tacks in beside me. The hay is warm to nestle in. Here, I think, I will sleep.

I shut my eyes hand-in-hand with the burning question, "Why did I ever marry Andrew?" For too long we've been a seam that's coming undone, stitch-by-stitch. He doesn't even sound the same anymore. And I'm not sure, other than our address, that there's any common ground left. When I met him that day at the hospital he had a voice that promised to take care of you and he seemed like a carefree soul drifting gently on a tide – not fighting to be anywhere, anywhen, just here, then away, then here again. That's what I liked, the untangled nature of our meetings, to start with they almost seemed like happy accidents, bumping-into's. We didn't have set times at set corners. He didn't call, I didn't answer. He found Willow's one day, that was OK, and gradually the occasional became next week, then tomorrow.

He made Nana laugh. He said he *preferred* elderflower champagne. Nana thought he was charming, and he was. Then his job had a three-month posting to Paris. Did I want to come? Just a random idea – an experience to take – a why not. Of course! Nana and Willow both agreed. We should never have returned – Paris was our paradise. It was a dream to cling to in bad times, a fantasy we thought we could carry on back in London. We lived in the land of make-believe; he worked, we climbed the Eiffel Tower, gazed at the *Mona Lisa*, wandered the boulevards and made Jesse. We should never have come home, we should have stayed as runaways. At home his parents fumed, Caroline waited with her huge diamond ring, a thing that had completely slipped his mind and hadn't been mentioned to me.

Finally, when Jesse had arrived, when Caroline had departed, and his parents had been silenced, I did say yes, it made sense, then. And Amelia had exploded into planning mania: she even booked the Dorchester; 200 hundred for a sitdown lunch and evening buffet. She made an appointment with Jenny Packham, sure that I would turn up in something "unsuitable" otherwise. Ms Packham was very understanding when I phoned to decline.

I ignored her colour schemes, I ignored the summons to attend a wine sampling, let's face it, they didn't really need me. I'm sure a more suitable bride could have been found even at short notice. The day after her great invite mailing, a Saturday in September, the 12th, I met Andrew on Richmond Green. "I've got someone I want you to meet, wanna come?"

He followed me through the little lanes full of things that only Amelia could afford to buy, and on up the High Street, round the one-way system to the Registrar's Offices. Willow and "a bloke" she'd met the previous Friday were waiting for us, she clutched a big bunch of ox-eye daisies held together with string.

"So," I stopped and turned to Andrew, "we could wait until October for a hideous circus, ring mastered by your mother, or … we could go today and see the nice Registrar and in ten minutes time you can call me Mrs Wolfe. What d'you think?"

He laughed as if I were joking. "Really?" Maybe he counted to ten. "Go on then. But what about rings and…"

"I don't want to be labelled – I don't know about you."

"OK!"

"Great."

After the ceremony we walked back across Marble Hill Park, found a bench without a wino and shared a magnum of champagne (not elderflower for once) with Willow. No one remembered much about the rest of the evening, only the eruption the next day sticks in my mind! It makes me laugh still: poor Amelia, she'd even bought the hat. I loved that Andrew, the one that could throw life in the air and see how it landed, the one that didn't conform. Marrying that Andrew made perfect sense.

I can't sleep in the hay, it's scratchy on my face and the swallows have woken up at full volume, there's no peace to be had. I decide to have a catch up with Alys for a while.

August 10th 1898

I'm beginning to wonder if I can do this. Tis so very lonely, nights are worse, sometimes when the wind blows this way down through the elms I can hear the noises coming from the big house. The parties, the music, the place seems to have come back to life since she arrived. The Judge would hear none of that nonsense after her ladyship passed on, never music – not a note. I walked to the edge of Hollow's Wood last night – Pengarrow looked like a Christmas tree with all its lights.

Davey Morgan comes by every day even though I told

312

*him to stay away. Why are you bein' so kind I ask him
but he just shrugs an' says he wants to help me, but why
I ask, an' he just blushes like a maiden. I'll marry ya
Alys Thomas he tells me this morn, well I fell over the
bucket in surprise! Be gone with you, you're soft in the
head Davey Morgan!*

*Aye he says, but think about it Alys – it makes sense.
An' for some reason that's all I've been thinking of all
day. It makes sense – it does mean I could show me face
again in the village, make an appearance at Chapel. But
I don't love him, don't even like him, big brute of a
thing, hands like shovels, rough as the road to
Tavernspite, not like Auden's hands...But I ain't never
going to feel Auden's hands again...*

*Oh but I could never lay with that Davey Morgan,
never!*

*I always dreamed of marrying someone I loved, I
dreamed of the dress, the flowers I'd carry. You don't
marry someone cos it makes sense, do you?*

Her words leave me with a shiver; she's an unnerving echo.

Pengarrow is waking, lights flicker, someone turns on a
tap, water flees to the drains. And like a big bell clanging in
my head I remember yesterday when Rufus arrived already
knowing the place. With all of Andrews's idiotic plans I had
completely forgotten. I'm going to have to find him and
drag this out of him.

Chapter forty

1½ up. Flour S.R.   **DUMPLINGS**
3 oz. Suet
Soda Salt
Mix dry, then add water gradually, until dough.

Oh-my-God, Dad's gone totally mad! He's gonna get a new job like Granddad. Crap, we'll have to sit through even more dull, dull talking and standing still for more photos. How embarrassing. I thought gettin' away from all that was why we moved here. At tea last night everything went wrong which did mean we didn't have to eat the mingin' fish thing. Someone's got to get rid of Mrs George she's a *rubbish* cooker. Dad was really stupid, I bet if Grandma hadn't been there he wouldn't have told Mum nothing about his new job.

Guess this means he's gonna be in London with Granddad even more. What's the point moving in down here, then? This morning he's like trying to be nice, wantin' to ride or go fishing, but I don't believe him – don't want to be with him. I mean who's gonna look after me when he goes, is Mum up to it? I bloody hope Grandma isn't stayin', I mean she's all right for a bit, but I couldn't live with her and neither could Mum. Maybe me and Mum can go back to London. I tried to find her to ask her but she's gone back to sleep Grandma said. She spends all her time asleep. The summer holidays are going to be *well* dull if this goes on.

The only person I could find was Granddad, didn't think he'd be up this early. It's not that I don't like him or nothing it's just if you get on your own with him, he's like a teacher, he has to explain how everything is – how everything works, and he puts in loads and loads of rules – its boring. Never play Monopoly with him, he tells you off for spendin' your money, which is the whole point, derrrr. Anyway he was going through loads of old stuff he found in the library – old photos and stuff, some of it was actually quite cool. Granddad says hundreds of years ago – like in olden times – Grandma had a relative that actually owned this house, he was going on a bit I didn't hear all of it cos I was listening to my iPod – only with one headphone though – Dad gets well upset if you talk to him and listen to music, he says that you can't concentrate on two things at once! Well that's wrong, cos I can talk to him, watch telly, still listen to my iPod *and* do homework. Anyway don't think Granddad even noticed.

So Granddad shows me a picture of a massive wedding at Pengarrow like a million years ago. You should see what everyone was wearing! This man that got married was like my great, great, great, great uncle or something, Auden Llewellyn-Rhys Granddad said he was called, and he married this minger called Isabella. Granddad says she was a Lady. "Derr, I can tell that Granddad," I told him. "She's got a dress on!" He was goin' on about some big battle, not one with guns and stuff but people rowing I think – so not a battle at all – anyway some row over the people who thought they owned this house – the Morgans – and Grandma. Well it looks like Grandma won cos here we are. Bet the other people are pissed off with Grandma taking Pengarrow off them.

I asked Granddad if I could keep the picture. I thought Mum would like it, might cheer her up, she likes olden stuff – she could put it in Alys's book cos it goes with all the things already in there. Granddad was well chuffed.

"Glad to see you taking an interest in your heritage, my boy," he goes. So I didn't tell him it was for Mum, cos he then gave me a tenner for what he calls "tuck". *Result!*

So I go and find Mum. She's not asleep. Not in the kitchen, well who would be with dragon lady Mrs G taking over. The kitchen looks like a Jurassic Park lab, everythin' is shiny. Mum will hate it. Thought I'd try the stables cos she likes it in the hay there – she hides from Dad and Grandma. I didn't find her but got a surprise – Nye was there! He was frightened, shakin in a corner covered in hay. He was *actually* shakin! I could hear his teeth shivering. And he was sweaty. I didn't know what to do, I wanted Alys but you can never find her and I couldn't find Mum either. Grandma would make everything worse. Great … everyone's vanished.

"Nye," I said. "Nye, you OK mate?" and he kept on shakin'. "Look, d'you want help or something?" I thought what would Mum do if I freaked out, cos sometimes, since Jesse died, I have nightmares – like mega ones not baby stuff about monsters, but guns, it's always guns. And when it happens Mum sits with me and sometimes she makes hot chocolate. So I say, "D'you want hot chocolate?" and he stops shakin' and looks at me weird then goes back to shakin'.

I'm stuck. Can't just stand there so I sit down with him. Then he starts crying, felt *well* embarrassed! "What's wrong?" I said and I waited. Then after ages he says, "They're going to get me." And he shakes more. "Who's gonna get you?" I say.

"They're gonna make me go back, I can't go back, I can't..." He starts shoutin' and I have to tell him to cool it otherwise Grandma's gonna find us. "Go back where?" I ask him. "The Front..." He says, then he starts crying again. "D'you know what it's like in them trenches – the noise and the stench and the blood all messed up with the mud. The mud is everywhere like you were wearing the stuff, it gets in yer eyes, yer mouth, you eat it, its everywhere... And bodies lying where they fall, rats, eating out the eyes and the smell, everywhere, the stink of death. I can't go back." And he grabs me and starts shaking me till my teeth are rattlin' like his. "Don't let them take me, don't let them, you hear, you gotta save me, you hear, don't let them come for me!"

I can't think how I'm gonna sort this on my own, I pull away from him a bit but he grabs on tighter so I say. "Stay here." He panics and grabs on even harder. "I'm comin' back, I promise." Only hot chocolate is gonna sort this, I run back inside prayin' Mrs G hasn't turned up yet. She's not in the kitchen, so I hunt the hot chocolate thinking she's probably chucked it cos it's bad for you or somethin' but I find some. Can't make it like Mum, I make a bit of a mess, but clear out before the kitchen dragon turns up. I can hear her now shoutin' at me to come back and tidy up – like, she's the one who's paid to help; not me lady! I spill most of it on the way but at least there's some left, it looks like mud and I hope this doesn't set Nye off again about his trenches.

He doesn't say thanks or nothin' but he does drink it.

Think it was a bit hot cos he spits the first bit out. At least by the time he's finished he ain't shakin' any more.

Then I have the best idea yet! Nye's about the same size as Jesse, and I'm sure Jess won't mind, so I tell Nye we gotta disguise him then these guys who are coming for him won't know him, cos he can wear some of Jesse's stuff! Brilliant or *what*? Nye doesn't think so, moron, but I talk him round. I get him up to the den without Grandma or Dad or Granddad or Mum seeing us. I've hid some of Jesse's stuff that I thought was quite cool up there – before Grandma chucked it all out. I was right (of course) Nye is totally the same size as Jesse. And then I have the most mega brainwave, get Jesse to dress up in Nye's stuff then when these guys come looking for him, Jesse can be like a decoy and run off in the woods so they follow him and then Nye can escape. Happy days! Sometimes I'm brilliant! Just need Jess to show up.

Nye looks normal, he looks like Jess, he looks too much like Jess: I feel a bit weird. No sign of Jesse, natch. I shove Nye's old stuff in my bag, he needs to wash it cos it stinks. We decide to go back to his place. He's chilled a bit, but keeps on about all this stuff that happened in the trenches, it's gross, wish he'd stop. I try to listen. Got all my stuff together and was just stuffing that old photo in the pocket when Nye grabs it. "I know these people!" he says, "How d'you get hold of this?" I thought: weird, cos on the back of the photo it says 12th September 1898. He looks at me and points to the man in the middle, "That bastard there, he's Auden Llewellyn-Rhys, owned this

320

house an' all you can see that way and that. Show it to Ma, she'll tell you."

"Why's he a bastard?" I say, but he won't tell. I hear Dad coming in, he shouts up askin' if I wanna go riding. Nye starts sweatin', I can see he's scared again. We lie low till Dad gives up shoutin' and goes back outside. The front door slams and Nye shoots up in the air, landing with his arms over his head shoutin' at me that the shells are comin'. "Take cover!" he yells pulling me to the floor. I'm like, Nye we're inside – what shells? But he won't let me go. We gotta get out before anyone comes and finds us.

Chapter forty-one

In between the comings and goings of the kitchen, before the arrival of the non-cook, Mrs George, I sneak back inside to brew up one of Alys's teas. It looks like someone has already passed through; Mrs G's shiny surfaces are dusted with cocoa, and there's a big brown splash in the door-way that looks like Finn's handiwork. The tea instructions nestle far back in Alys's happier years. "A Soothing brew" it says as I read the ingredients:

Camomile
Lemon balm
Shot of alcohol (Brandy)
Motherwort
Lavender

The cup foams and smokes, its fumes calming. Expensive-sounding shoes clip down the staircase, echoing along the hallway, warning me of an incoming threat. I slip out of the back door and scramble up through the gardens as quickly as a scalding mug of tea will allow. Passing through the herb garden and vegetable patch I climb up through the orchard. I haven't come up this far often. Already I've climbed higher than the roofs and chimney stacks of Pengarrow, and now have a clear view across the valley to the farm opposite which is wide awake and working briskly. A tiny dot of a man rides a quad, chasing sheep; they pour through a gate like grains of rice. And right at the topmost part of the garden, where Pengarrow land ends, stands a chestnut tree that's been watching over the valley for hundreds of years. A circular bench built for another generation sits like a choker around the trunk. From here you can gaze out at the rest of Wales starting its day.

The tea has cooled enough to sip, its flavours lull my mind, giving space for thoughts to form and they're all Andrew-shaped. I lean my head back against the bark of the tree wishing I could soak up the slow rhythm of its heart. The branches above me net in a web of protection, the leaves whisper "Shhh" in a hardly-there breeze. Somewhere below, Finn is calling.

"What do I do, Nana?" I ask her with my eyes closed against the real day. I can hear her humming but she's too engrossed in her tune to answer. Behind her gentle song Ma whispers, "Not so clever now, eh, Evelyn?" I sweep her aside physically – knocking Alys's book to the ground. Papers, mementos, little torn notes, scatter in sycamore seed circles, I scrabble to catch them before the smallest of breezes floats them away. The pile in my hand is as crisp and fragile as dry autumn leaves. Beneath a recipe for damson jam I'm holding a letter from Auden Llewellyn-Rhys. The notepaper has been screwed into a tiny, angry ball at some point, creases scar its surface. These words have made it across oceans – Auden wrote this from Ladysmith Garrison, Natal, South Africa; it's dated November 1899.

My Dearest Alys,

Please, I pray, give these my feeble words a cursory glance. Dear Alys, I have no right to ask anything of you, I have behaved as a coward. I do not ask for your

325

forgiveness, for I do not deserve it, but here in these pages
I hope to atone for my behaviour…

I can read no further, his words sicken me, shutting my eyes against the morning I turn back to Nana's song that hums inside my head. Jesse comes, sits down beside me, I don't open my eyes – I don't want him to go. "When will Grandma and Granddad go?" he asks. "Soon, I hope, sweetheart … I've missed you." He mumbles some "Yeah well's." I understand his meaning. From a small child he's been nervous of Andrew's parents. Andrew blamed me for this indoctrination against them, but Jesse felt their threat as much as me. It's funny, Finn takes Rufus and Amelia in his stride – doesn't look for their cunning – accepts their weasel words, very much like Andrew.

I know I'm losing the strength to fight them off, the constant war and self-protection is exhausting, the thought of running away repeats in a circular chant inside my head. And I can hear Amelia Wolfe jeering, "That's right run away, just like your mother." I wonder how much she really knows of Ma's disappearence; I'm amazed that she's never bothered to look further than my version of events, in fact no one really has. At least there's something I can be grateful to Ma for; her unreliability, neglect, alcohol and drug-fuelled binges. Because I've found that no one hunts very thoroughly for a badly behaved person.

The crack of a twig snaps me awake. Andrew stands in the sun, darkening the day. His hands are shoved in his pockets, his shoulders hunched – the fight has left his silhouette. He stands there for a long time, I can't read his face, his thoughts, he's a black cut-out.

Eventually he flops to the bench and throws his head back against the tree, studying the overhead branches for an opening line. His hand finds mine, covering it, warming it. I turn my head slightly gazing at his profile. It's worn rough with our life; his once-black stubbled jaw sparkles quartz-like with silver. A single tear slides down over his cheekbone, leaving a shining trail. He looks broken and dishevelled, almost unrecognisable. For a moment my anger is muted. I slide across the splintery slats of the bench until my head rests in the hollow below his collarbone. If I could rip us from this life and weld us permanently together like now, with no scheming, no betrayals, no interfering parents, rewind right to the beginning, to Paris… That is the man that I could hold onto in a storm until the day I die. I breathe him in, wanting to fill all my senses with him and listen to all the memories of the times he's told me he loves me, I replay some in time to the beat of his heart. I need him back.

Gently he rubs his lips across the top of my skull warming my head; he's breathing me in too. "I love you, Evie." He whispers so quietly that I only hear it through my bones. He withdraws his hand to wrap his arm around my shoulder holding me to his ribs. I want to draw out this moment like the final chord of a symphony that hovers around the upper circle before the audience erupts in praise. I remember this embrace, the strength of it, from Nana's funeral, from the days after I gave birth to Jesse, then Finn, their first days at school and always it was accompanied with: "We'll get through this, Evie – you and me." But there's too much, this time I fear, for the pair of us to get through. He's pulling in one direction, I'm stuck fast in the past – surely we will be ripped apart, won't we? Our only hope is to stay like this, linked, tangled around one another till all the wounds are soothed.

We breathe in time. Far away, a thousand miles across to the other side of the valley the breeze carries the sound of the farmer still collecting sheep, a dog calls out, builders arrive to carry on their destruction of Pengarrow, somewhere a lawn is being cut. I rest on Andrew's chest, his head rests on mine; we are sealed. When he speaks his voice comes from inside him, I listen to his words as vibrations that echo round his chest cavity. He sounds the same as the day the ambulance guys took Nana away. He had Jesse in the crook of one arm and he held me to him with the other as I cried out my childhood, watching Nana blue-light away through Richmond.

"Come home with me Evie, we're a family now, we have to be together, that's how it is…" He held me all the way to his flat and didn't seem to ever let go through all the funeral preparations, the service, so quiet, so small, just Andrew Jesse, Willow and me. He was there, grown on to my side. For once I didn't need to be brave, I didn't have to sit at the window hoping comfort would stroll down the road and scoop me up. I didn't have to make do with second-hand consoling, because however much I loved my Nana, it was Ma's arms I craved, arms that never did open wide enough for long enough. Not like Andrew, he stayed until I could stand again, run again, without support. He filled the cavern in my life and for a long time that raw wound closed a little each year, almost healed, until Jesse was ripped from us and that cavern broke open all over again.

He'd started to speak, to tell me something, I pulled myself back into his arms from all the yesterdays. "The House ... Pengarrow ... another thing I should have told you, explained. But I thought telling you would over-complicate things. I just wanted to make you better... It was stupid, no selfish... Can you forgive me, Evie, for not including you?"

An angry voice erupts from the hurt place inside me before I can calm it, "Include? When do you ever do that these days?"

He sighs heavily. A silence stretches out. He blows through his lips, as Jess would when he couldn't be arsed to do whatever needed to be done. I fear my outburst may have cut the thin ribbon of communication between us – the silence spreads. Then he begins so softly that I think I am reading his memories.

"When I was a child I spent my summers down here. There was an old lady who used to be the housekeeper, a Mrs Morgan, I think. D'you know I was convinced she was some kind of witch, sounds silly now. But she had this knack of appearing, poof, just like that! Then you would turn to ask her something and she'd clean vanished – most strange! Ahh, but what a cook!" He inhales as if he smells her food right there. I copy him and can taste the bread-baking air that's followed us up the garden. "I've still never tasted anything like it to this day. Just the simplest of things, bread, butter and home made jam ... heavenly." He's talking about Alys, surely. I feel my pulse racing slightly. "I always thought she looked after the place for my parents but it was her family that owned it ... or thought they owned it." He stares off into the distance, through the view in front of him to his childhood..." To me this place is heaven, it's like a secret world that has never changed. Everything has been here – as it is – for hundreds of years. Imagine that, Evie, a hundred years ago some other couple may have sat here watching that farm over there with this very same tree keeping them cool. I always thought of this as my paradise – an escape from school, from rules, from behaving oneself, you know, achieving top marks, not being a disappointment to anyone... Go on laugh at me, I know I sound foolish."

I squeeze his arm, understanding completely; Nana always gave me a chance of paradise, a place where everyday stopped and fantasy took over, maybe not on such a grand scale as here at Pengarrow but a paradise all the same.

"Even Father loved it here. He always took an entire fortnight's holiday and together we would fish, and camp, hike in the Preselis, swim in the river – real Enid Blyton stuff! I had him all to myself – just the two of us. Oh, it was magical. He wasn't the man you see now; he was like some wise older brother. I don't know, it's hard to explain. It truly was the best part of my year; I felt like he belonged only to me... It kept me going when they sent me back to school."

"And yet you wanted to send Jesse off, knowing how

lonely it was, knowing how much you missed your parents…"

"It seemed like a last option. But this is what I wanted for our boys – I wanted heaven for them – and for you." He sweeps his arms across the view. "When Mother told me that their years of legal wrangles over ownership had finally finished and that Mother and Father had been restored as rightful owners of Pengarrow… When they suggested it to me – to us – I just couldn't stop. I *had* to be here, can you see, it overwhelmed me? I thought that if we could be here then the magic of Pengarrow could mend us; we could be in heaven, Evie. I thought it might even make the pain of losing Jesse less of an agony."

I lift my head, kissing his jaw. His heart beats faster with his confession. "But why not tell me all this, why not just be honest about it?" I can't resist asking.

"You wouldn't have come to see it, if you knew it was part of my family's inheritance." The bluntness of his answer is a looking glass for me to view my stubbornness in.

Chapter forty-two

I wasn't being a weirdo or anythin' but I spied on Mum and Dad. I just needed their help with Nye. I'd been searching for them for ages, shoutin' out. No one answered. I thought any moment Granddad is gonna show and find Nye. What I really wanted to be doing was to hang with Dad, and Mum – go riding or something, maybe go to the beach, do some surfing. That would've been totally cool. I kinda told Luke I'd already started to learn, and he was well impressed, says he's gonna come down and stay in the holidays cos there's nowhere to surf in London.

Anyway, couldn't find anyone, not Mum, or Dad, or Alys so I went up the garden to search and there they were. At first I thought errr when I saw them cuddlin', but they weren't arguing which was good, actually they weren't doing anything, just sitting under the big tree. I liked seeing them like that – together – it's not happened for ages. It's a totally cool place to have a tree house cos you could see for miles. You could spy all over Hollow's Wood then when that gun-nutter appeared you could shoot him, say if you had a catapult or something.

So I was kinda bored by now. It sounds babyish but I thought I'd like play commandos and sneak up on them through the grass – leap up and shout, make 'em jump. I should've just walked up cos I really did need to get Mum's help with Nye. I get close enough, only a couple of metres away – grown-ups can be so blind sometimes. And I can hear all that Dad's saying – he's like been coming to Pengarrow, he says, since he was a kid. I didn't know that! And he's talking about this old witch that used to live here, sounds as mad as Alys does. And talking about fun stuff Grandad did, so maybe he was cool once, although...

Then Dad starts telling Mum history stuff, the same stuff that Granddad has been tellin' me in the library – about great, great, great great like a million times great Grandfathers or uncles. And all the time he holds onto Mum. Anyway, one of them was like a gangsta (Granddad didn't say anything about him but dad does). He hung people and stuff, and one died in a war, and gave Pengarrow away then took it back, I couldn't understand it all, but then Mum starts getting all angry and they start fighting. And then just to make everything a thousand times worse bloody Grandma shows up, then the shouting really kicked off.

I didn't want to listen. It freaked me out, I mean if that was Jesse and me shouting them things, shit we'd have been in trouble for weeks. I backed out, was glad now they'd not seen me. I raced back to the den. I dragged Nye downstairs, ran faster than Usain Bolt across the yard and literally dived into the trees before anyone saw us. "Made it!" I go to high five Nye. He doesn't do high fives. "You go first." I tell him cos I'm not sure I remember the way. I just hope that psycho with the gun ain't about. I want to warn Nye but I don't want him shakin' and hidin' if that guy shows up so I don't say.

His house isn't half as far in the day as it is at night. Guess that's because you can see where you're going. Alys comes charging out, doesn't say nothin' to me but grabs Nye in a big hug and starts tellin' him she thought they'd got him. I wanted to say – Not now lady, I only just got him chilled – but I don't think she'd have listened. They go to go in their house and I'm stood there like a total loser, when Nye remembers I'm there. He pulls me by my bag and the whole lot comes out. There's clothes and stuff everywhere, and the stupid photo Granddad gave me. Alys sees it, grabs it then starts yellin'.

"Where did you get this?" she's yellin and, "How dare you bring that bitch into my house." Shit, I thought she was gonna kill me. I couldn't get a word out, she was epic, man! Thank God Mum turned up!

Chapter forty-three

"So what happened to the people who thought Pengarrow was theirs? I mean the old lady that showed us around, was she one of them – a Morgan?" I try to keep the scorn out of my voice "…Oh God, tell me your mother didn't kick her out…"

"Please don't start, Evie. Let's just talk, eh?"

His words annoy me, I want to retaliate, but the worn-out heaviness of his voice stops me. "OK. Tell me. I want to hear." I move in tighter to his side as he pulls his arm around me, his lips brushing the top of my head again. Somewhere Finn is still calling.

Andrew sighs, settling his breathing. "Are you sitting comfortably?" Knowing I must force down my anger, if we are ever to move forward I must bite my tongue. I wriggle a bit trying to play the game. "Then I shall begin… Once upon a time… And happily ever after…"

"That comes at the end, stupid." I nudge him in the ribs.

"OK, OK. So the story goes – and this, I must point out – is Mother's version, so just go with it… My Great-Great-Great-Grandparents moved here from London in eighteen something or other, they came for the coal. He owned mines here, she embroidered as far as I can understand, and was extremely sickly, eventually dying from the fever. The old man was heart broken, shut up most of the house, retired from mining and only popped out occasionally to sit as a local magistrate, taking his grief out on the village hooligans. Actually, I'm ashamed to say he was cruel – keen on hanging…" I shudder involuntarily. "I feel I should apologise to the whole village on his behalf. People don't forget around here. In fact, can you see that field over there, the one with the sheep in," I lift my head to look out, a coldness creeping through me. "Well, that oak standing on its own – see it – is said to be the hanging tree they used to swing the poor souls he'd sentenced, well, so father says."

"What was his name?" I whisper, already knowing. I'm not sure how much more I want to hear.

"D'you know I have absolutely no idea, they just called him the Judge." I can't stop myself pulling away from Andrew, I make out as if I'm studying the field. I feel sick.

"So where was I?" He continues. "Let's not dwell on the macabre. The Judge and his wife had a son Auden – Auden Llewellyn-Rhys." I whisper his names as Andrew speaks them. "By the time he became a young man he'd supposedly fallen in love with a local girl – I think she might have worked here," he waves at Pengarrow, "in the kitchens or something. Anyway, Mother said she was a gold digger, after nothing but the family's fortune. You can imagine the uproar that it caused!"

I can, I'm immediately back in that marquee staring at the horror on Amelia's face as Andrew introduces me as her new daughter-in-law. "But she's a waitress," Amelia had cried. "I just asked her for another glass of Champagne!" My heart beats again at the speed that it did as I ran as fast and as far away as I could from all those haughty faces staring down at me, their glare telling me I didn't belong.

"A familiar story," I mutter. "I wonder if your mother considered that Auden might've been a complete bastard, roaming around seducing innocent young girls for pleasure?"

"I'm only repeating family folklore! D'you want me to go on?"

I shrug which he takes as a yes. "Go on, tell me what Amelia *thought* went on." I utter begrudgingly.

"So, Auden announces to his father that he wants to marry this kitchen girl, imagine the fireworks?"

I wonder whether the Judge offered "the kitchen girl" a fat cheque to disappear the same way Amelia did to me. "Ha – was it a bit like you telling your parents that we were getting married? Let's hope he chose somewhere quieter than a bloody polo match."

"Am I going to have to apologise for that for the rest of my life?"

"Oh much, much longer – I will never forgive you for that, ever."

"Evie, let it go – don't dig up old wounds." He crushes me in his arms and I wonder if he's trying to squeeze out that memory, make it float away. "Right where was I? Oh yes, Auden and the kitchen girl…"

"Alys, her name was Alys, she wasn't just some 'kitchen girl'. She was a real person with a name and feelings. Alys Morgan."

He sits back to look at me. "How d'you know that?"

"It's all in here," I turn and tap the cover of Alys's journal beside me on the seat.

"What on earth's that?"

"A diary, well sort of, it's like a journal, like a scrapbook of Alys's life here at Pengarrow."

"Where did you find it?"

340

"It found me. After you went back to London that first time, it turned up with…" I was going to say with Alys, but she is my secret.

"You should show that to Mother, she'd find it fascinating."

"I don't think she would."

"No? So, you know the rest of the story then?"

"Not totally, just parts, Alys's diary isn't complete. Tell me your – sorry – your mother's version."

"Well. I think Mother said the girl – sorry, Alys – got pregnant, nobody's sure because she married a local miner's son not long after Auden married the wealthy daughter of some family friend, a Lady Isabella…" A convenient 'Caroline' waiting in the wings, I make sure the words stay as thoughts. "…And Alys and her husband were given an estate cottage in Hollow's Wood by all accounts so Auden and the Judge can't have been completely evil."

"What? Nonsense! Alys was kicked out by everyone, including her own mother! She was only a teenager, not much older than Jesse, homeless, abandoned by her lover and pregnant. I would say that a cottage was the least Auden could do."

"So she was pregnant? It was Auden's? Good God, no wonder the Judge married him off to Lady Isabella so quickly! They had a baby about the same time as Alys – my Great-Great-Grandmother… Was Alys's child a boy?" Andrew whispers.

"Yes, she called him Nye… Nye Morgan." I want to tell him that he's beautiful, that he looks just like Jesse.

341

"God, this gets worse." Andrew scratches at a pain that's creased his forehead. "So this, this, Nye could be my half Great-Uncle – this is getting complicated." He shakes his head trying to clear it. "Because not long after his daughter was born, Auden posted himself off to Africa to fight the Boers, got himself killed – the idiot – and Lady Isabella disappeared to grieve back in London. Which is where the disagreement began…" I can hardly bear to listen. My mind is filled with Alys's grief, I feel her pain, words and sentences from her book whisper from beneath the covers making sure that I sense each and every second of her agony. I'm sure wood smoke, from Alys's cottage hangs around the trees at the edge of the garden. And there, behind the branches, a shadow shape, an Alys shape, listens, making sure her story is heard, making sure I tell it, defend it.

Andrew stumbles on, but there's now confusion in his voice as his tale untangles and disintegrates. "It's said that Auden, feeling guilty I guess at jilting this servant – sorry, Alys – supposedly wrote a letter to her, in which the Morgans claim he said that he had signed over the deeds to Pengarrow so she would have a secure income and home. I thought that all sounded very far-fetched, I mean, the solicitors could find no record, although they supposedly had a flood and lost many of their records … but now that you say Alys's child was Auden's son … well it makes sense, makes the Morgan's claim more authentic." He stares into the trees, at the point where the shadow watches. I will him to see her. His silence stretches out, works its way around Alys's story. "So this might not be our house after all. Oh

God, what a bloody mess." He drops his head into his hands, rubbing his stubble.

Like a thump on the head, I realise I know this, I've read this letter. "I've seen the letter! It's true, it exists!" I start to scrabble through the pages of Alys's book. "But what about Lady Isabella's child, wouldn't they have been an heir?"

"She had a girl and the Victorians weren't so enlightened on women's rights, I think that still makes your Nye top dog…"

I hadn't heard her, hadn't seen her, but with an angry burst of words Amelia storms into our day, "What *are* you talking about?"

"Mother!" Andrew jumps from the bench as if scolded. "I was just telling Evie the story of Pengarrow. She's found an old diary that tells what really happened here. And a letter…" He moves to give her Alys's book "…I think there may have been an awful mistake."

"Mistake! Rubbish. The only *mistake* was allowing those filthy squatters to live freely on *our* land for so long! Do you know how much that law suit cost your Father?"

"But the servant girl … Alys, I mean, her son was Auden's, his name was Nye…"

"I'm not interested in his name. I've heard all this before from the Morgans. How convenient that the supposed deeds should be lost in a flood. Pure fantasy! And Nye Morgan was the real heir? Ha! Nye Morgan was nothing but a coward! An army deserter. You wouldn't catch a member of our family behaving that way!"

I can't stop myself, "That's not true…"

343

"Of course it is. They shot him right after his Court Martial, and the Army don't usually make mistakes. He was just like the rest of that lazy good-for-nothing bunch – did a bunk after his leave and refused to return to the front, to do his bit."

"But that's a lie too!" I'm shouting in Amelia's face, a speck of my saliva glistens on her cheek, but not once does she blink. She holds my glare. I try again "He was only a boy, just sixteen…" She snorts, a short, disdainful sound, it says my protest is as worthless as a servant girl's. She turns her back on me.

"Enough of this ridiculous nonsense. Andrew, Caroline has been on the phone, darling." Her voice is calm, back under control, as if nothing has passed between us. "You're needed in head office. It's very good news by all accounts. I've packed you some overnight things…"

"No!" I shout through Amelia's back. "Andrew, you can't go back – not now!" I watch him across the barrier of Amelia, his worlds spinning behind his eyes, we're tearing him in two.

She turns on me then. "For God's sake woman, stop it! You're childish, selfish and spoilt. You've ruined everthing for too long. Let him go. Stop holding him back!"

"Mother, that's enough." He utters, with no strength in his words.

"No, Andrew. Something must be said. *She* needs to understand once and for all. Your father and I have stood back and let you make a mess of your life for long enough! If only you'd stayed with Caroline… You'd be a minister by now, maybe even…" Her voice is shrill, piercing, and in my head she's joined by Ma, by Caroline, by all those who agree that I am a tiresome obstacle, a nothing.

"Mother! Jesse and Finn are not a 'mess'. Surely you can't think that?" Hurt bleeds into his tone.

Momentarily she pauses but then, "They are not a disaster, but what you allowed them to be *is* disastrous. Finn is barely educated, practically feral, and he's in a completely unsafe environment, because *she* doesn't believe in private—"

"Oh for God's sake don't start on that one again." I can't believe, now, with all this going on, she has to start talking about the school thing.

"Don't start?" Her voice is high, thin, loud. "You listen to me, now – you with your ludicrous ideas, you'd have us all living in a commune. Constantly preaching, 'We're all equal'! Ha! Well we aren't, we're not equal – *we* are civilised*,*" she waves between her and Andrew. "*We* don't allow our children to shoot each other. Let that be on your conscience Evelyn, you sent our boy to that place, that excuse for a school, your decision, no one else's, because you wouldn't listen to us."

"You think where Jesse went to school caused his death?" I don't believe what I'm hearing.

"Of course it did! How could you think anything else? Let's face it Evelyn, they don't shoot each other at Eton! Rufus and I won't stand by any longer watching you destroy Finn and Andrew like you did Jesse. You are ruining Andrew's life, Andrew's career. These silly breakdowns – your drinking – you're an embarrassment!" And there it is, her ugly thoughts writhe in front of me. I killed Jesse, that's what they think. I killed him. I look to Andrew who's gaping cartoonly. He says nothing. I wait. Nothing.

"You think I'm responsible for Jesse's death? Andrew?" I ask him in a whisper. I watch him think over all the dirty words that lie spent between us. Has Amelia given sound and shape to the something held in Andrew's heart? I think I see it – he blames me too. Anger rolls into a rock that I throw with all the force I can. "I didn't kill Jesse ... I wasn't the one who called the police..."

I didn't see her move, I just felt the burn of her hand as it crashed across my cheek, right on the place where Caroline had thrown her ring so very long ago, leaving that tiny crescent scar that must be acting as a target. Sound bursts into my ear. Amelia seethes; years of frustration erupt from her. She's exposed, gone is the cold calculation, the frozen stares. Stunned I stumble backwards, I know I must walk away, because at that very moment I want to rip her apart, tear hair from her head, spit and scream away her accusations.

"Mother!" Andrew cries. "Evelyn! Stop." Andrew catches the back of my sleeve. I snatch my arm away.

"Let her go, Andrew, she's a deluded, rambling mad woman." Her arm wraps through his, coaxing him away. "What you did – calling the police, turning in those awful drug dealers, was brave, courageous. Caroline is waiting for you, darling." I thought he would tell her to shut up, or go to hell even, but I couldn't believe it when he spoke...

"Quiet Mother. I can't think with you two fighting like

346

alley cats… Tell Caroline I'll be there by this evening … a few things to sort—"

"You're going?" I stare at him in disbelief. "You're going to her?"

"I'm not going to *her*. I have no choice but to go if I'm to make it as an MP. Don't make it impossible for me. Can't you think of *me* for a change? Every time I need support you make a scene and now you're quarrelling with Mother…" His voice rises with each word; something has come undone in him, breaking his surface, bursting out of him.

"She hit me, for fuck sake, you saw her! You seriously expect me to stand by and let you go off to play *Yes, Minister* with your daddy?" I'm laughing at him, but there's not a note of humour in me. "If you go, Andrew, that's it. I won't be here – *we* won't be here when you get back."

"Don't threaten me Evelyn. You're sick. I try to understand that. I try to understand your drinking, your delusions, your depression… But this is my big break, for once this has to be about me…"

"How many times do I have to tell you, I'm grieving for Jess, that doesn't make me mad… Why did I believe all your stupid, lying stories about 'new starts'? You've never said anything about being an MP before, about guns – where's all that come from?"

"From me – from losing Jesse."

"That's bollocks and you know it. It's come from your father. And you've stuck us down here so we're out of the way, so no one can see your crazy wife, so you and Caroline can waltz off and play Prime Ministers."

"How many times do I have to tell you it's got nothing to do with Caroline?"

"Many, many more cos I don't believe a word you're saying."

"Andrew, darling, can't you see it's no use. She's never going to understand you…" Amelia coos, reaching up to stroke away a strand of his hair.

"Oh I understand all right. I'm the scapegoat – I, basically, killed Jesse. So your conscience is clear, tuck me out of sight and slide Caroline into my place."

Amelia pulls him, the pressure turning him away slightly. "Andrew, you can't go." I'm running out of energy to shout anymore, I'm at the point that's saying give up *they* have won. Her grip on his arm is the end of my marriage, if she pulls any harder he will come away with her and she will have torn him from me. It will be over. I know I cannot live a Westminster life, a life with no front door to shut out the world. I do not want to be the news again. I don't want to think about how I behave, I want to own my family, allow it to be whatever it needs to be. I've seen Amelia's gold-fish-bowl existence; the plastic falseness, the air-kissing parties and fake networking friendships. I can't play those Party games. I am real, I am bad, and dirty and rude and honest; I can't act, I can't pretend and I won't lie.

She moves her hand from his elbow reaching up higher to rest it on his shoulder, a more possessive gesture, she leans her head into his arm and whispers, "Come on, darling." I hear his thoughts – choosing, deciding, each minute movement a stride toward *their* world. I thought he had the courage to walk far enough away that there would be no going back to them. How wrong I was. Andrew was just playing at being ordinary – being free; he's Establishment and they don't allow deserters. From nowhere Auden Llewellyn-Rhys wanders into my thoughts. I see him at that party watching Alys serve, and then stepping up to his father to obey his command to marry Isabella. No courage I want to scream at both of them. No courage. They're the cowards, not Nye.

"I'll take Finn, we'll go back home." I mutter. I sound pathetic.

"You won't," Amelia butts in. "You can't blackmail Andrew like that. Finn will be here when you return, darling. You, Evelyn can go where you want!"

"For God's sake, stop this!" Andrew shouts at us both. He inhales deeply and carries on mechanically. "It would be better if you stayed, at least until I come back – I can't make you – but it's only for two days, and you and I obviously need to work this out. Don't, please, try to take Finn, Evie, he needs stability, he needs our support. I *will* have to stop you if you do, understand that." Andrew's voice is quiet, but final. His decision made – it's them. I hear the sound of our wedding certificate tearing in half, the sound of promises being torn up all around me.

"I'll be gone when you get back. Finn and I will find our own place." I repeat. But they walk away, he watches me over his shoulder, a laser sight line that doesn't break until they dip down and into the house.

"I won't let her take our Finn, darling," I hear Amelia

349

reassuring Andrew as they disappear, "I won't allow her to ruin your life any further. We mustn't keep making excuses for her, she's clearly insane … just like her mother. These things are hereditary you know…"

I drop to the ground where I stand, the bones of my legs liquid. Tears run from my breaking heart down my face. The birds sing on happy with the shiny day. Leaves overhead uselessly hush me. The oak on its own in the field below glares back up at me; my marriage swinging dead from its boughs. After a while Andrew's car starts, he's off to his proper world, his home. The engine fades up the lane, we're finally driven apart. I won't see him as my husband again; he is lost to me, taken away, gone. I fall back into the grass, staring up into the endless blue that reflects back the nothing that I am.

Chapter forty-four

Silence folds and wraps around me, drawing me down. I lie flat pushing myself into the grass, the very earth, hoping that it will engulf me. Then all that will be left is a patch of primroses flowering over me in spring, a bright and jolly reminder to those who sit on the lovers' bench, that here below your feet lies Evelyn Wolfe. Like a shield from the pain I clutch Alys's book to me, wrapping my arms around it, pulling it into my chest as armour. I want to absorb some of Alys's strength, so I can get up and carry on; take Finn and go. But where, where is the "go back to" place? Back to Nana's, or to Willow's my forgotten lost-touch-with friend, to the London noise that drowns out thoughts? I imagine myself sitting on Jesse's bench in Marble Hill Park, Alys's words with me; I will start on the first page and read right through to her last, learning her inside out, teaching Jesse and Finn about her.

A black ache pounds inside my skull, like smoke it spreads and occupies the space where rationality should be. This morning I thought I would argue out Andrew's ridiculous plan with him. I imagined it would be ugly, that we wouldn't get to the end of it, that we would drag it between us as a smouldering burden for days, maybe weeks. I was sure, arrogantly so, that there was a path through this. Yet here I am without him, he's gone – with our marriage and probably custody of my son – and I don't have any idea what happens next. I watch myself finding a train station, with cases, with Finn. We get back to London, to Nana's, to a ruin, a place that hasn't been lived in for years. Builders want to pull it down, develop it, they write to me offering sums with ridiculous amounts of zeros… If only that could be my answer, but the builders will dig – dig deep. I don't want them disturbing Ma.

So I'm back to the beginning again, my child and I, a ruin and Ma. In exasperation I throw my arms out wide onto the grass and run the blades between my fingers. The sun burns orange through my eyelids. I'm paralysed. No ideas, no plans, because that's what Andrew did for me and our family, filled in the empty spaces, put in holidays where they should be, asked people to dinner when it was our turn, found the interesting film to see, the exhibition, the sleepover at the Science Museum; he knew Santa would be at Syon Park, and that the tallest Christmas trees were over Chessington way. I can see now how he helped me loosen the emotional knots I'd tied myself in; he knew the direction we should be facing. How did he do all that, how did he have the energy to keep on hunting for all the things families do together? Even through this last year when we didn't want to do anything? I lay at the foot of the gaping abyss that is life without him, and it yawns in the same way that life without Jesse does.

If I could run after him, down the M4 and over the bridge I would, I would pull him from the car and hold him to me so he could never get away again, I would hide him from *them* and keep him safe just for Finn and me, feast on his time and attention, greedily.

A shadow falls over my burnt orange lids, a shoe crunches down on my right fingertips.

"So…" The word is deeply rumbled and drawn out to

breaking point. Rufus Wolfe, a bully. He moves the toe of his shoe slightly crushing my fingertips a little harder. "Just wanted to make absolutely clear, my dear girl, that Finn will be staying here. You know, just in case you had any more ridiculous ideas…" I pull my hand, he presses down harder. "Don't want to involve any authorities, do we, I'm sure they don't need to know how unfit you are as a mother, with that little drinking problem you seem to have developed?" He presses down once more, then moves his foot away. I scramble up immediately, grasping my throbbing fingers.

"Are you threatening me?" I quaver, annoyed that I can't sound in control.

"Oh, absolutely."

"Finn is my son too, I have every right…"

"You have no rights." He throws a heavy envelope at me, "I've just bought them."

"Money again! You think you can buy Finn now?"

"No, but I'm pretty sure that I can buy someone as desperate as you will be." I can't speak; rage has swollen my throat, my mouth flaps without words. I switch from sound to action, ripping notes, bright sharp £50 ones, from the envelope he's just insulted me with.

"I'm not for sale, you bastard!" I yell in his face and throw the money as confetti. Concern briefly passes over his carefully bred features, but as thousands and thousands of pounds flutter about him and away on the breeze he regains his smug, arrogant leer. I want him to shout, to bellow and roar, I want something to latch on to that I can fight, but as always I slip on his smoothness. He is the master of control:

that day at the polo match – the very first time we met, his frozen blue eyes didn't even blink. It's one of my most chilling memories, even deeper than the scar from the redundant engagement ring Caroline threw, deeper even than the scorching humiliation. He just stared at me, sizing me up and finding me instantly lacking, inferior and totally unsuitable for his family's needs. In that stare he dismissed me, adding my name to the list of things that would have to be dealt with. And today he's here to finally succeed in crossing me off that list.

Why, I need to know, does he hate me, loathe and detest me? Was it really such a heinous crime to have married his son, to have produced his grandchildren? Hasn't time eased any of these sores? Did he not see Andrew's happiness in years past, how contented we were as a family? I can't comprehend this man. He is of another species, robotically locked into a pre-programmed mission that I may not thwart. He is about power, hierarchy, inheritance and class.

"Finished?" He inquires with a slight tilt of his head. "Don't come begging for more when you're crawling around in some gutter, as you inevitably will be. That was an awful lot of bottles of gin you've just thrown away." He begins to turn.

"I'm not an alcoholic…" I don't even know why I'm trying to defend myself.

"Dear girl, of course you are, your mother was, and, by the sounds of it, so was your grandmother. You people just can't help yourselves. It's how you deal with your guilt, your responsibility for Jesse's death. You hide away at the bottom of a bottle."

I grab at his departing arm, incensed. As he looks down his expression is pure disgust. Gripping tighter, I'm exhilarated to see a reaction at last. I pull myself close to him, breathing words in his face. "I didn't kill Jesse. I'm not the one to blame. Look at your own family, because you have no idea who I am or who my family is. You're not worthy to even utter their names." He flinches with every syllable. Unable to bear my closeness he throws out his arm that I'm clinging to catching me off balance, I stumble backwards hitting the ground. Ever the predator he looms over me.

"Foolish girl. I know all there is to know! Did you think I would allow you into our lives without having your background checked out first? I know all about your sordid little family. I know your mother was arrested for drug possession, when and where she served her sentence for dealing. I know she was a washed-up, out of work, alcoholic. Did *you* know that Evelyn?"

Air is sucked from my lungs. Nana never mentioned prison. All this time I thought … I mean she came back … but then…

"No, I thought not. And where is she now Evelyn? She seems to have disappeared! Perhaps one of my chaps could dig around see if she turns up, they could start in that ruin on the edge of Marble Hill Park…"

I barely hear his words over my thundering heart. He can't know … he's bluffing. No one was there … she fell, it was an accident…

I scrabble crab-like, away, my bruised fingers bump into

Alys's book which I snatch up in front of me, shielding me from his awful accusations. Somehow I stumble to my feet travelling backwards as fast as I can.

"That's right, run away Evelyn, run away – hide. And don't come back, vanish just like that mother of yours." I fall and tumble down the garden, never taking my eyes from Rufus Wolfe's victorious face. I reach a gate in the garden wall and wrenching it open I finally turn to run. I take a last glance over my shoulder. I think he says goodbye but pumping blood is all I hear.

I don't know where I'm running to but my feet do, they know the way to sanctuary. Across the front yard to the trees, sightless I stumble down a path. Rufus Wolfe's voice runs beside me, *murderer, murderer, murderer* it pounds, I dare not look back. As branches catch and snap I glance left, right, sure he's hired that Shadow Man to hunt me down. My legs burn, my breathing hurts, I try to speed up, but fall down banks, jumping and tumbling over fallen tree trunks. The smell of garlic is everywhere – intense and choking, as strong as the day Jesse lay dying in my arms, blood from the bullet wound in his stomach running through my fingers. The air was too thick for him to breathe laden with school-run, rush-hour fumes, with stale fried take-away, kebabs and curry, with the burnt garlic stench from the Indian.

On I run, fleeing from memories, from Rufus Wolfe, from Ma staring up at me from down in that trench. Suddenly the path tilts steeply up, bends sharply, the stream appears and there is Alys shouting at Finn, "Why did you bring that bitch here?"

Chapter forty-five

I've never been so glad to see my mum – she looked well wild, I thought the Shadow Man was chasing her cos she looked like she was running for her life! She couldn't even speak, her face was red, she was crying.

Alys was going mental, shredding Granddad's photo into snow, and shouting at me: "Why did you bring that bitch here?" Nye was no help, down on the ground, hands over his ears, rockin'. Anyone could see he was well scared, he was like shakin' all over and I think he was crying. And then, oh my God this is so gross, he pissed himself! Truly, I saw it, his trousers went dark then it ran out all over his shoes. He didn't even notice! Just squatting an' rocking an' pissing all over his feet.

Then Mum's shoutin' on at me we gotta go, "run away" she's saying. The whole place is mad – I don't know what to do, I'm like freakin' out. And, I'm like: "Mum, stop shoutin'." Then she just grabbed me, like tackled me to the ground. She was shakin' all over too. I wished I'd never come here, never listened to Nye, cos comin' to his house was a stupid idea – everyone's mental. I'm not even bothered who's in the stupid photo any more.

Finally, everyone chills a bit. Alys goes inside. At least she stops shoutin'. Mum gets Nye in, he stinks. Mum doesn't even notice. We get into the cottage and manage to jam the door shut, Nye just runs off, then, Mum, typical, blacks out again. I can't tell if it's one of her drinking black outs – she doesn't smell or nothing. I know, mental, but she does, but she said nothing, one minute shes draggin' Nye through the door, next minute she's on the floor and

I'm like left on my own. I do as Dad told me and prop her up in a corner so that if she's sick she won't choke on the vom. Normally she comes round quick, thinks she's been doing all this stuff, and you have to tell her that it's a dream, like she's the baby and she's had nightmares. This time she's out for ages. I even slapped her face, like I've seen Dad do. Didn't work and it felt bad. So I waited, and waited. I wasn't on my own but it was like being on my own. That was when they came. I heard them, heard them outside the door...

Chapter forty-six

I thought my lungs might explode as I crashed up to Alys's. I thanked God Finn was here safe and away from them – the Wolfes – so it took a second to take in the situation: Alys screaming at Finn, shredding paper everywhere, Nye dressed as Jesse, cowering on the ground. I couldn't stop myself shouting out to Finn, all I could think was that we must go, get out now – while we could – run away.

Finn turns, looks at me, but his relief washes away, my panic frightening him. He's surrounded by hysteria and I'm just adding to it. I check behind once more, no gunmen, no Rufus Wolfe – not yet, but time is racing away. I have to calm down, I have to make sense, I *have* to stop scaring Finn. I lunge for him sending us both crashing to the ground, feeling our bodies beating together as I hold him too tightly.

Somewhere a twig snaps I hear it over Nye's low moaning. I drag Finn to his feet. We have to hide. Alys has disappeared into the cottage, its door yawns darkly. We scramble up the bank to her gate past Nye still crouching in mud, I can't leave him, I pull at the hood of his sweatshirt – he falls. Grasping him, he flinches but I hold him to me. His hair is damp, stuck down to his skull, months from the last time it was washed. He stinks of urine and dirt. His body is bones hung with Jesse clothes. I root for his face and lift it to mine, "Nye," I whisper. He lifts his head and his eyes are the colour of horror. I nod to Finn and gently we extract him from the ground. I hold him to my body reassuring him we mean no harm. As he rises, his weight, what there is of it, falls into me, between us we drag and coax him up the garden path hauling him into the cottage.

I slam the door behind us wishing there were a boulder to keep them all out.

Here inside something dark and oaky is cooking, dragging the flavours from the iron pot that it's bubbling in. The room is murky, the air wood smoke. Alys lurks the other side of a dividing wall, trying to control her breathing, battling sobs. We settle Nye softly into a kitchen chair, but the moment I release my hold he springs free, scrabbling up the ladder that disappears through the ceiling. His feet scuttle across above us and silence themselves in a corner. I look at Finn, whose eyes bulge and shine in the dimness. "I didn't mean anything," he repeats in a whisper. He hesitates then makes for the door, "Stop!" I shout, but he carries on out to the path, I watch him collect the scattered pieces of confetti. When he has a palm full he returns, sprinkling his find on the table.

"Grandad's gonna go mad." He explains about Rufus's photograph and tries to sort the pieces into an image. Alys moves behind the wall, Finn sweeps the fragments back into his hand fear darting across his face. He holds out the bits of paper to me in panic, I take them and tuck them inside Alys's book just as she appears in the room. Her hair is wild and escaping, forming a red glow around her head, her eyes are swollen. Finn is sprung, ready to run, watching Alys. In a voice so different from her usual song she whispers to the floor.

"That picture… Seeing her… Brings it back… No one told me, see. Sunday, like all Sundays, we went to chapel and the minister says for us all to pray, pray for *her*, he tells us, Auden's dead – killed fighting some war in a place nobody's heard of. No one told me though. But they told *her*. Weeks I waited, weeks and they knew but no one thought to tell me…" Her voice melts into the smoke. I wait for her to continue and the air between us is painful and mourning.

"He wrote me a'fore he died. Must've known what was coming." Her voice is a rasping whisper drawn from a place of pain. "He said he was sorry. Sorry! Can you believe that? But that's not enough…" she raises her head looking at me through a web of red hair. "Is it?" I shake my head. "Then he says he's giving me the house! The whole of Pengarrow for me an' Nye! What rubbish! How's that gonna be, now, us from down 'ere walking where the Ladies do? Not that they're any better than us, mind. Nonsense Auden Llewellyn-Rhys, more of your nonsense! I don't want some guilty handout – don't want to live where he lived with *her*. And what would folk 'ere say, eh? What do we want with ten bedrooms? Ha! But Monday morn, old Morris – the Judge's man comes knocking. 'Tis mine, he says, like he can't believe them words he's saying to me, hands me a jailers bunch o keys, 'tis mine…" She stares off into space where she watches her memories replay. "Sit." she mutters, coming to, she sniffs wiping her face up her sleeve and snatches a bottle the colour of blood from the windowsill, banging it down on the table between us. She slops thick dark liquid into the glasses and lifts hers. "To men, may the dirty, lying bastards rot in hell!" She cracks her glass against mine and downs the contents. "Come on girl, get it down yer." I lift the glass to my lips breathing in autumn stewed up with sugar. The drink is warm and burning.

"To lying, *scheming* bastards." I add offering my glass for a refill.

"Mmmm, scheming, I'll take that yes, dirty, lying, scheming, *cheating* bastards!"

"Now you're talking; dirty, lying, scheming, cheating bastards, yes but what about the snivelling cowards that run back to Daddy the moment things get tough, eh? Here's to them all." I drain my second glass, my aches and pains turn to tingles even my crushed fingers calm their throbbing. Nye moves again above us, Finn must have gone to him. Alys stares into her glass.

"Coward? Good word that, coward. Auden was a coward an' I never saw it. Known him, man an' boy, I did. Chased us round the orchard pulled our plaits till hair came out in his hand! He was sweet on Megan Mathews then, "Ahh Megan *bach*," he teased, "marry me and I'll make you queen of Wales." She died that summer. The fever, took them all, Lady Mary – Auden's mam, our Dewi, Megan an' two of her sisters, one was only a *babi* mind. Ten we were, changed everything that summer. The Judge sent Auden away to some fine school for gentlemen in London town, he was all grown up when he came back. Proper snooty." She hums softly.

"Did you love him?"

"Love, ha! What's love, 'tis just a folly for foolish little girls? My *cariad* they whisper, Oh Alys, *bach*, ha, nonsense it is!" She carries on her humming and Nana joins in quietly from the dark. "Once I had dreams … once I thought… But love doesn't put a square meal on the table or a roof over our head now does it?" She throws the remains of her glass down her throat and refills, her words begin to round off and run together in a way I recognise. She lurches forward staring straight at me. "The trouble with men, see, is they're unreliable… When things take a turn for the worst, off they go and get themselves killed, Auden, my Davey Morgan and now … now my boy…" She drinks again and retreats back into her chair staring into the gloom. "You're very quiet for someone who turned up like a mad woman." She mutters to the glass in her hand. "No tongue in yer head?"

"Sorry, I didn't know about Davey…"

"Davey Morgan, mad fool. 'I'll take care of you Alys, that boy of yours needs a father.' Turned his back on the sea for us – reckoned the mines here were safer. 'Get to come home of a night,' he said. And safe he was when that mine blew d'you know, but oh no he couldn't come home to his wife and *babi*, no, no, he has to go back down that mine to rescue the others … but … there we are, that's menfolk for you… A hero, they called him. And what do I want with a dead hero? And now," she's shouting, "now they're going to take Nye. He's a boy, shouldn't even be fighting! A deserter they're calling him so back he goes they say."

"No, Alys, you can stop this," I find my voice, "You can prove he's too young, show the army his birth certificate, then they *can't* send him back. He'll be safe. You can save him."

"Who's going to listen to me? Who am I supposed to tell?"

"I have no idea, but we can start with the police."

"Police, ha! They're the ones that want to lock him up for poachin' tha's what he ran away for in the first place! All that rubbish he wrote about following the other village idiots, thought I didn't know…"

"Better he's alive and locked up here, than lying dead in France. Where's his birth certificate, Alys?" She nods at her journal. I grab the book, throw open the cover scattering scraps of paper. The letter from Auden in the Transvaal sits on top, I take that and carry on, Alys joins in pulling notes out from between pages, discarding them on the floor.

"Here it is!" She waves the certificate in the air. "Now you take it, Evelyn Wolfe, they'll listen to you." She forces the paper into my hand. "They're coming for him. He's a boy I've told 'em, just a boy, but they're coming anyhow. You save my boy. You save him." Her red swollen eyes bore into mine. Me, save him, I want to shout at her, I can't, I can't save myself, I couldn't save my own son.

"Alys, they're after me…" I stumble "I have to go, I have to go fast…"

"Who's coming for you, Mum?" Finn demands from the shadows. "Are you awake now?" A small part of my brain reminds the rest of me to behave as a responsible adult, the mad muddle shouts it down and bursts out of my mouth.

"Granddad has people… He wants to keep you … but … but I have to go, I need to hide…"

"What d'you mean?" His face is fear. "You can't leave without me. Don't – don't go, Mum! Take me with you!" He throws himself at me, I catch him, holding on tight.

"My darling, of course. But it's just us, Finn – no Dad, understand? We're on our own. Oh God I'm scared … I'm so scared of being without you…"

Thundering sounds at the door, we all visibly jump. No one had heard anyone approach.

Chapter forty-seven

"Who's in there? This is private land. Show yourself." That nightmare voice, it's shadow-man. He thumps again on the door. "Come out, I said." Then mutters, "Bloody poachers." It sounds like he tries to kick the door, streams of dust pour from the ceiling but the door sticks fast. The kitchen melts to shadows, it's cold, the floor has muddied. I turn to look for Alys but the gloom has swallowed her. Finn grips onto my clothes. "It's him!" he whispers in terror.

Oh my God, it's the man with the gun! Why is Mum just sitting there. I'm scared. This must be how Nye feels, I've never been so shit scared, he's going to shoot us, if that door goes he's gonna shoot us. "Mum, Mum!"

Someone else is with him, the banging stops. "Bloody poachers again. Come out – bunch of cowards!" He carries on to someone else. "I've warned 'em, I'll get the police onto 'em this time. We'll shoot on that way, where the foxes have been seen." There's a muffled response we can't quite hear. "This is your last chance, come out now an' I won't call the police." We hold our breath for an eternity, till the crunch and snap of feet disappear into silence. A shot is fired over the cottage and a smack of wings instantly follows as birds scatter in panic. The next shot sounds further away, then two follow in quick succession further still. We have to get out of here fast. I call out to Alys – she's gone. I clutch the two vital pieces of evidence; Nye's birth certificate and Auden's letter and grab her book from the floor where it lies in the mud. The ladder that Nye climbed has gone too, there's a gaping hole where half the ceiling has been eaten away. The cottage is a ruin, rooted and crumbling, the transformation is too crazy, too confusing. A holly tree claws through the space where the kitchen window was. Now is the time to run – we have to go. I pull Finn up, his face is white and he's shaking his head.

"No!" I tell Mum, but she doesn't hear. She's gonna make a run for it! You can hear them still shooting. Bang it goes, BANG. "I can't do this, I can't I'm too scared," I tell her. She says it's ok, that we need to go before they come back – bring the police.

I can't get the door open the ceiling has caved in jamming it – we're trapped! I whirl around the room hunting for an escape. The broken window filled with a holly tree is the only option. The space left is tiny, I reach back to grab onto Finn dragging him. All the time I urgently whisper to him, "We have to go now Finn, we have to go before they come for us." We're torn and scratched, brambles joining with the cruel leaves to catch and snare us. With the last of my strength I haul at Finn and finally he flops down into the mud beside me. Now which way do we run? In front the guns continue, behind leads to Pengarrow. To the side of the cottage the ground rears up so steeply I know we couldn't climb it, and across the stream lies a messy wood that opens onto fields, the gun men would see us.

Every bit of me hurts. My hands are bleeding. We should've stayed inside – now there's nowhere to run, only into the guns. Any minute now they'll come back for us. "Which way, Mum? Which way?"

Back the Pengarrow way is our only option. If we hear someone we'll hide. I grab onto Finn again and pull him towards the stream. He understands, I let go and run, stuffing the book under my arm, crushing the papers firmly in my fist. The guns go off again, the deafening noise bouncing off the gullies in the wood. I'm sure I hear Nye calling, "Wait… I'm coming." I glance back over my shoulder, stumbling over a root but I can't make him out. The trees close in, darkening at the edges. My heart pounds with my running feet, a pain wells and builds threatening to break my skull in two, I focus on moving faster. I check Finn is still behind me, he is, the whiteness of his face like a flashlight in the gloom. I think I catch Nye, chasing behind us, arms thrown in protection over his head. Tripping I turn to look forward, my vision narrows to a small point on the track ahead, a figure looms at the top of the incline we're racing up, sun suddenly breaks through the trees burning the person out. We need to get out of sight. I duck down the bank, Finn follows. Nye doesn't see and runs on, I manage to grab his coat, pulling him down with us. He slides tumbling beneath me. A shot explodes right over our heads.

My legs drag uselessly. "Run!" I urge them. I'm falling, earth, mud rushes up to slam me in the face. Dazed I struggle to look up – the figure is still walking towards us, the blazing light behind obscuring their identity. Finn is close, calling out. He pulls on my foot, a sharp burning pain shoots up my leg; I reach down and Finn's hand touches mine. I hold onto him. Nye is sprawled beside me his hands still over his head, "Don't shoot!" he moans. The figure is nearly above us peering down the bank. With all the effort I have left I try to focus on it. My breathing roars like waves over pebbles, I hear the shouts of men, Alys is pleading with me to save her boy, Finn calls out, but they're all muffled. Nye moans again. "You're safe now, I got you," I soothe him and call out to Alys, "I saved your boy." The figure is above me now. He begins to crouch down, to reach out to me, I see the toes of his trainers – I know them. The jeans that hang down over the cracked white leather are wet and mud soaked, the hem fraying into a grimy fringe. He squats, stretching out his hand, I drop Alys's book and touch his fingertips. They close round my hand and his skin is warm against mine as he pulls. A long way off Finn calls me, pulling me back down, tugging my other arm. I try but can't hold onto him any longer. I let go of the pieces of paper I'm still holding, I let go of Finn and let Jesse pull me to my feet.

~~Alys Morgan~~
~~Evelyn Wolfe~~

Finn Wolfe

September 12th

She's gone. They said she was ill, might die. She's gone for ages. I think it's a not coming back gone.

People say shit loads of rubbish to you when really bad stuff happens. They think they know how you're feeling but they don't. Like when Jesse died, so I was sort of ready for it.

"She'll get better soon." "She's in the best place." "Have to look after her when she comes home." Like how am I gonna do that when I'm miles away at shit-minster school? I heard Granddad tell one reporter: "We just want our beloved daughter back with us as soon as possible." Liar – he doesn't even like Mum, she told me he was sending police to get her! Of course now he says that was her illness talking, says he'd never say stuff like that. Everything is down to her illness now. So if she was so ill why didn't they look after her? All they said was she's mad, said she saw things and thought things and drank too much. I asked Dad, he reckons he tried but now she needs doctors. He doesn't want to talk about all the Pengarrow stuff.

When she let go my hand, in Hollows Wood, when the gamekeeper's shot hit her, I shouted at her to stay with me but she was still trying to get away – going on about "saving your boy" or my boy or whatever and I begged her to stay with me but she said that it hurt too much and I thought it was cos of her leg, but maybe it was the stuff going on in her head. She let go of my hand and grabbed Jesse's. I saw him standing in the sun, he'd come for Mum cos he always made her better – happier. Dad says all the crazy stuff she did, cutting her hair off, running away, blacking out was her being ill. I tried talking to Dad but he won't talk. So I told Dad that I saw Alys as well and Jesse and Nye Morgan – he told me I'd grow out of it! Like I was playing games. I thought thanks Dad, now I'm thinking maybe I'm crazy like Mum.

And now she's stuck in a "special place" they call it. Jess has gone too – disappeared – done a total runner, they thought, him and Mum, that I didn't see but I did. I saw them, standing there together. Grandma's calling it a breakdown – its not – she chose Jesse – she could've held onto me. Dad's trying to make it up to me but I know, I'm not a stupid kid anymore.

Anyway I don't look for them now. Don't want to see them anymore. I shut out her voice, all that "I'm always with you, Finn." What use is words – I need her here not in my head? Sometimes I read what she wrote in Alys's book. Well it's not hers any more it's mine. Sometimes though, if I touch Mum's words, I can feel her, I can I'm not makin' it up.

September 21st – Nye's name is finished on the war memorial in Llaneglwys Graban.

Western Telegraph are going to interview me cos I helped Nye Morgan. I proved, with his birth certificate, that he was sixteen, so the army couldn't make him fight. They shouldn't have court martialled him. They have to do a big apology to the Morgans. I'm making Dad take me to the war memorial although he doesn't want to go. He said he'd never go again. I asked if we could look at Pengarrow and he shouted at me for even asking – I only wanted to check Red was OK, seeing as Dad just gave him to Morgan the Milk – like he did Pengarrow. He didn't even ask if I minded, just said there's nowhere to keep a horse in London, not now he's sending me away to school. "School doesn't have stables," he said. "So send me to one that does!" I told him and he walked away.

September 25th Tea at Willow's.

Gave Willow mum's letters that I found in Alys's book. They made Willow cry, which was dumb. I thought they'd make her happy. And she gave me some of Mum's things, things from when she lived with her Nana in Marble Hill Park. We lived near there when Jesse was alive before we went to Wales, it's stuff Dad doesn't know about, stuff Mum left with Willow for "safe keeping", weird old necklaces, some stinkin old ballet shoes, pictures of her and Willow dancing, totally uncool, but I kinda like them. And her Nana's old house is mine and Mum's now, Willow said it was Jesse's as well, but he's not here and neither is Mum at the moment so it's all mine and I have to think what to do with it. Live in it I told her, then I can go back to my old school, but of course I'm too young and the place is too old, like falling down. What do you do with broken old houses? Sell them to builders Willow said.

September 26th – Sleep over at Aunty Caroline's.

September 27th – Sleep over at Aunty Caroline's

September 28th – Caroline's
She's not my aunty I told Dad, I don't have any real aunties or uncles or cousins or even a brother or a proper mum any more actually.

October 1st – First day at 'Shit'minster school, not going.

October 2nd – Hate it.

October 3rd – Hate it even more.
Can't sleep,
Don't like my room.
Don't like the Housemaster.
Don't like the people in my House.
Don't like the food.
So don't like the homework – First-bloody-World-War, don't like history.

October 6th – Dad sold *my* house to builders. I can have the money from it but can't have it till I'm 21. It's all invested. He's acting on my behalf. Whatever. Totally useless.
Still hate school.
Still hate the food.
Still hate the people.
Hate the way the old woman walks up and down the corridor all night checkin' on you, she's some kinda of night warden I guess, always singing stupid stuff. Shut up I wanna tell her. Sebastian in the next room says he's never seen her – div.

October 10th – Result! First history essay back, A*. Sir said it was like I'd actually been in the trenches, felt the shells coming over, like I knew what shell shock felt like. Ha, I didn't tell him that I just copied it all from Nye Morgan's letters! Sir said I have real empathy for the subject, whatever that is, so I told him I knew someone who'd just come back from the war. Sir told me off for being "impudent", sent me to the Housemaster, took back the five points he'd just given me.

Still got the A* though.

October 13th – Freaked out – the old woman was only sitting on the end of my bed when I woke up in the night. She said I'd called out and she'd come to check on me. She's been looking at my diary. She's spying on me for the history teacher. She said I could call her Nana if I liked like my mum did she said. No thanks I thought. Told her she didn't know my mum and she laughed.

October 23rd

OMG. Luke txt'd me this link. Is this your house, mate? he said.

BUILDERS UNEARTH BODY

Builders demolishing a house in the Marble Hill Park area have discovered human remains. The property previously owned by Evelyn Wolfe, daughter-in-law of Rufus Wolfe, MP, has not been inhabited for over twenty years. Police can't say whether the death was suspicious at this time…

Shit, got to stop writing, the old woman's in the corridor I can hear her. Weird, she's singing the song Mum used to sing to get me to sleep…

"We'll meet again, don't know where,
don't know when…"

Acknowledgements

Creating this story – bringing it to life, has been a long and wandering task that's not just been about the words written, crossed out, and written again, but about all those people who have encouraged and supported me in this quite amazing experience. One of the most important of those is my dear friend and fellow writer Peter Phillips: without his fearsome red pen, bottomless pot of commas and challenging questions (and even the odd bar chart) this story would probably still be a mumbling mess. Also the belief, advice and guidance from Jane Belli ensured that I made it across the finishing page.

I'm very grateful to Marcia Willets for her invaluable guidance on untangling the publishing world and its peculiar habits, her advice and reassurance were much appreciated. It's a daunting thing, as a new writer, to hand over your words to another to read so, I would like to say thank you Joan Moon and Susan Brace for your time and gentle feedback. And, as this is my first novel, I would like to take this opportunity to mention a few people who helped me to get started, to put my pen to paper; Gwynne Barnes, Christine Pinch and Bob Reeves thank you. Of course, none of this would have been possible without the patience of my family, my husband and children, who inspire me daily.

Finally, a huge thank you to Caroline Oakley and the team at Honno who have taken my dream and turned it into a reality.

ABOUT THE AUTHOR

Originally from the New Forest Helen Lewis has lived with her family in Pembrokeshire for 11 years. She trained as a graphic designer at The Faculty of Art, Southampton and worked in studios in London before setting up her own consultancy. Helen has been writing for ten years and has had short stories published in anthologies and national magazines. This is her debut novel.

You can find Helen at: http://www.helen-lewis.co.uk/blog or https://www.facebook.com/helenlewisauthor
and on Twitter: @hedlew

ABOUT HONNO

Honno Welsh Women's Press was set up in 1986 by a group of women who felt strongly that women in Wales needed wider opportunities to see their writing in print and to become involved in the publishing process. Our aim is to develop the writing talents of women in Wales, give them new and exciting opportunities to see their work published and often to give them their first 'break' as a writer. Honno is registered as a community co-operative. Any profit that Honno makes is invested in the publishing programme. Women from Wales and around the world have expressed their support for Honno. Each supporter has a vote at the Annual General Meeting. For more information and to buy our publications, please write to Honno at the address below, or visit our website: www.honno.co.uk

Honno, 14 Creative Units, Aberystwyth Arts Centre
Aberystwyth, Ceredigion SY23 3GL

Honno Friends

We are very grateful for the support of the Honno Friends: Jane Aaron, Annette Ecuyere, Audrey Jones, Gwyneth Tyson Roberts, Beryl Roberts, Jenny Sabine.

For more information on how you can become a Honno Friend, see: http://www.honno.co.uk/friends.php